IMPOSSIBLE CHILDREN

ROBERT YUNE

SARABANDE BOOKS
LOUISVILLE, KY

Library of Congress Cataloging-in-Publication Data

Names: Yune, Robert, 1981– author.
Title: Impossible children : stories / by Robert Yune.
Description: First edition. | Louisville, KY : Sarabande Books, 2019
Identifiers: LCCN 2019006338 (print) | LCCN 2019009015 (ebook)
ISBN 9781946448415 (ebook) | ISBN 9781946448408 (pbk. : acid-free paper)
Subjects: LCSH: Korean Americans—Fiction.
Classification: LCC PS3625.U54 (ebook) | LCC PS3625.U54 A6 2019 (print)
DDC 813/.6—dc23
LC record available at https://lccn.loc.gov/2019006338

Cover and interior design by Alban Fischer.
Cover art © AdobeStock.
Manufactured in Canada.
This book is printed on acid-free paper.
Sarabande Books is a nonprofit literary organization.

This project is supported in part by the National Endowment for the Arts. The
Kentucky Arts Council, the state arts agency, supports Sarabande Books with
state tax dollars and federal funding from the National Endowment for the Arts.

TO EVERYONE WHO HAS EVER WORKED FOR
A SMALL PRESS OR A LITERARY JOURNAL.

CONTENTS

FOREWORD

ohn Berger once wrote that the "constant stranger must continually travel." Robert Yune's magnificent and richly assured debut, *Impossible Children*, takes us across the United States, from New Jersey to Michigan to Alaska, portraying the lives of the itinerant, the wanderers, and the lost. Many of the stories focus on the experience of Korean Americans, though one of the many striking aspects of this book is that it never stays within the borders of a single culture or community, but rather continuously expands across landscapes that are at once familiar and yet difficult to categorize in simple terms.

"I wasn't aware of resonant frequencies, how the right vibrating pitch can shake buildings apart. I was ten and all I knew was that our father was surrendering us." So begins the hilarious and heartbreaking story "Princeton," which is about two young brothers, recent immigrants, who must navigate not only a new country but a new kind of family: their father, needing to find work, has left them in the care of a doctor he met once years ago in Korea. The story excels in its ability to disorient and defamiliarize as the sons run wild through the doctor's house, distracting themselves from the fact that their father has temporarily abandoned them. In another,

"Solitude City," a woman living in Alaska is called back across the country when her sister goes missing. What begins as a story about a search evolves into a daughter coming to terms with her wealthy father and the empire he has built.

This is a collection that is both precise—in language, in imagery and tone, revealing key moments in a life—and vast in geography, events, and the heart. The stories are infused with a loneliness and melancholy that reminds me of a Wong Kar-wai film, saturated in reds and blues, a book that isn't afraid to be at times slow and patient—but, like Wong Kar-wai, this book is also a triumph of sly humor and endless, joyful surprises. Children and adults alike behave very badly, and we delight in their unwise actions and choices. We also root for them as they all, whether they were born in this country or are an immigrant to it, attempt to form a sense of home.

Like Stuart Dybek's *The Coast of Chicago* or Edward P. Jones's *Lost in the City*, the stories—through a fully realized community—embody and evoke generations, history, and the history of war and migration. And like Dybek and Jones, what is ultimately revealed, through the characters' isolations and solitudes, is a moving portrait of the unbreakable bonds of family. One of the book's greatest achievements is in its sense of accumulation. Each story shines; but in its arrangement, Yune has created a deeply rewarding narrative that reads like a map of our time.

I keep coming back to the empire that the father in "Solitude City" has spent his life building. It is embodied in a skyscraper, "a monolith of glass and steel" that looms over Lake Michigan. It stands at the very center of these stories, both literally and figuratively, becoming a kind of foreboding lighthouse many of these characters sail toward.

Yet I doubt very much that Yune intended for us to travel solely toward this tower. What he has built here, and what we enter, from the first sentence of *Impossible Children*, is an achingly beautiful, many-roomed house, not only peopled with all of us, now, but also with the ghosts that have shaped us and the ones that help propel us into the future.

PAUL YOON
Cambridge, MA
April 2017

Jondaemal

(n.) Formal aspects of Korean speech used to demonstrate respect, especially to strangers, elders, and authority figures

HONEYMOON

Nearing the end of their honeymoon, Sunja and her husband Jung-ho hiked up Jangsan Mountain. The trails were steeper and rockier than they'd expected, but they were eager to prove their resilience—to each other and to the world. Neither complained. As they passed through a pine grove, Sunja heard distant music: flutes soaring over the mournful vibrato of a Korean zither. "Which means," she declared, "there must be a temple nearby." Meditating together seemed like an auspicious way to begin their marriage. While she was there, she could pray for a son or two. Also, she'd packed her new camera, and it would be nice if its first photograph was holy. She wasn't superstitious, but considering the thick blanket of forests sounds, the patient way her new husband helped her over the boulders beside the shallow waterfall, the summit's promise of Busan stretched out below them—everything felt vaguely symbolic. The trails were poorly marked, and they branched out in a way that defied logic.

Jung-ho couldn't hear the music or pretended not to just to tease her. They'd stopped to rest near a shallow creek when an American couple burst through some underbrush. They wore white spandex pants and headbands decorated with neon rectangles. At least in

America, the couple were slightly ahead of their time, fashion-wise. Sunja and her husband wore light outfits of mostly rayon and carried wooden walking sticks. Jung-ho offered the foreign couple his canteen. His English had grown a little rusty, but he didn't really need it—from the slightly crazed expressions on the Americans' faces, they'd been lost so long that they'd worried about ever seeing another human. Sunja, who'd just finished law school, prided herself on efficiency. In no time, she'd sketched them a map and refilled their canteens, but the Americans' gratitude shone brightest on her husband's language skills.

Bowing deeply before taking his leave, the American man pointed in the distance and asked, "By the way, what do those triangle signs say?"

Jung-ho squinted at the signs. "Warning land mines," he said in English. It took the Americans a few seconds to understand. From their expressions, they'd clearly ventured beyond the fences and inadvertently stumbled into a history lesson.

"Did they pass a temple on their way here? Do they at least hear the music?" Jung-ho relaxed his face into an easy smile, pretending not to hear. The American couple, their faces still a little frozen in shock, showed a newfound interest in things they didn't understand. "Would it help if you explained that they're *American* land mines?" Sunja asked.

PRINCETON

I wasn't aware of resonant frequencies, how the right vibrating pitch can shake buildings apart. I was ten and all I knew was that our father was surrendering us. We had the sense of being carried to the end of the world, to this new, forested edge of New Jersey. My brother and I were too young. Our grandfather and family friends tried to shield us during recent disasters: the divorce, naturalization, Dad's job search. We wanted to believe their assurances, so we folded our panic deep into our suitcases.

An unpaved section of road jarred us from our stupor. We bounced as our father gripped the steering wheel in surprise. None of us expected dirt roads in America—not in the early nineties, the height of history and progress. Then, a mansion appeared like the ones we'd seen on television, colonial and white with a phalanx of trees on either side. The front door opened and the doctor walked down the driveway to meet us. He and my father hugged and watched with vague disapproval as my brother Tommy and I dragged our luggage to the door. A few minutes later, the doctor's wife came out to help us.

"Prove yourselves," our father said by way of farewell. Then he added in Korean, "Behave or I'll kill you." Once he found stable employment, he would be able to afford to bring over our grandfather, who was subsisting on noodles and broth in an unheated apartment near Busan. My father was a proud man, the eldest son drowning in filial piety. Our grandfather was a patient man except with his own family, and currents of his anger had pulled us into the present situation. Tommy and I could see the tension in my father's neck as he shifted into reverse and backed down the driveway, giving our hosts a terse wave.

The doctor's wife smiled at us as if to say, *Everything's fine,* but we knew better. Our father wasn't going far in his search for a new job, but there was something ominous about his departure, as if everyone sensed his journey didn't guarantee success. That unease followed us as we lugged our scuffed vinyl suitcases to the guest room upstairs. Tommy was twelve and I was ten—we were basically human wrecking balls, but I distinctly remember how carefully he avoided banging his suitcase against the walls or scraping it against the hardwood stairs. I trailed behind him, following his lead. Our hosts' names were Paul and Leslie Hrisak, according to the mail in the basket that sat on the bottom swirl of the banister.

We'd met white people in Busan—our father would sometimes bring them over for dinner—but living with them was another matter. These two seemed as odd as their names. After we unpacked, scattering our clothes around the guest room and fighting over who got which identical bed, our hosts called us to the dining room downstairs.

Paul wore a crisp white cotton dress shirt with an orange tie, and Leslie a pastel yellow dress with puffy sleeves. As we passed under the archway into the dining room, the first thing I noticed was the room's dimness: the windows and screen door let in some watery evening light, and wall sconces bearing electric candles were just bright enough to highlight a pair of neatly trussed Cornish hens, which steamed wildly next to Fiestaware bowls heaped with cranberry chutney and peas. Beast that he was, Tommy seemed to take this in stride, but meals in Korea, especially after my parents started sleeping in separate rooms, mostly consisted of Sterno-sized offerings of mackerel and pork dumped over rice. On special occasions, Dad would serve *budae-jjigae*, a stew consisting of instant noodles, hot dogs, Spam, kimchi, and cheese. He claimed to have invented it, but everyone knew that such an unholy combination could only result from starving Koreans raiding the dumpsters of American military bases after the war. Dad would serve it in our fanciest stone bowls with a bitter cluster of leaves as a garnish.

There were no garnishes, sardonic or otherwise, at the Hrisaks' table. Out of polite efficiency, they had already served us: on my plate were two medieval-sized dark-meat drumsticks, along with a perfect mound of mashed potatoes holding a dam of gravy. Tommy had a similarly sized portion—looking back, it was obvious our hosts didn't have children, but as I fidgeted with the cloth napkin on my lap and stared at that plate, it seemed more of a challenge than an offering.

"What's wrong?" Paul said. The lighting emphasized his deep sockets, inset with the bluest eyes I'd ever seen in person. Icy. Even adults who didn't know him as the chief of surgery at Princeton General became self-conscious about their posture and grammar around him, though retirement seemed to have left him with slower vowels and a barely perceptible slouch. Leslie's posture was impeccable and persistent, as if it were part of a job she'd never retire from.

"I think they're just tired," she said. "Right, boys?"

Tommy and I were both good Korean Presbyterians—the same way decorum had been instilled in our hosts, religion had been beaten into us. We waited with our heads bowed, breathing in the fog of poultry as the gravy on our plates congealed.

"Let's begin, shall we?" Paul said, passing his wife a bowl of carrots.

And just like that, without grace but with a certain American grace—a blustery dedication to forging ahead—our first real meal in this new country commenced.

After dinner, Tommy and I bolted upstairs, leaving the Hrisaks to clean up the leftovers and make some recalculations about portion sizes. Over the next few days, we adjusted to each other quickly, the Hrisaks bending their routines and giving us space as we reverted to our natural states. I filched like a magpie while our hosts worked side by side to prepare meals and scrub our muddy handprints off the walls. On our fourth night in their mansion, I emptied my pockets onto the bedsheet. I'd collected a #1 Ticonderoga pencil, some photographs, heart-shaped paper clips, a black marble. The thievery was thrilling enough, but as I mentally cataloged the items, I got the sense that the photographs weren't merely trinkets—their combination of paper, gloss, and image held some deep revelation. Who were these strange Americans we were living with?

It would be a long night. My brother was sitting cross-legged and gawking at the nude tribeswomen in one of Paul's *National Geographic* magazines. Tommy had a bowl of popcorn, which he occasionally lifted to his mouth like a horse gumming oats from a bucket. His focus on these tasks meant peace, for the moment.

The first photograph came from Paul's office, frame and all: it was a shot of the doctor holding me when I was maybe four years old. He was wearing a suit with a wide lemon-yellow tie and had just tossed me high into the air. We were maybe at a park, a field of tall grass in the background. He was visiting Busan as part of a university exchange program; my father served as his guide and interpreter. Paul was pale, with white hair, even then. He wasn't a tall man, but he was blessed with the face of an American aristocrat—imagine the captain of Yale's lacrosse team at his fortieth class reunion. In the photo, he was laughing, his attentive gaze fixed on the amazing flying boy.

A few other pictures popped out when I slid open the frame, mostly old people I didn't recognize. One was a Polaroid, presumably some distant Hrisak relative. The face was marred by fingerprints now permanently burned into the paper, but it belonged to an elderly white man with fierce bushy eyebrows. The lens had focused on his open mouth, bellowing at the height of some electric madness. I leaned the photo against the lamp on my nightstand and let him face the window. His silent scream joined feathery insect sounds and peeper frogs, a desperate struggle for survival against the matte black outside.

The Bakelite flip clock read 10:50 p.m. "Hey fatty." My brother had silently moved to stand next to my bed. "Where did you get those from?" he said, jerking his chin toward my treasures. He was about a foot taller but slim, a sinewy mass of twitching muscles. We were dressed nicely enough in denim shorts and pastel polo shirts, but we both had the same unfortunate haircuts. The most popular style at the time was a crew cut plus a rat tail, but the haircuts we were permitted were more like flattops, which we maintained with a waxy hair gel. Our first night in the mansion, Tommy discovered the gel was flammable: I woke to see a glowing orange disk glide under me and hit the wall. We scrambled under the bed and extinguished the flames just in time.

I slid the stack of photographs behind me. "The doctor's wife gave them to me," I said.

"You're a freaking liar," he shot back, shining a flashlight in my eyes. I squinted, suddenly tired. The flashlight clicked off and he vanished, replaced by a reddish afterimage and a stabbing pain. "The doctor's gonna find out," he said, his voice ominous as the room's colors strained and settled like a developing photograph.

"You're gonna tell?"

"Doctor's gonna find out."

"Gonna tattle?"

"You're done for," he kept saying.

"Tattle tale tit . . ." I'd overheard neighborhood kids scream-chanting this rhyme.

"Shut up now. I'm going to bed," he said.

"Went and had a fit—" He threw the entire bowl of popcorn, which landed on my bedspread, kernels mixing in with my artifacts. "Damn it," I said, hopping to the floor.

"Serves you right, thief." He pulled the covers over his face.

I brushed away the popcorn and rearranged the photographs. I had to rely on moonlight, which meant standing in front of the window, which was locked open to let the late summer breeze in. I worked quickly, aware that a thin screen was the only protection from scissor-faced insects and other nighttime horrors. There was a shrieking noise and wind chimes—Tommy said no, he couldn't hear anything. "And shut up, too." From outside, a crashing sound and a booming, disembodied voice sent me scrambling to bed, the thin bedsheet fluttering hot and wet over my face.

It was around nine a.m. when the curtains parted with the snap of sparrow wings and the room burst with light. "Dr. Hrisak wants you up for chores," Leslie said, patting my arm. I suspected they referred to each other as "Dr. Hrisak" and "Mrs. Hrisak" even when we weren't around. We thought they were odd, but it was easier to follow their directions—don't curse, don't bring animals inside, wear shirts to the dinner table—and we mostly obeyed.

I stomped down the wooden stairs and slumped over the table. Leslie sat beside me, peering over horn-rimmed reading glasses at the *New York Times* as I ate my cereal slowly, stalling, until the doctor walked in. He sat across from me and placed a napkin on his lap, even though he wasn't eating.

Paul was in his sixties and hard of hearing. Raising our voices to adults was as unthinkable as calling them by their first names—we didn't like repeating ourselves, and we'd shy away when moved closer to hear better. It was easier to avoid him, and there were so many distractions: wrestling in the backyard, trying to shove each other into the pond, and accompanying Leslie on trips to the grocery store. This particular morning, she must have insisted on some meaningful interaction between the men in the house. The Hrisaks were hosting their annual summer party that week, so our job was to beautify the grounds by pulling weeds. The garden was surrounded by a chain-link fence to thwart deer, with a path through the middle made of rotting boards. Paul looked strangely underdressed in cargo shorts and a white tank top. It was already unbearably hot, the insects flying into our hair, sleeves, ears. I wiped the sweat from my forehead and pulled at a dandelion, but the stem broke off and the root remained in the soil. Shrugging, I tossed the leaves in the bucket. The doctor saved the finest tomatoes in a plastic Cool Whip container. The rest he mashed into the dirt with his foot.

"There's a beast in here," Tommy said, holding up a small brown frog. He bounced it a few times in his hand.

With some effort, Paul stood up and walked over. "That's a toad. *Bufo americanus*. A native of the New World and of course plentiful here in Princeton." At times like these, he spoke as if addressing a note-taking class of lesser surgeons. "There has been talk of changing the nomenclature." He laughed to himself. "And perhaps they will. Simpler language for a simpler era."

"We need a hero to slay this beast," Tommy said. He turned it over and stabbed at it with his finger.

"The only beast to be slain here is indolence," declared Paul.

"Hey Jason, you want to take a picture?"

"I do not," I said, glaring at my brother.

"Jason's a photographer. A idealogerrr. He takes pictures," Tommy said in a singsong voice, emphasizing the word "takes." After a windup, he pretended to pitch the toad to me and I flinched. I gave him a look that said, *You got me, OK, now stop.* The doctor kneeled and frowned at a tomato plant, fussing with its leaves.

I launched a dirt clod square at Tommy's chest, but it hit him in the neck, a spray of dirt flying into his nose and eyes. He snorted and stamped like a brain-damaged bull, then scoured the ground for rocks.

"Enough," Paul warned.

"Did Jason tell you about his collection?" Tommy asked, brushing off his shirt.

"Tell the doctor what you've been doing with his magazines," I screamed, pointing at Tommy. "And why you stole those photographs and hid them under my bed." Tommy's face reddened. He threw his bucket across the garden, opened his mouth to scream, and abruptly collapsed. The toad flung itself from his hand as the doctor sprinted over. In his last seconds of consciousness, Tommy was laid over the doctor's lap like the *Pietà*, his eyes wide, mouth open as if chewing on a gigantic question. He reached out for me, and that gesture shocked me even more than his face. I stood frozen for a few seconds before remembering to grab his hand. By then, the doctor was shouting at me, and my brother's eyes were closed.

"Get help," Paul repeated. I ran into the house without a word. It must have looked like I was going to call Leslie, or the hospital. Really, I was sprinting upstairs to our bedroom to hide the evidence, that black-magic photograph I'd snuck under Tommy's pillow—which had, for all I knew, just killed him.

Tommy survived his brush with the dark arts. He'd actually had a panic attack and fainted. If I'd arranged my curses just right, perhaps he would have turned into a toad. Or we could have switched places: he'd be the fat kleptomaniac and I'd be the expert at making fart noises with my hands. That evening, our dad called. Wherever he was, there was a symphony of noise in the background. I pictured a diner, complete with dinging bells and clattering plates. The classifieds were spread in front of him, opportunity after opportunity circled and crossed out. "All is well—that's what everyone says. Tell the truth about your brother," he demanded. I looked around the kitchen for help but found none.

"All *is* well," I replied, quickly passing the phone back to Tommy, who smirked down at me from a tall stool and swung his legs to kick my chair. In front of him was a wooden bowl of cherry tomatoes. He made a whistling noise as he tossed one in the air and caught it in his mouth. "Anxiety" was the diagnosis from the hospital. The doctors recommended rest in a calm environment for the next few days. His face broad and innocent, Tommy asked when he could return to his work in the garden.

Even though Paul wanted me to continue weeding, Leslie

intervened and said we brothers should spend some time together. So there we were, facing each other at the thick oak kitchen table. Tommy picked up the heavy magnifying glass Paul used to read the newspaper and examined me through it. "Dad said only room in the new house for the eldest," he said, blinking a gigantic bloodshot eye.

"Liar."

"And he's gonna get me a freaking wheelchair 'cause of all my anxieties. And then I'm gonna run your fat ass over with it."

"Hardly," I said, looking down at my lap. I flipped through the *New York Times* on the table, searching for the funny pages.

"You're gonna live in the forest and eat toads. *Buffoonus americanos*. But someday, a toad will eat *you*."

"Shut up . . . hospital boy," I said. It felt cheap and mean, but I didn't take it back.

"Dad said he's coming back for me next week. Maybe no one's coming for you," he said, standing to examine a family of wooden elephants displayed on the bookshelf behind us. He walked out of the room, leaving me to ponder the very real possibility that even the doctor and his wife might vanish and the fruit in the bowls on the table would rot and I would wait there forever.

The next week, Tommy took his revenge. After all, he'd fainted like a character in a Victorian novel—in front of our host, no less. Also, he'd begged me with his eyes, and all I'd given was a horrified stare. I picked out the rocks he snuck into my food and didn't tell anyone when I woke to find him putting my hand in a bowl of warm pond water. I think it was water, anyway. But as the week went on, and my sympathy dwindled, I began plotting.

. . .

It happened when we were in Paul's study, playing a game he'd invented: whoever went the longest without speaking would win a little metal penlight that vaguely resembled a lightsaber. After a period of silent taunting, we opted to ignore each other. Tommy stood on a chair, trying to reach the anatomy books at the top of the shelves. I stared out the window at the forest outside, reviewing my strategy. The doctor was somewhere upstairs.

I didn't have anything to lose. There were two doors to the study, and since Paul was upstairs, he'd have to come through the closed door nearest us. It was perfect. I strolled over to the desk and unearthed a cigar box that was mostly hidden by a stack of magazines. Now I had Tommy's attention. I slid a cigar from the box and with some effort bit off the tip, like I'd seen in a cartoon. I spit the tobacco into the wastebasket and wiped my mouth. There was a Zippo in the desk drawer and I flicked it open. "What the frig are you doing?" Tommy whispered. A few moments later, I heard Paul creaking slowly down the stairs on his bad knees. But Tommy didn't seem to care. He kept flapping his hands in excitement. After I held a finger to my lips, he sat down, mesmerized. Usually, he was the daring and impulsive one. I ran the cigar under my nose, relishing the freshness of the experience, along with the exotic scent. I grabbed a lighter and the cigar crackled over the flame. *My insane little brother,* Tommy mouthed. He was immensely proud of me, even if pride was only one of several emotions he was trying to contain. I closed my eyes like a jazz saxophonist and placed the cigar between my lips.

"What's going on in there?" came Paul's voice. He must have smelled it and was now really hoofing it across the hall. I raised my eyebrows and took another puff. My brother looked at the door, then at me. The moment the door handle turned, I tossed the burning cigar into my brother's lap and bolted through the empty door.

Leslie drove a purple sedan. Normally, I would have been embarrassed to ride in such a girly-colored vehicle, but today I sat with my back straight, taking in the world from the backseat. A tuft of Paul's white hair rose above his headrest like a cloud. I loved my new flashlight but couldn't see the beam in the sunlight, so I pressed my forehead to the cool window and watched the scenery.

She steered through a grid of mansions and thick trees. "There's Einstein's old home," she said, slowing as we passed a little white house with a big porch. It was too small and plain, I decided, searching instead for a solid-gold palace shaped like a mushroom cloud. We turned the corner and Paul pointed to a baseball field. He began to ask a question but caught himself.

"You don't play baseball, do you?" he asked. I said no, that was my brother. I could barely walk up a flight of stairs without panting. Tommy was rotting at home doing his punishment—I couldn't wait to tell him about this drive. The air smelled like freshly mowed grass and someone was burning a woodpile in a distant backyard. Paul closed his eyes again. I rolled down the window and let the wind tug at my fingers.

It was around noon and the sun would have been a problem anywhere else. But this was Princeton, where the surfaces were ancient. The town absorbed rather than reflected the light, and there was a softness to the old houses, like the smoothest sea glass or worn pages of a book.

Scattered mansions gave way to green fields, streaks of yellow wheat at the borders. Leslie drove a few miles on a rutted dirt road. "We used to buy all our veggies here when I was a girl," she said as the air got dustier. She had mannish short hair and was wearing a pink dress with white flowers on it. At the farm, Paul gave me money and let me pay for the vegetables—the responsibility was part of my reward, he said.

We took a different route home. The scenery was almost enough for me to forget about my father's job search. He'd been gone over a week, during which we'd almost burned down the Hrisak's house and forced an emergency room visit. Our grandfather was still stranded in Korea, but Leslie's purple car outpaced those worries. Out the window were scenes I'd only seen on TV. Without even trying, I'd discovered the peace and harmony my father was ultimately searching for.

After carrying the corn, squash, and other veggies to the kitchen, I checked on Tommy, who glared up at me, then turned back to his essay on integrity and honesty. In the margin, he wrote, *I'm going to frigging kill you you turkey turd burger.* Like a TV cop during a traffic stop, I clicked on the flashlight and aimed the beam at his eyes.

Later that day, Leslie consolidated boxes in the attic. Hoping to find more baubles and trinkets, I volunteered to help. In a few hours, at the opposite end of the attic, there were only cobweb-shadows over a wide patch of floorboards. Dust floated in the sunlight, creating a haze—if I squinted, it seemed like the boxes were simply evaporating.

She wore a purple bandanna, and from pictures I'd seen, she didn't look much older than she had on her wedding day. Her hair was long hair then, down to her waist. She was a small woman. I could see it in her wrists and fingers as she lifted wine glasses to the light. They had a date etched on their bowls, but before I could read it, she wrapped them in brown paper and set them in a smaller box. Watching her repeat this simple action, I forgot about my father for a while. But he surfaced again as we slid the packed box across the room. "What happens when my father comes back?" I asked, meaning, *What happens if he can't find a job or can only afford to take one of us with him?*

"Well," she answered carefully, "the paperwork's finished, so once he's employed, he'll bring your grandfather over from Korea. And you'll all move in together, I suppose." I'd almost expected her to say, *I know you don't like your family. If you want, you can move in with us.* But it was impossible—Princeton was too foreign, too old, too fragile for someone like me. Leslie stood over me, then grabbed my hands. Without thinking, I held on and let her pull me to my feet. "We're having a party tomorrow," she said. "Let's forget everything else, shall we?"

We spent the rest of the afternoon shucking corn. After we finished, I retreated to the living room to slouch in my favorite chair. It faced a brass bowl filled with dusty firewood, placed where a TV should have been. When cars passed in front of the windows, its seams and dents shifted. I watched, idly speculating about all the millionaires driving past. The drapes were porous, the outside world blissfully muted.

On the wall above my chair hung a red-and-white rug depicting rows of alien-like stick figures holding hands. The carpet was light brown. There were magazines on the coffee table, but they were filled with big words and tedious charts. Aside from the brass bowl, the only interesting object in the room was a flea trap, a glowing bulb above a tray of sticky paper. A few unlucky fleas and beetles twitched on it, their free legs waving.

Tommy entered the room with a bored, predatory look in his eyes. He glanced at the flea trap, then at me. I left quickly.

In the living room, I could pretend to read magazines, but it would only be a matter of time before Paul spotted me wandering and assigned a chore. I considered my options and headed right into the lion's den.

"Bored?" he asked, looking up from his desk. I shook my head. He laughed. "Of course not." I stared at the cigar-sized hole burned into the carpet.

"Tommy wanted to know if there were chores he could do," I said.

"Tommy said that, did he? What a thoughtful brother you are."

I backed away slowly, realizing I didn't have much of a plan now that I was in the doctor's study. My new plan was to back out of the room. "Work is . . . important for a man," he said finally. "It's a shame I don't have anything for you."

My eyes fixed on a blue-and-white striped bowl at the top of a display cabinet. It was about the size of a salad bowl. There were more colorful pieces surrounding it, but they didn't hold my attention. "You like pottery?" Paul asked, as if he were about to offer a gift. I nodded. "You have good taste," he said, walking over to the cabinet. He lifted the bowl from its stand and shook a dead spider from it. "This might well be the capstone of my collection. Anasazi." He raised his voice as he switched into teaching mode. "The Anasazi were American Indians who lived in the Mesa Verde, near New Mexico. Leslie attended college there. The best archeological minds are still trying to figure out how these people lived, considering the lack of vegetation in the area. No one knows where they buried their dead. They've unearthed small burial sites but not enough for such a large settlement. There were cliff dwellings—have you learned about this in school yet?" I shook my head. "The Anasazi are also notable because one day they simply . . ." He held his hand out in a fist, tightened and opened it, shaking particles of nothing onto the carpet.

"Vanished?" I said.

"About the same time this bowl was made, actually. 1100 AD."

"And they just left that behind?" I asked.

"Among other artifacts."

"Why did they vanish?"

"Ah. Another mystery. Some scholars believe there was a drought. Or disease. Some . . . intrepid explorer recently found evidence of cannibalism among the tribe. This . . . claim could always be fiction, something to scare up grant money."

"Cannibals." This wasn't history. It couldn't be. The ground under my feet never felt solid, but I'd never imagined entire tribes of people could disappear overnight.

"They left behind carvings, but no one can decipher them. I've come to believe this bowl came from a dubious source," he said, holding it so I could see the pattern inside. Four pencil-thin blue stripes curved toward a vanishing point in the center. It certainly didn't look more than eight hundred years old, but the pattern was impeccable, the lines so straight it was hard to imagine they'd been painted by a human hand. I was suddenly impatient to hold it, to trace my fingers along its pale slopes.

"This may be the only surviving spirit bowl. Usually when the craftsman died, his kinsmen smashed the bowl to set his spirit free. Dubious, as I said, that this one is still intact. The man I bought it from has since gone the way of the Anasazi, so to speak." He laughed.

"Can I hold it?" I asked.

With some effort, he put the bowl back on its stand in the cabinet.

Tommy strode into the room. "What's shakin'?" he said. I wasn't about to give away my new secret, but I couldn't think of a distraction. I'd need Paul to play along, too.

"Come help me set the table," Leslie called to us from down the hall.

During the party, I snuck down to the basement and stole a bottle of port, mostly because I'd admired its crystal decanter. I really began to covet it when Paul noticed my interest and moved it atop the liquor cabinet, but it was easily reachable by standing on a chair. Like I said, the Hrisaks didn't have kids.

I switched on the fluorescent magnifying light above the desk Paul used to tie flies, revealing stacks of clear plastic containers filled with feathery objects and metal tools. If my father didn't return, I could be an assistant. Paul could say, "Tweezer-thingy," and I would place it in his palm. I took a sip of the port and tried to keep a straight face. My mouth burned as I swallowed, my throat convulsing against the liquid. *This stuff's gone bad,* I thought. But I'd already made the effort to get the bottle, so I had to follow through. I took a less enthusiastic sip, listening to the party above. I could make out the light classical music wafting through the cherrywood speakers. I sat at the desk and loosened my tie, pressing my back against the chair. Tommy would be too busy charming the other guests to notice my absence. But the doctor wouldn't. I walked up the stairs, feeling queasy.

While the basement had been cool and smelled like dry wood with a whiff of ancient motor oil, the first floor was oppressively humid, the air a clash of perfumes and sweat. A bald man carrying a stockpot full of steaming corn speed-walked past me in the hall. The loud conversations and symphony music drove me from room to room. Inside Paul's study, a white bowl warming under halogen display lights quietly waited for me, but this evening, the door was locked. I put my ear to the door and heard a faint humming, as if people inside were having a hushed argument. A passing party guest shot me a disapproving look and I reluctantly left.

There were enough people that no one really noticed me. Some waved or tried to introduce themselves, but I just nodded and walked on like I was looking for something. By this point, I felt the liquor in my brain, and I had to concentrate to keep from stumbling. Color swirled around me, the pinks and yellows of the women's late-summer dresses.

I drifted, at the mercy of gravity and my own tired legs. Tommy was holding a snifter of grape juice, chatting with some older men. "Here's my little brother," he said, grabbing me by the shoulders. I shook free with porcine grace and fled the room. It felt like a liquid weight was coalescing in my head, weighing it down, and my neck strained to carry it. *Left foot, right, neck straight, don't panic,* I repeated to myself.

The anticipation, the crowd, the music—it all told me this party was supposed to be my first step into the adult world, but I'd screwed it up. My drunken stumbling would lead to prolonged stumbling through the years to come, and there was nothing I could do about it.

I found myself on the back porch, gripping the edge of a picnic table to remain upright. The cool breeze licked at my eyeballs as I watched the crowd inside the house through the screen door. Inside, Paul rarely paused to chat, though the guests waved and shook his hand as he passed. He was smiling, or at least doing his best. He slid open the screen door and sat across from me without saying a word. Looking back, I think he was about to ask whether I was having fun, but the answer must have been clear. There were a couple of smokers outside, but they didn't notice us. The breeze already a distant memory, humidity crept beneath my shirt. I loosened my tie again and sat on my hands, pressing them against the slats in the bench. Paul sighed and stood up slowly, trying to hide the pain in his knees. As he passed, he put his hand on my shoulder as if to say, *I know how you feel,* then returned to the crowd.

Tommy was too busy entertaining guests to remember that *we* were guests, but I knew we didn't belong and wouldn't stay much longer. Somewhere in the wilds of New Jersey, our father's search was drawing to a close. Even if he didn't find a job, Tommy and I couldn't stay in this moneyed purgatory forever.

I'd been lying in the warm grass for hours, maybe, when someone lifted and carried me into the house.

"Are you a cannibal?" I asked. The man shifted me in his arms and I heard Paul's voice.

"Truly your father's son. I hope you remember this."

I said something like, "Please don't kill me," and may have offered up my brother as an alternative. But beyond this easy betrayal, I didn't say much. The trip to my room must have taken just a few minutes.

"Damn, you're heavy," Paul said. His knees popped as he set me down on the bed. Shrill insect noises floated through the window. He put his hand on my forehead. It was huge and cold and after a few seconds everything went quiet. The sickness and tension flowed away—only calm and sleep remained.

"Left foot, right foot, head straight, don't panic," I mumbled, out of habit. He laughed quietly and left. After he flicked off the light, the room was still faintly illuminated by the tiki lights near the deck. Tommy must have been outside chatting with guests because his laughter, careless and loud, drifted up through the window.

. . .

I woke around six a.m. with a slight headache. The inside of my mouth tasted like a carcass soaked in methanol. From what I'd seen in movies, I'd expected a blinding hangover. I poured myself some cereal. It was nice eating alone. I could sit and think all I wanted without interruption. As the sun rose, I worked a little in the garden. I knew some kind of Old Testament punishment was coming but somehow wasn't worried. I'd survived the party and that was enough. No one mentioned anything at lunch and I considered the possibility that my drunkenness at the party went unnoticed. I slumped on a leather recliner in the living room, guilt sharpening my senses—upstairs, Leslie sorted through what seemed like centuries of memorabilia in the attic, throwing away so much. The doctor held court in the garden, holding tomatoes to the sky and lecturing to an invisible class. Tommy threw rocks at ducks in the pond and did pushups until he puked. None of this was unusual that summer, but now I could see the true shape of things, trace the outlines of each sad world.

My grandfather called, ostensibly to see how we were, and there was a loud buzz on the telephone line. Paul frowned when I answered our grandfather's questions in Korean, so I switched to English. "How is America?" he asked. He was really asking, *When can I join you?* His voice was tight, but only I could hear. He asked about my grades and my father, and I replied, "Grades perfect, father good," both of which were lies, since it was summer and I hadn't heard from Dad in four days. "We're having big fun here," I said, handing off the phone to Paul and leaving my grandfather to wonder why I'd started talking like a B-movie Indian. "Heap big trouble" pretty accurately described what I was carrying on my shoulders. It felt like the low hum from that long distance call never quite left my ears.

. . .

International calls were expensive back then, but maybe our grandfather's was worth it, since it expedited my father's search—or maybe Paul let slip that that during our dad's two-week absence, his twelve-year-old had to be rushed to the ER and his ten-year-old had gotten drunk. The night before my father arrived, Tommy and I pretended to clean while the Hrisaks actually cleaned. Dad would arrive in time for dinner and would share his news then. "Everything will work out." The Hrisaks seemed to genuinely believe this. My family knew it wasn't true: we'd fled a nation that was ripped in half—and we were from the good half. That night, the doctor's study was unlocked. Realizing it might be my last chance, I touched the spirit bowl and instantly regretted it. The blue lines, slightly indented, were spaced as far apart as my fingers. The surface was slightly damp, and the whole bowl vibrated quietly. When I managed to set it back into the cabinet, my hands continued its trembling.

Dinner the next day. I watched my father eat, my chubby hands gripping the table. Something had been welling in my chest for the past week. "Everything will work out" didn't change the fact that my father had returned with bad posture and a flat, joyless smile. How many people in New Jersey needed Korean interpreters? My chest tightened and I could hardly breathe as Dad cleared his throat and stood. Everyone else waited calmly. I took a few breaths, drawing nothing. My heart pounded in my ears, and I scrabbled from the room.

In the doctor's study, I stopped in front of the cabinet to catch my breath. Everyone else had shaken off their surprise and started to follow me, but I didn't care. I stood on the bottom shelf and grabbed it, the heat and glory of the bowl cradled in my hands.

"What do you have there, Jason?" my father said. Apparently he didn't know anything about pottery. Maybe he thought I was hungry and wanted cereal. "Where you going, tiger?" he asked as I exited the room. *Tie-guh.*

"Oh my God," Paul began. "Jason—"

I ran through the kitchen, pushing their hands away. Now came the real yelling and commotion. "He's lost it. Call a SWAT team," Tommy yelled. Because Princeton had lots of those.

Upstairs, in our bedroom, I scrambled out the open window, onto the gable, balancing myself with a leg on either side. It was starting to get dark out; the grass below was indigo. The stars emerged in constellations I'd never seen before. I held the bowl in both hands and caught my breath, greedily sucking in the night air.

"He's here," Leslie said. She took a step into my room. "What are you doing with that, darling?" My father jogged a little as he approached the window.

"Snipers," Tommy suggested.

That's me on the roof. I've summited Mount Princeton and know exactly what I'm doing. The bowl is between my sweating hands—it's charged somehow, the current shaking my heart until all I hear is the rush of my blood. I can see my family though the bedroom window, advancing. My feet slip a little on the shingles as I back away toward the gutter. Everything stops except the ringing in my ears. And as the world leans toward this rooftop in Princeton, anticipating my next move, I hurl down the bowl and it smashes with a crisp rattling sound, the pieces cascading onto the lawn below. The universe exhales. Then my foot slips, my leg following, and then my chest slams against the roof, my fingers scraping at the rough shingles as gravity takes over.

. . .

I don't remember the impact, or much until the hospital. In the waiting room, my father made his announcement: he'd used his connections to secure a job at a university near Toledo. The doctors made their own announcement to the family: I had a couple bruised ribs and a broken wrist. Later that evening, my father made me haul my luggage from the Hrisaks' to his car, my hospital bracelet flapping as I dragged my suitcase with one hand. Paul stayed inside, but Leslie emerged and waved as we pulled out of the driveway. I was the only one who spotted her in time to return the farewell.

The drive to Ohio reminds me of my relationship with my father, and my life in general: a winding, fevered glide punctuated by my father demanding, "Why?" *What the fuck is wrong with you?* He'd been asking since the hospital, and I still didn't have an answer. The first few times, he actually turned to face me.

I still didn't have an answer days later, after my father maneuvered the car through a small development of nearly identical single-story houses, each with green vinyl siding. It was late evening, and the road was freshly paved, the sidewalks lined with maidenhair saplings. Instinctively, I knew one of these houses was ours. In Busan, we lived in the shadow of the mountains. There was a flatness to this American neighborhood that extended to the crew-cut lawns, the grimly efficient symmetry of the cul-de-sac's layout. "This was supposed to be a surprise," our father grumbled as he pulled in front of a house.

"What?" Tommy whined, sounding like he'd just woken up. The front door flew open and in the doorway stood the silhouette of my grandfather. Even from the car, I recognized the slight stoop, hands behind his back in a vaguely martial pose. I could picture his gray stubble, his eyes shut into neat little arches as he flashed a smile. Life in postwar Korea had left him with teeth like Indian corn, but in moments like these, he didn't care who saw. He flicked on the porch light and waved to us, beckoning. He didn't know I was in a cast, or that my father was stewing in a brine of shame and confusion over his strained relationship with Paul. I realized my father meant this moment was supposed to be a *happy* surprise. He probably thought I'd ruined it.

Maybe I had—in some ways, I never left that rooftop in Princeton. Even now, I can picture the curve of that white bowl, the way it rested in my hands, begging for me to curl my fingers around the rim and slam my palms together. Smashing it brought holy silence, but I didn't consider the cost. Even as my father switched off the engine and the headlights winked out, I sat listening to the tick of the engine. My grandfather was smiling because he believed he could start anew, buoyed by the hot blood of his grandsons and the piety of his son. I wondered if the spirit I'd released by smashing the bowl would follow us across this new threshold. None of us could yet make sense of what happened in New Jersey, but I couldn't shake the notion that our time in Princeton revealed how little we understood or even liked each other. We were, in fact, broken beyond repair. As I opened the door and stepped from the car, my cast glowing in the streetlight, I wondered if we'd spend the rest of our lives gathering up the shards.

THE TIDES OF ALDERAAN

Maybe it's because he's in a church, but Jason suddenly wants to confess that he doesn't love *Star Wars*. He might not even like the movies. Any of them. Saying this out loud would be sacrilege to friends and most of the other middle schoolers. *But come on,* he wants to say. The first movie came out in the seventies. There's been so much good sci-fi since then. Honestly, the haircuts are bad. Luke is kind of whiny.

He knows he shouldn't be thinking about *Star Wars* during his grandfather's funeral. The man was an officer in the ROK Marine Corps during the war, and he deserves better. "I'm one of the few who still fit in their uniforms, so lay me out in it," he'd announce during Chuseok, then Thanksgiving, which he referred to as "Turkey Chuseok." Sometimes he'd wink at Jason, who'd always wished to be skinny. Now, his grandfather is laid in state in his crisp greenish dress uniform, a grid of colored bars pinned above the jacket pocket. Jason has only seen the uniform hanging in a closet, and the shoulders and sleeves drape a little too loosely over his grandfather's frame. Jason doesn't know what the bars signify, and of course it's too late to ask.

At home, there's an epic legacy of the man's telescopes and ham

radio antennae and model trains and *Popular Mechanics* issues waiting in the basement. Jason's brain is cluttered with questions. How
will his family manage?

Then: Luke Skywalker's adoptive parents lived on a moisture farm.
What is that, exactly? You can't eat moisture. How do you sell it?
Star Wars is such a weird cult. This is the first open-casket funeral
Jason's ever attended, and he feels uncomfortable with his family in
the front row. They have the clearest view. It's strange that there's
no choir in the church, though Mozart's Requiem Mass is playing
through hidden speakers in the ceiling. It just floats down from
nowhere, and the pew is vibrating with his father's sobs. The man
in the casket doesn't look like Jason's grandfather. His lips were
never that color.

There's one thing *Star Wars* got right: if you were awesome
enough, you returned as a blue ghost. If this were a *Star Wars* movie,
the casket would contain only the uniform. His grandfather would be
standing in front of it, glowing faintly, hands clasped in front of him.
The first thing he'd say is, *Jason, it's okay that you're not crying. I know
this is strange. But believe me, I'm missing you just as much. . . . See your
family next to you— seeing isn't the same as watching. I love you. You are
not alone in this.*

Jason realizes he's been holding his breath, and he inhales with
a vibrating, skidding noise, like a folding chair being dragged across
the floor. He's seated in his pew, and he leans forward, reaching out,
trying to brace himself against the back of a pew, except there isn't
anything in front of him, just a wide expanse of gray carpet, then a
casket and thick scent-clouds of yellow chrysanthemums.

His father notices and leans hard against Jason's shoulder,
breathing slow enough for the boy to follow. In that moment, Jason

doesn't need to look up at his father to see him. It isn't much, and this small moment of comfort feels like the most any father could do in that moment, like it's all the universe will allow. Jason sucks in another breath and thinks it's good enough. It has to be.

CLEAR BLUE MICHIGAN SKY

Sometimes, office ladies visit our scrapyard. It's better than ice cream or the blues, watching us and realizing life could be worse. So welcome to evening shift at GM: Gauntlet of Monotony to us, General Motors to you. This particular office lady is watching the cranes lift and sort hot metal pipes. It's almost like an art exhibit, kinetic sculpture, and there's a lot to admire, from the barnlike warehouses to miles of steel rails. If she waits long enough, a cargo train will steam through the yard.

Steelhead arrives as the shift begins and flicks a cigarette at the office lady's shoes. She hops back. Mr. Head is a new breed of American peasant, a punching bag of a man with a dry, cracked face and a white mustache colored from smoking. He's in his early fifties, never left Michigan and damn proud of it. "You got no business here," he says by way of hello. But if she hears, she doesn't acknowledge. I like her a little more, wish she hadn't flinched.

"She's just looking," I say.

"Who says I was talking to her?" he replies. This is the longest conversation I've had with Steelhead in months. The last one happened in the cafeteria, where our entire sector had gathered during a power outage. The cafeteria had aux power and a television to distract us. I was watching a news report about miners trapped by a cave-in when he walked over. "That's what's special about America," he said, jerking his face to the screen, where rescue workers peered into the hole and a reporter rattled off worst-case scenarios.

"What?" I asked, annoyed. I'd just dropped out of college, just started at GM. I'd started my shift hungover and now this.

"That's what makes this country special. Folks look out for each other." He nodded and stepped back as if waiting for applause. The mood was sour in the cafeteria. Things dropped as the outage continued—production quotas, bonuses, civility. It was a hot day in June, hotter with everyone in one room, and blood rushed to my face. I should have let it go, but I followed the news better than he did.

"Know what's funny about you?" I asked. "The worse this country treats you, the harder you wave your flag. Even with how often they lay you off, I bet you still drive a GM car."

"Truck," he said. He swallowed, and his throat tightened a little. How dare I impugn the beloved factory, which at this moment was literally draining our paychecks. To him, it was like I was peeing on the flag. *You dumbass kid,* his face said.

Darnell, my buddy from the paint division, pulled me back. "Come on, now." People were gathering around us to get a better view.

"Our president passed NAFTA and the union bent over and took it. Didn't you hear? GM means Going to Mexico. How long, you think? *Uno* years till Jorge gets your job? *Dos?*" I flashed two fingers like a peace sign. "Keep waving your flag, *amigo.*"

"What am I supposed to do?" He called me several *f* words. Then his neck was hot, my hands closing around gristle and bone. It was all Darnell and some others could do to pull us apart, red and coughing, before the foreman saw. Violence toward a coworker means instant termination.

The woman toes Steelhead's cigarette butt, rolls it under her shoe a couple times. She isn't from the offices. She's been here too long and she's wearing jeans. It was her shirt that threw me off, white with a round collar. She's in her fifties, one-twenty pounds, tops. "I'm your new partner," she says, her voice turning up at the end so it sounds like a question.

"Guess even the hiring folks have a quota," Steelhead says. "Another thing this company can't afford." Maybe I shook some sense into him after all. All these men in the scrapyard. I'm amazed management tolerated it this long. For a while, it was white-only, then they sent me. And now we have a woman.

I can work, the expression on her face says. But other than that, she doesn't respond. I check her papers and shake her hand when she offers it. "Paige." I should say something comforting. All this time, she's been wondering why she got sent here, who she pissed off.

Here's Slow Mike, the last member of the afternoon crew. He has doughy white skin, an epic belly, and dark gray hair buzzed into a crew cut. I wouldn't trust him for directions out of here, but he's a steady worker and we talk Red Wings during the season and off.

The four of us are standing in the heart of the scrapyard, a concrete platform the size of a high school gym, covered by a tin roof. Outside, there's scaffolding with a lighting rig—from a distance, the yard resembles a concert stage. Around us lies a square mile of windblown junk, three yellow cranes sorting everything into piles. We keep our beer hidden and the yard clean for the safety inspectors.

There's the murky smell of spent hydraulic fluid around my half of the workspace, which basically consists of a waist-high worktable.

They worked the real men in this country to death, someone grumbled the other week at a union meeting. I ponder this as I start my shift. Per usual, my worktable is upside down. One of the legs is gone, thrown across the yard. It's a sturdy table, iron, and it must take two men to dismantle it—one to hold while the other hammers. "Just day shift saying hello," I tell Paige. Of course, they leave Steelhead's alone. I've put in a report to have the whole thing rewelded, but it might be decades before the Maintenance shoprats get to it. A few weeks ago, I showed up early with a chain wrench and asked the day shift boys to kindly stop molesting my table. They filed an incident report and I got mandatory anger management. But not enough.

"Union. The word suggests solidarity, right?" I ask as I flip over the table.

"Unity," Paige replies. In the end, we all spend forty-plus hours in this stinking heap, and we all have to meet quota. Fighting outdated machinery? Check. A healthy mistrust of our corporate monarchs? Check. Budding to full-blown alcoholism? Checkcheckcheck. One would think we'd trample each other to help our fallen. But when you're struggling to fix your table, the union gathers to watch. It's folks on smoke breaks first, then bored assistant foremen. Sometimes they'll yell something helpful like "C'mon kid," or "Kid don't know his ass from a hole in the ground." During my sixty-day preunion "apprenticeship," they'd flick cigarettes at me. But now, men like Steelhead watch in silent judgment. That's what's special about GM.

. . .

As I rivet my table leg back on, another phrase runs through my mind: *Sabotage is a dismissible offense, and any persons responsible will face SEVERE legal and civil penalties.* That's the only thing I remember from the orientation manual. It seemed so absurd, like the signs on hair dryers warning Do Not Use While Bathing!!! A Beastie Boys song also came to mind. *I'm Buddy Rich when I fly off the handle.*

Paige wants to help. Our shift runs from 3:30 p.m. to 11:30 p.m. and I'm in for a long afternoon. I've fixed the worktable, so I explain the job. "I split these driveshafts. Yes ma'am, been doing it the fourteen months I've been here." They're cylindrical, thick like old cannons. I ask her, "What do they smell like?" She leans in and makes a face.

"Garbage. Like after a clambake?" Which is to say they smell like rotten flesh.

"It's my job to drill through the rivets, separate these into two smaller pieces," I tell her. This is not as simple as it sounds—in most cases, they're fused together in what I can only imagine was a spectacular wreck. Sometimes it takes a hammer and a chisel.

She still wants to help. I drop a wooden pallet on the worktable. After I stack enough disassembled shafts on it, an orbiting forklift moves the pallet to the outer yard. "Can you pick that up?" I say, nodding to a driveshaft. She bends down and gives it a good effort, even lifts one end a few inches. Eventually, she shakes her head. I lift and set it down on the table. "Know what broken chalk looks like?" She doesn't believe me, so I pull down my goggles and set the drill to a rivet. She doesn't know whether to cover her eyes or ears. I pull back the sleeve on my uniform to show off my braces. Blue, to match my uniform.

Slow Mike introduces himself. He brings her a pair of goggles and earplugs. What a gentleman. "This is Tommy," he says, motioning to me. "Tommy Gun, Tomcat."

"Stop that," I say. Mike punches me in the arm, horseplay, and jiggles his fat quickly to his side of the yard. I drill a couple rivets and when I look up, she's watching intently. I slip on the last one, the bit glancing off and tattooing the cylinder. "Want to make yourself useful?" She nods. "I don't mean to be rude, but there's not much you can do. You haven't worked long at GM, have you?" She shakes her head. I wonder what kind of work she did in the past, if any. Her hands are smooth with clear, varnished nails. Pretty as the foreman's.

"The most important thing is to look busy. Can you look really focused, maybe a little . . ." Stressed. She can, furrowing her brow. The look comes easy to her. Her hair is brownish and frizzy, which somehow enhances the expression. I empty my toolbox and hand it to her. "Walk around—anywhere in the yard, but keep that face when people come around. If anyone asks, I sent you on a critical mission." She gives a sort of salute and then she's off. I'm back to work. At the end of the shift when we're in line to clock out, Steelhead shoots me a glance that says, *Now we're both babysitters*. But I don't mind. Ninety percent of the time, it's like she's not even there.

I've learned to cruise-control through a shift, but deviations throw me off. "You said you went to college? Here in Michigan?" Paige asks. I don't remember telling her that, but I have been drinking more than usual lately. I nod, focusing on the job. But my eyes are sending little waves that say, *Back off*. She scratches her neck. "So why did you leave?" What she means is *How did a smart Oriental like you end up here?* Most of my white coworkers asked the same thing when I started, just in different ways. This question often hung unspoken in the air: a double take, an upraised eyebrow, a voice pitched up to a pitying tone.

I could pretend to not hear over the drill. I could tell her I'm here to smash and stack, not to answer personal questions. I haven't looked up, but her eyes are pressing down on the top of my head. She hates being ignored, especially by the dirty, interchangeable men she's been tossed in with. I shake my head, split the driveshaft and move it to the pallet, all without looking up.

Two more driveshafts and she could lift a Vandura with the energy she's exerting on top of my skull. "I guess I brought it up first," I say, finally looking at her. I tell her it was Parents' Day at college, a couple years ago. My father drove hours upstate to visit. And so there he was, big-shouldered in the frame of my dorm room, a few gray hairs on the back of his head. There were some flakes of plaster on his shoulders. I brushed them off, afraid someone would think it was dandruff. He said he'd been wiring a hallway light. "It needed done. End of story." I felt a little less embarrassed—no student in that building would have attempted such a task.

Standing there, my father took in the plastic furniture, the graduation party photographs my roommate and I pinned to our bulletin boards (*See, I have friends back home!*). Maybe he wondered if I was homesick. He definitely noticed the thin gray carpeting, stacked pizza boxes and mostly cleaned-up barf. The concrete hallways were in dire need of paint. *The Silence of the Lambs* had recently come out, so the poster with the surprised moth-mouthed woman hung crooked in every other room, the masking tape visible.

Instead of his usual jeans, worn-out sweater and dress shoes, he wore dark slacks I'd never seen before and a dress shirt covered by a corduroy blazer. "How often do you wash your sheets?" was all he said. My grandfather served in the ROK during the Korean War, and that earned him a golden ticket to America. He was old and tired of subsisting among the rubble, so my father gave up his life in Busan to bring us to America. Then, my father gave up everything he'd scrabbled together here just to pay my college tuition. Dad didn't seem comfortable in the dorm. A trio of international students clad in leather pants and impeccable denim jackets brushed past us and continued down the hall.

My father had been a researcher at a university in Seoul, something to do with chemicals. He'd learned English from his father's friends after the war and occasionally dabbled as a translator. That hobby became his career in America, and universities in the Midwest traded him like a farm-league player. One time, I asked why he hadn't pursued a research position, but it seemed like he didn't want to discuss it. "They think differently over here" was all he said, meaning the work culture in America is strange, the processes and logic impossibly foreign.

As I'm sitting in the office, it occurs to me that my father would never have survived at GM. The work culture here is stranger than anything in academia. For example, instead of reprimanding me face-to-face, someone anonymously filled out a form, walked it down a carpeted hallway, and handed it over to a bureaucrat, who processed it as incident report: by doing Paige's job, which is the factory equivalent of helping an old lady across the street, I was accused of "failure to follow company procedures or otherwise impeding standard work practices." When I defend myself, the lady behind the desk tells me to take my sexist attitude "back to the fifties" as she tears off my copy of the canary sheet. I tell her I wasn't alive during the fifties and she says they're sending a rep to monitor my reeducation. She actually uses the word "reeducation." Which, tragically, means everyone in the salvage yard is doomed to sobriety.

Now, we lift driveshafts to the table together. Paige gets every other rivet, even though she can barely raise the drill and her entire body shakes like she's being electrocuted. I back away to give a clear view to Steelhead, who probably filed the complaint in the first place, and our dear comrade inspector. By Friday, the PC police retreat, grumbling, but no one reassigns Paige. She's getting nosebleeds daily and has taken to tying a sweatshirt around her waist. My numbers are abysmal and someone from the plant calls me into the office. A performance complaint will appear on my record. I have fourteen calendar days to appeal. I sign my name to acknowledge receipt, pressing hard on the carbon paper.

Three weeks and Paige hasn't quit. Got to respect that. We've worked it out so mostly she passes me tools. "Chisel," I say, and it's in my hand. Now all I need is someone to dab the sweat off my forehead. On the other side of the yard, Slow Mike lights one of Steelhead's Winstons.

The final step of the process is spraying the separated parts with rust remover. I let her do that, flip them, and she does the other side. It's just a mask and an aerosol can, but she's been watching me carefully and does a thorough job. Now that she's no longer a hindrance—or, to be fair, I've stopped viewing her as one—I've noticed new things about Paige. She's five foot with a short round face and gray eyes. Her hair's reddish brown, pulled back into a ponytail. She does have kids, two sons in high school. She doesn't offer photos and I don't ask. But she needs me to know that the eldest will attend Michigan State in the fall. And part of her will escape there with him.

■ ■ ■

"She gets beat" is how women explain it around here, nodding to a female shoprat with another broken nose. "Got fed a shut-up sandwich," Steelhead would say. But you can see it in the flinch when you lean in to talk, then the shame. And the apologies, always the apologies. Paige isn't the only one sent here to work off the old man's bar tab, not in a factory town close to Detroit. Mostly, we pretend not to notice and tell ourselves we're being polite. But then there's that old blue-collar joke: What do you tell a woman with two black eyes? *Nothing, you just told her, twice.*

Right now, there's the most beautiful sky, fading lakewater to bruise, and you can see the last sunshine glint orange off the factory's rooftops. If you climb the lighting rig, you can see Detroit, but turn your head and a million taillights fly down the highways, everyone traveling somewhere lovely and exotic. Breathe deep and expand with it. But down in the steaming ruin of industry, we have our own pleasures. With a rush you feel in the hollow of your chest, the floodlights kick on and the scrapyard's a new universe of halogen and gleaming metal, highlighted caverns in the rows of stacked pipes. And it's something to behold, one's labor laid out, pallet after pallet, six rows high. "Look at that," I say to Paige and she turns her mournful gaze to the freeway. "All those cars and we made most of them." Steelhead flicks a cigarette. It arcs and bounces off the concrete, sparking when it hits the ground.

"Shouldn't we get back to work?" she says, glancing around nervously.

The next day, it's back to the heat. You find your own ways to cool off. Now that Darnell's fixed our box, we've got the Stones back, and Zeppelin, and the Guess Who. One thing we don't argue about is music. After a shift-record week of near-sobriety, rock 'n' roll is back. When you got a nice stagger worked up, the pain in your wrists, shoulders, lower back melts away while you evaporate another rivet into sparks. You got "Black Dog" or "No Sugar Tonight" washing over and the hours just roll by. You keep your numbers up, keep the bottles out of sight, and the safety fairies pretend they're not there.

"Do you like this music?" Paige asks. It's six and the civilized world is rushing back to their prefabs. I finish my MGD and open another. This beer is skunked, but I suck it down anyway. They've made quota for August, so the other side is doing calculations. If they work too fast, their quotas rise to impossible. If they work too slow, the office sends us a babysitter. It's a game everyone loses. Steelhead finds a Sharpie in his toolbox and bleeds some numbers onto a paper towel. He nods, pleased with the math, so they take a break. I don't blame them. You can actually watch the heat rise in waves, swirl off the concrete. If I wanted to, I could wring the smell of oil and hydraulic fluid from my hair. I wipe the sweat from my face and ask if Paige's ever been fishing. She nods. That's right, two sons. She puts on the mask and sprays down the stack, moving the can in a tight diagonal pattern. Her hands are less shaky, so naturally she's better at it. The storm in my head picks up speed, but I force my eyes to follow her until she's done. Slow Mike says I should go home. I open the cooler and rub a handful of ice-donuts on my head. They evaporate before they touch me and I'm dry again. Or that's what it feels like. I pop a couple in my mouth. "All these beers are skunked," I tell Mike. He tells Steelhead, who makes a shrugging motion and pops in an AC/DC cassette.

Fishing. I tell her, "My father used to listen to this kind of music when he drove during these long fishing trips to Lake Michigan.

When I was young. He wasn't really a classic rock guy, but maybe he liked the idea that all over the state, fathers were playing this music to their sons. Hey, can you play 'Free Bird'?" Steelhead turns up "Big Balls" and Slow Mike plays the air guitar as he leans down to grab a beer. "'Free Bird'!" Dad owned a red-and-white Sierra, and summer began when he put the camper shell on the back. On the drive to the lake, our fishing gear rattled in the back. And then it was the shore, two sons and their dad against the ocean, or the closest we could get to one. A seagull swooped down as I cast my line and I caught it right on the neck, reeled it in slow. I was fourteen. My father covered it with a blanket and removed the hook. He took my hands and wrapped them around the blanket. The fabric breathed like he'd created a new animal. *Throw it,* he said, and it felt like a firecracker going off in my hands as it clapped itself upward, trailing feathers and blood.

And here I am, released staggering into the world of men. "I caught a bird. No shit," I say. I'm hugging the lighting rig, dizzy as I grab another beer. Paige flinches out of my way, bumping the table's loose leg. There are maybe twenty-four driveshafts on it and the whole setup shakes—watching it, something bubbles up in my stomach. I step out of the way, catching my hand on the lighting rig. I look down and it's bleeding. Paige apologizes. I suck at the blood, the taste mixing with the skunked beer.

"Tell me you're okay," she says. I'd really like to, but my legs are carrying me to the bathroom. Fast.

"'Free Bird'!"

I heave in the stall, stumble to the sink, and splash some water on my face. In the mirror, I see the man at the urinal staring at my boots. I turn and he examines my face without really seeing me. "Christ, you stink," he says.

"What about it?" I reply, the words running together even though I'm trying to enunciate. Christ, this headache. My hair sticks to the back of my neck, heavy. It's the only thing I can feel right now.

"Some of you out there are trying so hard," he says quietly, looking over his shoulder.

"What about it?" I repeat. For a second, the pity in his voice hangs in the air. I'm about to apologize, to tilt my head and listen to his advice.

"Some of you need to try harder," he says, leaning a little into the urinal.

The grass is wet. Roll. The world flashes red and I'm afraid to open my eyes. Someone performed an autopsy on me and forgot to put everything back. There is a gaping chasm where my stomach should be.

"You okay, sir?" someone says hours later. It's the paperboy. Now I'm curled up in the patio chair on my porch. Last night, I probably couldn't get the key into the slot.

"What day is it?" I ask.

"Tuesday." That's good. "Free Bird": I remember parts of Monday.

"How old are you, paperboy?"

"Um, thirteen."

"Wait," I say. His father, waiting in the van, rolls down the window. Whatever happened to paperboys on bicycles? "What do you want to be when you grow up?"

"I'm just thirteen," he says, backing away. I follow him to the van. He gets in and slams the door.

"You got a great boy there," I say to the driver, who shifts into reverse but doesn't press the accelerator yet. "Don't screw it up," I say to the boy. I reach through the open window to shake the father's hand, but he pushes me to the ground and drives away.

I should have called off. My car is missing a headlight and someone else's paint is scratched ugly across my door. I should be hiding. The foreman shakes his head when I pass him to clock in. There's a sign-up sheet for overtime and I sign my name next to Saturday and Sunday, giving him the best *f-you* smile I can manage. I don't turn around, but I know he's watching me every step down the hallway. Nobody else wants to look at me.

Down in the yard, I apologize to Paige, who doesn't respond. There's paperwork sitting on the belly of my upside-down work-table. My performance complaint appeal is being considered—an inspector arrives next week.

Mike doesn't help reassemble the table and I don't ask. Nobody's happy that I'm bringing another babysitter around. Paige and I work in silence the first few hours, then she asks me how old I am. Nineteen, I tell her. She lets out a whistle like I said eleven. "Why aren't you in college?" We lift a driveshaft and she watches me dissolve rivets into donuts of shredded metal. The whistle sounds and it's first break. I usually go to the cafeteria and talk to Darnell and company, but today I lean against the lighting rig and close my eyes. Paige turns the radio down.

Slow Mike appears carrying a rivet gun. The hose drags behind him. "Steelhead says you can trade if you want."

"He can have my rivet gun when he pries it from my cold, dead fingers. Tell him that." Mike nods. He opens his mouth and hesitates. "What else did Steelhead say, Mike?"

"It's mean. He said if you need diapers—"

"Tell Steelhead to keep it up and I'll see him in the parking lot."

Mike walks over and delivers the message. Steelhead makes a saluting gesture and plays "Free Bird" on the stereo. He's been waiting all day for this.

Back to work. I name the college I attended as Paige and I return to the worktable. I know I can tell her the story or wait for her to ask smaller questions in her meek, polite tone. It's unsettling how much that tone irritates me. I can picture the different ways she'll nudge me toward the topic—the same way she made me talk about growing up in Ohio and Michigan. She wore me down until I taught her how to use almost everything in my toolbox, even though I doubt she'll ever use wire cutters or a micro torch. So I give in and finish the story.

Flashback to Parents' Day at college. After my father inspected my dorm, a girl presumably returning from the shower skipped down the hall wearing just flip-flops and a blue towel. We excused ourselves and I walked him across campus to show off my classrooms. He watched a bunch of guys my age play Frisbee on the lawn. Girls sunned themselves while reading Kant and Spinoza.

There was a class in session, but the doors were open, as usual. "That's your classroom?" my father asked quietly, leaning to peer into the lecture hall. I nodded and told him that's where I had Intro to Astronomy.

"It's like a movie theater. There must be over a hundred students in there," he said. He stepped closer, hovering in the doorway. "They're reading the paper," he said, gesturing at the students in the back. "They're actually doing the crossword." He shook his head and, turning away, said of the professor, "Who wears a bowtie?" I made an apologetic noise and accompanied him to his truck. We didn't speak much. He seemed overwhelmed by the energy of the campus, the tides of students as classes began and ended. I can only imagine the university he worked at was established in a Confucian tradition: rigid hierarchies of principal investigators and assistants, reverence for the past, respect for one's professors. By leaving Korea, he'd spared my brother and me two years of compulsory military service. "They think differently over here," he'd once said. On the way home, he'd stop at a Dunkin' Donuts and chew on the fact that his sacrifices over the years had lifted me to this campus. He'd blow on his coffee and tell himself it was all worth it.

"And that was the beginning of the end," I tell Paige. "About a month later, I arrived late to class for the third or tenth time and kind of slumped in the back. I was sick, and my roommate had spent the night clicking away at his word processor, so I'd gotten little sleep. When the professor handed out a pop quiz like I was in junior high, I just wrote my name, turned it over, and left."

Paige says nothing. She's wearing that worried expression, but now it's tinged with a timeless motherly pity. It's worse than Steelhead's judging contempt. "And then, as soon as I was outside the classroom, I realized I'd left my backpack and books under my chair. I couldn't bring myself to walk back in and get them. Can you imagine?" I add this bit to lighten the mood, but her expression doesn't change.

"Do you think it's still there? Your backpack?"

I return from lunch and my drill's not working, so I borrow Darnell's. After second break, *his* drill's not working. The bit has actually eaten into the chuck. Neither of us has seen this before, but he still can't help busting my balls. "One-man wrecking crew," he says. Maintenance fixes my drill. Something about the wires, but Darnell's is beyond repair. I promise to buy him a new chuck, even though he says to forget it. On the way home, I buy it anyway. Eighty dollars for that one little part. Good thing I signed up for overtime.

My buddy Sue, who works in the cafeteria, is seven months pregnant. This makes her tender toward Paige, who sometimes visits the cafeteria with me. "You ever wonder why she doesn't eat with you?" Sue asked. This was yesterday, and I hadn't. "That woman eats in the bathroom. In the stall. You can *hear* her." Sue dumped scalloped potatoes over my pork chops. "In her lunchbox, it's her comb that rattles when she walks. I've seen her a couple times take it out and sort of brush her hair with it. I tell you, it's a damn shame. And the guy that drops her off—*mean*." She was talking like I didn't already know and then it hit me. *What are you gonna do about this?* was what she was really saying.

"Why the bathroom?" I asked.

"So she can't talk to nobody or *tell*," she said as if I hadn't been listening. A few people lined up behind me, so I stood off to the side.

"Goddamn. I don't like going in those bathrooms even to—"

"All right," she said. "But you promise me you will find a way to help that woman." Later, during Sunday overtime, it's just me and Paige—even the crane operators are home. The doors to their cabs swing open. It's 5:30 p.m., lunch, and she's eating in the open yard. It's so quiet all you can hear is the rustling tarps that trap the wind and shake. In the distance, the cab shop sounds like a riot in a faraway zoo.

She hands me a plate—five sticks of celery filled with peanut butter and raisins. "No thanks," I say. Won't sit with my coffee and caffeine pills.

"I made them for you," she insists. Rough weekend—there's a bruise on her temple and a little dried blood in her hair. "The raisins spell your name," she says. Seeing that bruise softens something in me, and now it starts to ache. The letters got shaken a little, but *Tommy* is still there.

"They're really good," I say. She's somehow removed the strings. "Never had it like this before." She nods and eats her peanut butter sandwich, watching the bandage on my hand.

"So, you left school because of a pop quiz?" she asks.

"On top of everything else. It felt like I'd been herded into a large . . . playpen and given busywork." She gestures to the yard as if to say, *And what do you call this?*

"A high-paying job. You know how much I'll make in overtime today."

"You could be somebody."

"I am somebody. I can prove myself here as well as anywhere."

"You could really do something with yourself."

"All right," I say, meaning, *Enough.* She stops—for about a second.

"Have you seen the campus at Michigan State? It is nicer than nice. My Jeff and later Brian are going to be the first in our family to go to higher education. Ever." We've almost filled a pallet with salvaged metal. *Look at this,* I want to tell her. This is *work.* You can heft it, add it up at the end of the day. I want to take her up the lighting rig, show her the stacks and stacks of driveshafts and say, *Look, we fucking did this.*

I take a deep breath. I could really use a drink. "I didn't mean any offense. I'm sure Michigan State is a great school."

"They're good boys. They'll do well."

"Go Spartans. I'm okay here. I really am." She looks at me. "Look, my father went to college. Worked at one. We grew up in houses with uneven floors and black mold. He had his fate and I'm working on mine."

"Fate," she says flatly, and looks away toward something I'll never see. I can tell this discussion isn't over. Maybe if her face wasn't bruised, maybe if she didn't shy away when I lean in to talk, I could say what's in my heart: *If you want to save yourself, you can't do it through me.*

It's too quiet. There's a pile of industrial hose clamps at my feet. I grab one. It feels nice in my hand, even better when I throw it. "They belong over there anyway," I tell her, pointing out the other piles. "They're going to melt all this down," I say as I throw another one. I aim at the cranes, but they're too far away.

"Where will they go after we ship them out?" She points to the stack of disassembled driveshafts.

"Never thought about it."

She picks up a clamp, testing its weight. "Everybody's got a dream. My Jeffy has baseball. Full scholarship, maybe play for the Whitecaps someday." She leans back, draws up her knee like a pro and fires. The metal ring bounces off the pipes with a clean ping and spins when it lands.

"Nice." I ask if she ever played in a league and she just laughs. Throws another. Ticking sounds echo through the yard.

Well, the cops haven't hauled me away for DUI and there's nothing in the papers. I guess I'm in the clear. I still feel more dead than alive, even though it's been a few days and I haven't—well, I've had one beer. I should take a day off, but I shudder to think who Paige would have to work with.

I arrive at the yard and in my mind, a red flag pops up: today is my Performance Complaint Appeal Day. The inspector's butt is weirdly square, possibly from sitting. He has a walkie-talkie so Get Movin' can eject me from the premises soon as they find a reason.

This place has a million stories—family men turning a production line into a crime scene with blood-slicked metal, sparks, tubes spewing oil and air. Any vet from the cab shop to the paint division can tell you stories. It's the rules, the heat, the monotony. Sooner or later, no amount of Zeppelin or whiskey can hold it back. *Cryin' won't help you, prayin' won't do you no good.*

I tell the inspector I don't know why my rivet gun and drill have been acting up. It's not a bid for attention, I'm not mad at GM. I love General Motors like I love Garth Brooks and the flag. But lately, everything I touch seems to break. Yesterday, I took a swing at a driveshaft and the head of my hammer flew off.

"Gremlins," the man mutters. But no, he hasn't seen anyone messing with my toolbox. I've got a hot drill on my lap, tools in my hands, and a screwdriver in my mouth. I ask if he could please toss me some electrical tape. "Not my job," he says.

And today's a scorcher. The other definition for "August" means something worthy of reverence, and this heat is something you need to respect. It butts against you, wears you down like a boxer's jag.

Baseball, schmaseball. Here's my recurring daydream. I'm standing in the middle of Four Door. It's big as Tiger Stadium, and, by God, they've finally cleaned it. The floor looks like it's made of glass. Roger Smith and the foreman—even Sloan's ghost, glowing like a dead Jedi—are there. Darnell, Mike and Sue as well, dressed in denim tuxedos with their hair combed. For salvaging useful material from the jaws of chaos, our overlord Roger Smith hands me a trophy. It's gold plastic, a spiky-haired Calvin peeing on the Ford logo. They want a speech, and suddenly, I'm being carried on my coworkers' shoulders. Aloft, the heavy marble base rises toward the lights. Someone raises the microphone to my mouth. I clear my throat and tap it. There's one figure in the background, parting his way through the crowd. I squint and lean forward a little. Of course it's my father. I can't see his face, but I really want to. *It's an honor to receive this award. Really. I couldn't have done it without—*

"What award?" Paige asks. She looks concerned, but I wave it off.

He sees everything, the inspector. He has a little clipboard. Probably just doing a crossword, but Steelhead moseys over and confers with him. After first break, someone's soldered my toolbox lock shut. I trudge down to Paint to borrow Darnell's sledgehammer. This heat, and of course there's no breeze. I make my request ("Feel free to break and buy me a new hammer") and I'm off. Jesus, it's a hot one. I also borrow a pair of lock cutters ("Don't ask why I have these") and it feels good to watch them bite the lock. Someone took my micro torch and Allen wrenches. I tell the inspector to add that to his notes. He does, or at least he adds something. My instinct is to defend myself, but I can't think of anything to say. Besides, right now, it's a numbers game and my numbers aren't moving.

Paige accidentally knocks my water bottle over. I pick it up, two piss-warm sips left. She's really sorry, but I tell her it's okay. Christ, it's hot. Nobody'll want this driveshaft, not after I've blessed it with Darnell's big black hammer. Paige tells me she heard about a new scholarship GM's offering and I cut her off by getting back to work. This cylinder's jumping all over the yard, rolling, and it occurs to me that my shoulders are designed to swing like this. I gather it up and send it all down. Thor himself couldn't do better. Sounds like an unholy orchestra as it leaps and bounces off the concrete. The inspector's watching me the way people watch burning buildings.

Again. "Bring me another." I'm sliding a driveshaft from the table when something gives. There's a sickening crack as my worktable gives out. The pallet splinters and the driveshafts fall, bouncing off the ground in a dull metallic chord. The world drops and takes me with it. There are metal tubes where my legs used to be. I ponder this as if watching from a distance. This asphalt should be searing my back and legs, but I can't feel it. I'm getting up and they're trying to stop me, grabbing my arms while the crotch of my uniform spreads black. And here comes the shouting. Beneath my uniform, I picture a stringy white mass where my balls used to be, dripping down my legs.

Paige is crying and pulling at me. I pull back, mostly to get away from her. Steelhead's saying, "Listen, the table fell sideways, most of the heavy stuff went past you." I can stand, even though he hollers, "Don't move!" I can walk. Against my better judgment, I reach into my boxers and everything's intact. Part of the pallet must have cut into my thigh, but not an artery. Slow Mike pulls Paige away, sort of pets at her head.

I'm walking it off, in small circles like Steelhead says. I grab the light rig to hold myself up and tools rain down around me. Steelhead hands me his water bottle and I suck it down.

"Over here," the inspector says. I look over, slow motion, hair whipping into my eyes. There's my micro torch. Under Paige's purse. She freezes. Then she's back to crying, sort of hugging herself. I walk toward my toolbox and the inspector glances at the torch, then the table. He taps his clipboard against his leg. "Well, here's your gremlin," he says. The complaints I blamed on Steelhead. The broken tools.

"Well, I guess it wasn't just day shift having fun with me," I say, stumbling toward her. She flinches as usual but keeps her back straight as she faces me. "Was it funny? Was it a good time? And the whole time pretending to *be my buddy?*" I get louder.

"It wasn't all me. Okay, I just—I'm sorry. You know I didn't mean to hurt you. You just can't stay here. You need to go," she says. I stumble a little, not hearing her. *She wanted the pallet to fall on me.* I don't realize I've hit her until she's on the ground, her face turned away. Mike's yelling and people are saying not to move her, something about the neck. I exhale, ignoring the sharp pain in my knuckles. Sweat drips into my eyes, burning, then down my face.

They're carrying me now, all I can see are the factory's metal walls rushing by and Steelhead's boots. There's beef jerky on the inspector's breath. He's gripping my arm hard, Steelhead on the other side. My feet drag. "Wait," I say.

"You just put your hands on a woman, kid," Steelhead says. The inspector's walkie-talkie mumbles static. The hallway's dark until I hit sunlight again. I'm in motion and tumbling forward through the parking lot. Somewhere in the factory, paramedics are scrambling toward Paige, and someone's probably calling the cops. As I open my driver's-side door, the rush of raw heat sears my face. Paige must have gotten the idea when she saw me cut my hand. She stacked her tough love but couldn't control how it fell. If I could, I'd tell her, *Paige. I am so sorry. It wasn't me that hit you. I don't know who that person was.*

That static roars in my head as my car flies down the highway. As God sees it, a small, silver car flashing down I-75. Someday, my time in the union will feel like a fever dream. Paige will have forgiven me, my father will have forgiven me, and as I flick my new college ID between my fingers, I'll remember everything I don't miss about the factory. The phrase "second act" seems bright and durable as plastic.

That's the furthest my imagination can go right now. The cops might be waiting at my apartment, so I pass the exit.

Pushing away thoughts of my leg and the red pooling in my vinyl seats, I remember the last time I stood on the banks of the Detroit River next to my father. It was late evening and we were fishing for walleye. As usual, I hadn't caught a thing, and the long day, the dying light bouncing off the waves, the shrill buzz from the forest wore me down. As I stared into the water, I imagined what a fish must feel when it's pulled from the water—the intense rush as gravity turns upside down and the world drips away. That flash of light so bright it obliterates everything. Standing on that shore that day, I longed for that kind of release. Now, pressing the pedal and leaning into the car's acceleration, I'm beginning to understand what that light means—for that walleye and for me.

INDESTRUCTIBLE

He carefully prints "Steve Han" on the attendance sheet, even though it's not his real name, the one his mother repeated singsong as he took shape in her belly. "Steve" is easy to remember, easy to pronounce. Steve is the name of someone who plays well with others. His old name is preserved in the family register in South Korea, and he's happy to leave it there, as sturdy and patient as an earthenware jar. He passes the sheet to the teens in the row below him, who are debating Wi-Fi allergies. "No, EHS is for real. That lady in France was getting headaches and nausea and had to, like, move into the forest. Next year, it's going to be in the official manual . . . the one doctors use for diagnosis. Then, people with EHS will quality for disability."

"The DSM," Steve wants to whisper, but they've apparently moved on. A tall kid in a red baseball cap whips out his phone. He has strangely long sideburns—they're almost muttonchops.

"Any word on when the disability manual gets published?" The row of young men consult their phones but find nothing. "The Wi-Fi in here sucks," one of them mumbles, and someone replies, "That French lady should move in here."

Steve pictures someone living in this classroom, which is more of an auditorium. It's quiet enough, in the basement of a tall lime-stone building on a university campus near Toledo. In a sense, this room is his home from 10:00 to 11:50 a.m. Tuesdays and Thursdays. The purple carpet hides stains well enough, and one can hook a laptop up to the projector. The professor is using the screen to explain conceptual graphs, but one could easily beam a movie, invite a few friends over. The room's two hundred seats are filled to capacity, and each could double as a bed—there are dozens of students sleeping in them, even in the front row, mere feet from the professor.

When Steve was a teenager enrolled in Seoul National University, wearing a hat would have been unthinkable. Napping in front of your professor would have been tantamount to starting a food fight at a funeral reception. At times like this, Steve is hyperaware of being the oldest man in the room. The professor, a thin bespectacled Caucasian with an unruly dandelion-puff of gray hair, is probably in his late forties, and pointedly ignores the ocean of disrespect before him. Steve himself is tempted to smack the boys in the row ahead of him, who are busy entering reminders on their phones to have a doctor confirm their newfound allergy.

Steve realizes he's lost his place in the lecture. ECON 2810 isn't related to his major (Chemical Engineering), but it's a required course, and anything can be interesting and useful if approached with an open mind. And focus—he's not going to think about the teens in front of him racing other deadbeats to declare a fake illness. He hasn't needed the calculator on his desk, either, so he won't think about it, even though it's a Moon Electronics graphing calculator, purchased by his eldest, Tommy, who was thrilled to see the old man heading back to college. The projector is probably made by Moon Electronics, and there are undoubtedly Moon Electronics components in the phones the teenagers are now using to check their emails. Avoiding the specter of Edward Moon is as impossible as avoiding Wi-Fi, it seems.

Moon was an electronics tycoon about Steve's age, and undoubtedly the most successful Korean in America. Moon came from a wealthy family but arrived in the States suspiciously bereft of money or connections. Koreans said his name with a mix of admiration and disdain: *Edward (fucking) Moon.* He was, chiefly, an inventor—Steve pictured him in a basement workshop soldering a motherboard for the ninetieth time while his daughters toddled above him on the living room floor. In the eighties, Korean electronics were largely ignored or eclipsed by the Japanese, and each time Moon Electronics released a quirky new radio or video camera, the company sank a little deeper into bankruptcy.

In a serendipitous encounter no one could have ever foreseen, a music reporter asked Billy Idol, "How are you still punk rock?" Idol gave his famous sneer, grabbed the Moon MX-350 recorder from the reporter's hand, and smashed it on the ground, grinding it against the asphalt with his boot heel.

"That's how," Idol said. For most people, that was the story, but the fact that the recorder survived the experience was not lost on journalists. Months later, Moon turned Idol's quip into an ad campaign, *"That's how indestructible we are,"* and the rest was history.

Feeling less than indestructible, Steve quietly unzips his backpack and slides the graphing calculator into it before turning back to the professor's presentation. The glowing charts floating above the students' heads depict peaks and valleys, bell curves. Following the upward trajectories, Steve thinks of the campus, with its bell towers and comically large fireplaces. How it's awash in money, as are many of the students—the boys slouching in front of Steve dress casually in jeans and vintage tees, but anyone watching carefully can tell: these boys take in the world like they own it. When you spend the first eighteen years of your life rolling in money, the smell never quite washes out.

Steve contemplates distribution patterns, the way everything shakes out. Back when Korean electronics were a joke, Edward Moon's failure was the likeliest punchline. But Steve isn't laughing— he wants answers. What possessed the man to keep going? How many more tried his approach and failed? The students around him rustle as they rouse themselves to stuff their books into backpacks. The professor frowns and changes the slide. Fifteen minutes remain in the class. Steve's immigrant brain knows America is full of money—it sleeps beneath the campus lawns, it bursts from the sky with each peal of a church bell, it tumbles and rolls through storm drains. Why was it drawn to some but so much more elusive for others? Steve considers buying a tape recorder—if he could follow all of the professor's lectures, maybe he could catch the secret, too.

STOP HITTING YOURSELF

I

Every year, the Boy Scouts of America throw a delightful weeklong festival called Jamboree. Scouts from all over the nation gather and attend workshops to earn merit badges. I first heard of it when I was ten; by the time I turned eleven, it was painfully clear that the only summer camp my dad could afford was Ohio's version of Jamboree. Instead of camping next to scouts from Hawaii and New Mexico, we got boys from Dayton and Youngstown. I was not looking forward to it. I hated being a Boy Scout. Also, there would be other Asians there, possibly other Korean Americans. My father, brother, and I were from an all-white town and I enjoyed the small thrill of being exotic.

Our father stressed acting white. Had we settled elsewhere, this could have worked out beautifully: I picture us sitting in wicker lawn chairs, sipping umbrella drinks as our friends cheer their favorite racehorse to victory. But we'd immigrated from South Korea to a small town near Toledo and our father worked as a lowly research assistant at a local college. Where we lived, being white meant country music and sports. For my fourteen-year-old brother Tommy, this meant football. Which combined his two favorite things: hitting people and being rewarded. Before long, America rewarded him with weirdly defined muscles. There are only two types of fourteen-year-olds who have bulging triceps, and both are breathing heavily in a dark alley. I joined the Boy Scouts because I liked being away from my brother.

And my father. He had the gelled hair, parted to the side, and tortoiseshell spectacles of a professor in the background of a sci-fi movie, and he dressed well enough in short-sleeved dress shirts and striped ties. But the truth was, he was the lowly Oriental lab assistant who wore his "uniform" at home during the summer. No one, not even his sons, knew him as the man who'd sacrificed his marriage and his career to immigrate. And for the next week, most campers wouldn't know me as the kid whose single dad has the thick accent. I wouldn't have to throw away lunches made of "weird food" such as pickled daikon and fried rice. My hands practically trembled as I imagined myself as the chubby, dark-haired kid graciously accepted in the end partly because he'd stuck out so much at first.

My underwear and T-shirts were neatly folded in my pack, waiting patiently as I ate breakfast. Dad was outside loading the van. My brother sat at the table pretending to read the newspaper and probably said something like *Have fun at Girl Scout camp*. I probably called him a bastard and he probably attacked me. He was strong, two years older, and I was fat: if you're male and have a brother, you know what this means. At that age, he liked to throw me to the ground, take off one of his socks, and wrap it around my head, trying to tie it in a knot. This may have happened that morning.

"Boy, Dad's *shuuure* gonna miss you, Gayson. Your asthma and your bed-wetting."

I told him it was "Jason," as he well knew, and added, "I'll see you in hell, Tommy." I said this a lot when I was eleven.

It was a three-hour drive to the camp. My friends Mike and Clay sat in the back of the van with me. There was another kid with us, Jonathan. He was new, so of course we only included him when the scoutmaster forced us to. He played a video game. This was before cartridges and 3-D. Back then, a video game consisted of a plastic case, a motor, and a scrolling plastic sheet. It made an annoying whir like a camera rewinding, but the van mostly drowned it out. I was too cool to acknowledge my dad, too cool to think of anything else once Clay told us about the Rifle Shooting merit badge. Of course, we had to go to Rabbit Raising and Leatherwork stations, but none of them compared. "Twenty-two calibers," Clay said. Bolt-action, motherfuckers.

For those who have never fired a gun, I can't fully explain the attraction. It's not a rush of power, it doesn't make you feel like a god. It's not about violence—it's about the light smell of oil when you work the bolt to chamber a round. The smooth wood stock nudging you in the shoulder after each shot, a crisp report of cause and effect. After a few hundred rounds, there's this odd peaceful feeling as the world shrinks so it's just you, the target, smoke, and the promise of a bull's-eye.

They taught us gun safety, of course—that was probably the point of the merit badge. And of course it was supervised, on a gun range far away from camp. But we eventually got to shoot. A .22 round could fit inside most pen caps, but they were rockets to us. Bolt-action rifles, as I said, American-made, and if I remember correctly, you loaded seven rounds in a magazine, pulled the bolt, and fired downrange at paper targets. We must have looked like tiny soldiers with our beige uniforms and rifles. Readying ourselves, we leaned behind a wooden shelf at the range, and beside us were small dividers that held coffee cans full of ammo. Coffee cans—I'll never forget the heft of a tin can brimming with death.

The sixth and final day of camp, there was water in the tents from an overnight storm and our packs were mildewing. The novelty had worn off especially for the city kids, but we were all tired of eating hot dogs and campfire eggs off tinfoil. Had my father strolled past our tent carrying a tray of pungent kimchi or barbecued pork belly, I would have sprinted to it before noticing the other scouts holding their noses and waving away fumes of garlic and red bean paste. Taking in his slowly deflating posture, the tremble in his arms as he stoically held out the tray, his expression imploring, *Just try it, kids, it's better than Chinese*, I would have made a point of walking to the grill and biting into a soggy cheeseburger.

If there was a merit badge for shitty behavior, I wouldn't have been the only recipient. Jonathan, the little fucker playing video games on the drive to camp, was in my troop and also in my noon Rifle Shooting class. On the last day of camp, he stole a handful of bullets from the range. Little .22 shells, I bet they rattled pleasantly in his beige shorts' pockets. No one knows why he did that, and no one knows why later that night he walked up to our campfire and tossed them in. If there's ever a campfire with young boys around it, someone's always throwing something to the flames. No one noticed the bullets. At first.

Here's how a .22 bullet works: after the trigger is pulled, a striking pin hits the flat bottom of the cartridge. This ignites the gunpowder; the explosion propels the lead slug down the barrel. But when you throw a bullet into a fire, it settles, sits calmly, and explodes. The heat warps the lead, which fragments into shrapnel when the powder ignites.

So there I was, sitting by the campfire, sipping orange astronaut-Tang from an aluminum canteen and singing "If I Had a Hammer." Popcorn! I looked up from my little spiral-bound songbook to be greeted by molten shards of lead. The world shut off like an old TV and then I was in the hospital. "Those fragments look like teeth," my father said, examining the glowing X-ray of my skull. Little canines— doctors are still afraid to remove them.

I don't know what happened to Jonathan, whether charges were filed or not. Sometimes, when I'm fighting through another weeklong migraine or waiting in some therapist's office, I wonder why Jonathan threw that bullet into the fire. *What did he want?* As if any motive could be distilled to a single sentence. Maybe it was a science experiment, an attempt to bypass that clumsy delivery system of wood and metal, get right to the result. I imagine him digging his fingers into the can, feeling all that ribbed lead . So many possibilities, so many different paths they could take. Most of the time I can forgive him.

This concludes the most interesting chapter of my biography. I used it on prospective friends in high school and later in bars. "Really? You drank ten beers at your Alpha Sigma Pi party last night? One time, at Boy Scout camp . . ." But nowadays, I rarely talk about the bullet. I got tired of people looking for the scars (just one, a tiny white spot on my forehead near the hairline). I shrunk when I told it—became the story, and people tired of it. Also, buried in adulthood was the newfound realization of my own mortality. The bullet in my cerebral cortex was a prophecy of decline and madness, the scar a tiny memento mori. I stopped talking about the bullet, but how could one not obsess over it?

With all this talk of bars and bullets, you may have forgotten my ethnicity. There was a time I'd forgotten it myself, and that's what the second part of this story is about. My father was born in South Korea, a charming nation stalwartly facing nuclear annihilation. Kim Jong Il, missiles—you know the story. It's something they don't think about it until it flares up. It's like loss, an entire nation gone at the end of the war. The North severed at the thirty-eighth parallel, it returns unexpectedly now and then like the pain of a phantom limb. South Korea, *my* South Korea, felt much the same when it returned to me. Between us was a bullet, an ocean, and the mazy passage of time, but sooner or later, everything returns.

II

At his father's funeral, Bruce Lee—*the* Bruce Lee—crawled screaming down the church aisle on his hands and knees. This was the custom: to beg forgiveness, penance for being absent when his father died. Bruce Lee was twenty-five.

At twenty-two, I'd done my share of screaming and crawling, and now, armed with a bachelor's degree in communications and forty thousand in debt, I'd been released into the world, except without the trauma that shaped Bruce Lee. My father was still alive. "I'm surprised you made it this far," my brother said to me at my college graduation. My therapist and I discussed this incident for weeks and finally decided to pretend I didn't have a family. It was supposed to be a trial period, but a few days after its one-year anniversary, I called the house.

"Tommy," I said.

"Who is this?" he asked. I hung up and ignored how bad my hands were shaking.

This continued for weeks, and one Friday evening he showed up at my apartment. I was living in a studio apartment in Newark, where I worked as a receptionist for a law firm. The buzzer rang, I looked out my window, and there was Tommy, loitering on my front porch and probably wondering how many of my neighbors had guns tucked in their waistbands. I lived on the third floor and appeared so quickly it startled him.

Time had been generous. I didn't know where he'd been, but he hadn't spent the past two years on a couch drinking vodka and procrastinating. He was tall and thick like our father—his face filled out in that broad Korean way. His hair was longer, pulled back in a ponytail. It reminded me of how some Native American men wear theirs. He was clad in all black: leather jacket, jeans, and a pair of classic Wayfarers.

"You're mocking me," I didn't say, looking him up and down.

"You're a mess," he didn't say, and I silently thanked him for that. My apartment was in the broken-glass section of town and he seemed eager to head inside, become less of a target.

"I've, uh, been . . ." I stumbled over the words for a moment. *I've been looking . . .* We hugged stiffly and I couldn't tell if his thumping pats on the back were sarcastic or not.

"You look like shit," he said. I locked the door to the apartment building and walked over to his car, an orange Dodge Dart. I opened the door to the passenger side. He got in the driver's seat and the gang members across the street pushed themselves to a standing position, brushed off the stairs they'd been sitting on, and ambled toward us.

"Drive," I said, leaning back against the leather headrest. The car smelled like stale sweat and Big Mac farts.

"I just drove for nine hours."

I said I had something to show him. I had a vision of a special kind of road trip—something important would happen once we were in motion. We could figure out the logic afterward.

"What are we doing here?" Tommy asked. I'd driven the last few hours and we ended up spending the night at a bed-and-breakfast in Connecticut. I was wearing the same outfit I'd answered the door in: khakis and a navy-blue V-neck tee. Tommy was modeling an undershirt and a pair of nylon shorts he'd found in the trunk. We were seated in the living room downstairs around a thick oak table with a white lace tablecloth. The elderly white couples sported Peter Pan collars and polyester slacks and tried not to stare at us.

"Delighted to have you. Don't get much diversity around here," they didn't say, sipping their coffee.

"Gas. Do you know how much it costs?" Tommy asked.

"We're watching the leaves turn," I said, mostly to the small crowd sitting at the table.

"It's August," he said. The manager brought our food: Tommy had scrambled eggs on toast and I had the eggs Benedict. I washed mine down with three mugs of coffee and told the manager she was an exquisite cook. The coffee didn't seem to affect me. They cleared the plates, but no one left the table.

"Answer the question," Tommy said.

"Think about this: people with bullets in their heads usually have something in common," I said, drawing out the first few words.

"Death," Tommy replied. The room fell silent.

"Living ones, though. Think about it. Some act of violence, some unspeakable tragedy. They're survivors. Capital S. Survivors."

"Throwing bullets into a fire isn't—?"

"That was chance. Not directed specifically at me. Not cocked and aimed, not *Get on your knees, fool, or I'll—*"

"Why are we here?" Tommy asked. I pulled the Identity Chart from my wallet, written on a sheet of folded notebook paper. It was something my therapist and I made. I held it up. "Survivors have people they can go to. Support groups. People like them. Did you notice I'm the only one in my neighborhood—"

"Your 'hood? Frankly, I'm surprised . . . ," he sang out cheerfully, then stopped. *Surprised you made it this far.* I put the chart back in my wallet. Someone coughed. We finished our coffee and left.

III

Drive. White clapboard houses with turrets and stone churches with red doors slid by as we made our way through southern Connecticut on our way back to Jersey. Wild mustard and burdock sprang from asphalt lots beside the rural highway. Tommy had been driving for a few hours and it was about two o'clock. The conversation wobbled back to the topic of destinations. "There's nothing in Rhode Island, trust me," he said.

"Lobsters."

"Speaking of which, I choose where we eat lunch. You picked that gay hotel," he said.

"Gay? Was the bed-and-breakfast *gay*? I didn't know that—"

"Here," he said, slowing as we passed a Korean restaurant at the edge of a strip mall. He turned the car around and pulled up next to it. It looked expensive.

"How much money you got?" he asked.

"Check the door. Do they take cards?"

"Yeah," he said, squinting at the door.

"I kind of wanted spaghetti." Actually, I wanted to find an

expensive Italian restaurant in the hopes that Tommy would cover the bill. It turned out he worked as an industrial designer.

"That's interesting," he said, the Korean flyers flapping and the bells on the restaurant's door jingling as he swung it open.

The restaurant's lobby had a large fish tank and a bulletin board filled with religious pamphlets written in Hangul: blunt, austere lines and circles compared to China's pictograms or Japan's numerous alphabets.

Inside, everything was earth-toned. We'd arrived during the quiet pause between lunch and dinner. The hostess beamed a warm *Welcome, tourists* smile at us. For the first time in the trip, Tommy seemed at ease, joking with the hostess as she led us to our table. She pointed at the paintings and sculptures as if we were touring a condo we'd just bought. Finally, she seated us in the back of the restaurant in what seemed like a reserved section, surrounded by a carved wooden railing. Our table was ornate, carved dark cherry with white placemats. It gleamed pleasantly in the track lights.

I could only read half the menu. Our dad spoke the language at home, but as I grew up, I spent less and less time at home. Friends and teachers draped their hopes and expectations on me, their minor miracle boy. I didn't need anything else: not when it was sunny out, not when there was so much to buy. Korea. "Too much sadness," my father said when I asked why we'd left. His marriage was over. His country would never reunify. In America, he could lose himself in the jet stream of a new culture. Tommy was the supreme ultimate eldest child, but I was the one who fulfilled Dad's dream of leaving the old country and its baggage behind.

The waitress said a few things to me in their language, but Tommy intercepted, folding the words back into their conversation.

He was covering for me. I folded my hands on my lap and shaped my mouth into something resembling a smile. I ordered by pointing at a photo on the menu. From the look she gave me, I could tell my brother had excused me either as retarded or as a deaf-mute.

"You think you're doing me a favor," I said after she left.

"I think I'm doing *me* a favor," he said. I'd kept a few insulting phrases from our mother tongue and we traded those for awhile. I was about to switch to English when the restaurant's owner approached us. Tommy later said this happened to him all the time at Korean restaurants. The owner comes up and asks if you're Korean. I don't know why. Maybe you win a prize or something. The owner was thin, with silver hair at the temples. He had the gaunt face and shuffling walk of a recovering cancer patient.

"Are you Korean?" he said to me, although it sounded more like "Ah. You Korean."

"No," I said. He squinted, trying to reconcile my response with my face.

"Oh," he said. He looked around at the restaurant, at the expensively framed calligraphy paintings as if he'd never seen them before. Then, as if he had more important work waiting, he wandered off. The whole exchange was over in seconds.

"Because I'm not," I said to Tommy. I reached into my pocket for the Identity Chart but hesitated when I saw his expression. While we were arguing about something on the menu, he'd picked up a butter knife and waved it around as he called me an effeminate, mouth-breathing dogfucker in Hanguk-mal. But as the owner walked away, the expression on my brother's face—the playful anger melted away around something fierce and immovable.

When I was ten, he'd tried to decapitate me: tied a length of rope around my neck while I was sleeping, tied the other end around a

doorknob, got a running start, and kicked the door shut. He'd pre-
viously removed a tooth in the same fashion, and the sheer force
ripped me from the bed and dragged me across the hardwood floor.
Snot and tears, I looked up and saw him, arms folded, his expression
impassive and stony. For some reason, he was wearing only underwear: bright white, and from a strange cinematic angle, I pulled at
the rope and heaved until I could draw a breath. A few days later, I
returned the favor by pushing over a bookshelf near his head while
he was doing push-ups in the living room. Three more inches and
I would have had it. But these were everyday experiments, playful
in their violence. We put thought into them, yes, but never thought
much about them.

In the restaurant, though, there was a genuine malice I'd never
seen in my brother. My hands were always a little shaky, but I could
usually control it. I put them on my lap. When Dylan went electric,
the guy shouting "Judas" didn't really mean it. Tommy meant it; the
entire restaurant steeped in the ugliness. Forgetting the language was
one thing, but it was unthinkable to deny my heritage in this place,
here, with our homeland's bounty presented to us by a generous elder.
I was afraid he was actually going to drive that butter knife into my
throat. Blood spurting slow-motion in a chrysanthemum bloom. He
stood up slowly and walked past me—everything in me contracted.

"You're paying for this," he didn't say. He walked through the
restaurant, still holding the knife, and the bells on the door jangled
as he left.

"We're almost there," I said. We'd passed Saturday in silence and
careful small talk, and now it was Sunday morning. I had to be back
at work in less than twenty-four hours. Now was the time, mostly
because I figured he couldn't attack me and drive at the same time.

I unfolded the Identity Chart, smoothing it out on the dashboard. I explained to him that my therapist and I had collaborated on it, but it was mostly my idea. "This will require theory," I declared.

"Oh my God," Tommy said.

"Weininger studied gender. Jewish fellow, sort of."

"What does that mean, sort of?"

"He renounced being Jewish." Tommy said nothing.

"He also committed suicide at twenty-three. But anyway, Weininger believed not in purity and labels, but rather in the beauty of spectrums."

"Please stop," Tommy said.

"In order to heal from the trauma of adolescence and to face uncertain adulthood, I must first come to terms with my identity," I read, quoting the mission statement at the top of the chart. "All the answers are on this scale, which will help me figure out where I fit in regarding Korean and American culture," I said, pointing to the ladder-like figure on the chart. "On one end, there's pure Korean Americanness."

"Drawn in red crayon."

"Burgundy represents Korea. And see, I've listed things that are purely Korean. And see the nice color spectrum in between . . ."

"Pink. Cute," he said. He didn't look at the chart—or at me—for the rest of the conversation.

"And then Anglo-Saxon-ness, represented by this white color at the opposite end. Among the items I listed: "Angel food cake," "fly fishing," and "water polo." "So, I'm here," I said, tracing a circle with my finger in the middle of the chart, "adrift in this vague ocean . . ."

Eyes on the road, he shook his head. *How are we related?* the expression on his face said.

I said, "Look, just because you don't understand something

doesn't . . . Weininger influenced Freud. He might have been flawed and his ideas controversial, but that doesn't—"

"Shut up. You've spent your entire life obsessing over—"

"People like binaries, *this* or *that*. Black or white. Dark outlines around everything. But seriously, who's one hundred percent anything? Are you? Weininger challenged a lot—" Tommy drove the car across the grass median, bouncing, and into opposing traffic. A pickup truck swerved out of the way, honking.

"Okay, okay!" I said, raising my hands in surrender. He pressed down a little on the accelerator. I pleaded for reason and stuffed the Identity Chart back in my pocket. The highway wasn't busy, but a few more cars swerved out of our way. Tommy pulled back into the correct lane.

"Have you ever tried talking to people instead of studying them? You really should!" he shouted. He was angry.

"Thanks, Oprah," I wanted to say, but didn't.

"Wherever we're going . . ." There was a pause which lasted about a minute. "How is this mystery place I'm driving to going to solve your whiny . . . whatever issues?"

"Race. And identity."

"I don't see how . . ."

"Hence the Identity Chart," I didn't say. His anger calmed to irritation. I took a picture of him with my cell phone.

"Are you saying that you've never dealt with anything like this?" I asked.

He shook his head. "On the way home, I'm going to tell you what I really think about you," he said.

A few minutes later, we turned down a dirt road. The shocks on his car weren't great and he had to slow down dramatically. The road became an alley when copses of pine trees appeared on both sides. Finally, there was a gravel parking lot. Tommy pulled in next to a minivan. While we argued over whether we were in the right place, a man emerged from the minivan. He was a portly fellow wearing a thick blue coat, heavy lapels lined with polished brass buttons, and a tricornered hat. He also wore some kind of leather sash from which hung a decorative sword. His pants were white. He pulled a small snare drum from the back of the van, slid the door shut, and strolled down the hill, whistling.

"What the fuck?" Tommy said, each word a sentence. We exited his car and walked to the end of the parking lot. It was a historic landmark, according to the sign. The hill we stood on overlooked acres of tall Connecticut meadow. At the far end, near the forest, a broad rock wall spanned the length of the field. There was a stone path that led down to a campground dotted with dozens of canvas tents. We watched our blue drummer make his way down toward them. It was too far away to make out any people, but we could see smoke from the campfires.

"Well?" Tommy demanded, making a sweeping gesture with his hand. He waited for an answer.

"Mildred told me about this. The owner. At the bed-and-breakfast. Her son's into this." See, I do talk to people. "But look. The trees, the colonials we passed on the way here. Revolutionary War reenactors in Connecticut—these are the whitest people doing the whitest thing possible." It was either this or line dancing night at an Elks club in Vermont.

"Stereotypes," Tommy said.

"This isn't about stereotypes. It's about purity. And look at his neat tricornered hat," I said.

"So your white friends do this?" he asked.

"Where would you buy such a hat?"

"Do you even have any white friends? Or any—"

I retrieved the chart from my pocket. "They read books by dead Germans, but I need more. One has to go to extremes when calibrating an Identity Chart. I've already got the Korean part from the restaurant—that was by accident, but it worked out beautifully. After this, we can go celebrate in a Presbyterian church, practice Hwa Rang Do in a vat of kimchi."

"I think if I punched you hard enough, it would fix everything," Tommy said.

"The X on a map—*you are here*. People need to know their place in the world. Without it . . . everything's this gray mush," I said, practically shaking the Identity Chart at him.

"But where?" he mused.

"Take enough cynical steps backwards and everything looks silly," I said.

"I'm going to take some cynical steps away from you."

I followed him down the trail. The stone path ended in a broad field, where clusters of tents waited. Soldiers gathered and talked, dressed in period costume. The uniforms looked hot and uncomfortable; many soldiers sat fanning themselves in the shade of their tents. There was a flagpole near the camp where a bespectacled, panting man lectured a group on how to lower, fold, and raise the flag. I hadn't wanted to get this close, but Tommy pushed further into the camp.

"Here we go," he said. He walked over to a young woman in a white bonnet. She was thin and hollow-cheeked, with short blonde hair. She wore a long dress covered by an apron and tended to a cast-iron pot hanging over a small fire. *Tourists? Way out here? That's* what she must have been thinking as we approached her.

"What odd manner of dress," she said, staring at us. She looked at our shoes for a long time. Hers looked like moccasins. "Which colony are ye from?" I don't think she actually said "ye," but she had a strange accent, a flutter of soft vowels. Accurate for the region and time period, I suppose.

"Michigan," Tommy said.

"Oh my. Are ye loyalists?" She regarded us with convincing suspicion.

"Tell her you're a loyalist, Jay," Tommy said. I ignored him. A man carrying a long musket approached us. Her husband. He was wearing the same thick white pants as the rest of the soldiers, but instead of a military jacket, he wore a white collared shirt and brown vest. He greeted us warmly, shook our hands. He introduced himself as Bucky (he was missing both front teeth), and the cook, his wife Virginia. The beef stew smelled wonderful, thick. The camp was a maze of smells: food bubbling in cast iron, the lightness of smoke. In the breeze, the faint, acrid scent of gunpowder. I told Bucky we were doing a report for a class project. On period weaponry.

"Oh!" he said. "Well, you'll want to see this." He hoisted his gun and sort of cradled it with his arms. I took a picture with my cell phone. "Like hefting a fencepost," he said, resting it on his shoulder like a sentry. "This is a Brown Bess, carried over from Great Britain. Tower Armory, seventy-five-caliber muzzleloader."

"Seventy-five," I said. Bucky nodded.

"Add courage and ye have a revolution," Virginia said.

"Muzzleloader, meaning one loads from the end of the barrel." He sat down on a wooden camp chair and held the gun across his lap. Virginia produced a canvas bag and he pulled out a tube of paper the size of a shotgun shell. "Little known fact: a great number of patriots were missing their front teeth. Because—" He handed the tube to his wife, who stuck it in the side of her mouth and bit off the end.

"The fastest way is with the incisors," Virginia said.

"Can't whistle anymore," Bucky said. He pointed the musket at the ground. "This here is the flintlock." He poured a little black powder from the tube into a hammer-like contraption above the trigger. I zoned out as he gave a long description about how the firing mechanism worked, using the words "frizzen," "pan," and "ignite."

"You're not writing this down?" Virginia said.

"My cell phone's recording everything," I lied.

"They're good boys." Bucky tilted the barrel up—the gun in its entirety was over five feet tall, the stock carved from dark, stained walnut. He poured the rest of the powder into the barrel and pushed the paper cartridge down into the barrel with a ramrod. "Normally, one would include a lead ball with the cartridge, but we're not that dedicated in our reenacting."

"Not like the Civil War reenactors," Virginia drawled.

"What is the—" I was about to ask why they did this—*what was their motivation?*—when a bell rang out. Bucky and his wife turned toward a church near the edge of the woods. Virginia gathered not one but three camp chairs, and Bucky set the gun across them.

"It's five. Time for the safety meeting. Then we'll have some demonstrations," he said.

"So . . . we'll go back to the car," Tommy said.

"I'll gladly trade ye some stew to keep the fire going," Bucky said. Otherwise he had to put it out. Safety. Starting a fire with flint and tinder was odious, he said. I promised to keep the fire going. Bucky looked at his gun, but we made sure not to. "They're good boys," he repeated as he walked his wife through the campground. They met up with others and filed into the church.

"What the fuck," Tommy said after they were gone.

"Bucky and Virginia obviously don't have kids," I said, picking up the musket. It was surprisingly heavy, almost as tall as I was. It was a beautiful weapon, the first gun I'd held in over a decade. I missed the feel, the meticulous craftsmanship, the weight of it. I knew what had to be done the moment I saw it, but I couldn't speak it until now.

"I want you to shoot me," I said. I handed the gun to Tommy, suddenly feeling helpless without it. It didn't take much for him to point it at me. I peered into the eternal darkness of the barrel.

"Wait," he said. He glanced at the campground to see if anyone had stayed behind. The metal barrel glowed dully as we headed down the field and into a shaded patch near the forest.

"Man, this thing is heavy," Tommy said.

"So, wait . . ." I moved ten feet away from him, then fifteen.

"And you're sure this doesn't have a bullet in it?"

"They shoot lead balls, not bullets. And no, he only loaded a blank."

"Because they were talking about loading these with real bullets," he said. I'd been watching carefully, I told him. Obviously, it was loaded with a blank. This debate went on for a while.

"Wait, why am I doing this?" Tommy asked.

"This is going to solve everything. I didn't plan this, but it's perfect. People with bullets in their heads, remember that conversation? I have effect"—I pointed to the shrapnel in my brain—"but not cause. This . . . musket is *cause*. Oh my God, this is perfect."

"What?" Tommy said.

"It's like Chekhov's rifle." Per Chekhov, if act one of a play shows a rifle hanging on a wall, it must be fired by the end. Cause and effect, foreshadowing, etcetera. "*I'm* like that story. It must be fired," I declared. I started to explain Chekhov, but Tommy sighed and took out the rubber band that kept his hair in a ponytail. He lifted the gun, sort of shook his head to move the hair out of his eyes, and pointed the gun at my face. "If this is what you want," he said.

"Wait," I said, taking a few steps backward.

"I thought so," he said.

"What?"

"Ready?" Tommy yelled. I could feel the air stir, a breeze from the forest. I spread my arms and took a deep breath. I was ready.

"We're going to prison for this. Or, at least I am. You'll probably be dead."

"If this doesn't happen, I will never have this chance. Again. Courage."

"God damn it."

"*Courage.*"

He said something I didn't understand.

"Go," I said. He seemed about to protest when his eyes widened at something over my shoulder. I thought he was joking, so I didn't look.

"I love you," he said, and pulled the trigger.

A man wrapped in smoke, that's the main thing I remember. I'd fallen, knocked backward by the rush of everything. The shot's deep thunder still echoed off the hills, inside my skull. The smell of gunpowder: it felt like I'd been inside the explosion. On the ground beside me were flaming ribbons of paper. *I love you.* Everything echoed.

"Do you feel reborn?" Tommy yelled as if I were really far away.

"I don't know," I said, but no sound came out. Everything looked new.

Tommy was shouting something. Had been for who knows how long. "Run! You fucker!" I looked over my shoulder. Apparently, the safety meeting was over and everyone had been calmly exiting the church—until they heard the shot. Now, torches and pitchforks, they were running down the hill. Toward us. "Get up!"

I had a perfectly reasonable explanation and we had friends in the group. Surely they would understand. Surely I would be able to explain. I somehow managed to stand and then followed my best judgment: I ran the fuck away, up the hill toward the car.

Tommy and I aren't speaking now (for the record, this is entirely his fault), but I can picture myself someday calling him and hanging up. You make progress with identity one day at a time. And I am making progress: I destroyed the Identity Chart in a ceremony with my therapist, sent it burning down the Delaware on a raft made of Popsicle sticks. It was cathartic.

But when I look back on that weekend, I think it's funny, the seemingly immovable objects we carry, and what can knock them loose. And as I picture my brother moments before our getaway, running up the hillside and holding that awkward musket aloft, I think: it's funny, the things you hold on to.

THE THIRTY-EIGHTH PARALLEL

The day I proposed to my girlfriend, I wasn't any particular ethnicity—I was simply a twenty-three-year-old whose brain had been addled by dopamine, stirred up by breezes along the river valley trail during hikes with Emma. The scent of fresh grass and wildflowers during our picnics. We'd returned to WMU for an alumni weekend, and Kalamazoo was practically misted with nostalgia. Emma loved the story of how I'd been a "nontraditional student" at WMU after a short career at GM. She always pictured the auto plant in *8 Mile* when I told the story, although that movie's about a white rapper, and I'm neither.

When I proposed, Emma wasn't simply a white girl, although her aggressively *nordique* features tended to inspire unease in her brown colleagues. She'd never admit it even if she noticed, but I'm talking the slightly upturned nose, the malamute eyes. The kind of face to fuel a million indigenous nightmares. The evening I proposed, we'd stumbled away from something called a Stampede Tailgate and found ourselves in a new college bar called the Zoo Saloon.

"Smells like a zoo," Emma said, slurring her words enough that the bouncer checking our IDs hesitated. I relaxed my face until it took on the sober, comforting contours of the stereotype: *Don't worry, honored sir, I'll keep an eye on her.* He stamped our hands and waved us on. Inside, the sawdust smell from the doorway gave way to a faint whiff of vomit.

It wasn't long before we'd drunk enough Miller High Life that we were back to our old habit of peeling labels off the bottles, rolling the paper, and feeding it into the tabletop candleholders. And there was a group of roaring drunks around us, other alums, mostly potbellied day traders decked out in Bronco brown and gold. Since we're talking colors, they were white. Still are, presumably. Even though my inhibitions and dignity were floating away on a river of cheap beer, it did not escape my notice that once the Hollister-clad Chinese bro peaced out, I inherited the position of "sole nonwhite ambassador." Which was unfortunate for everyone, really.

I didn't capitalize on my new position. After all, I hadn't woken up that morning and declared to the bathroom mirror, "Time to start another day as a Korean American." Just like I hadn't told myself I'd propose that night. In the bar, some magic hour began or ended as the lights dimmed and a DJ set up turntables. The hip-hop he played was so loud, it felt like the deranged heartbeat of the bar itself, then the whole weekend, just thumping through us.

Someone in our group admitted to working for GM, so of course Emma wanted me to tell my stories about the salvage yard. It's not quite a Scandinavian accent, but a brash roundness to her vowels emerges when she's drunk. As I saw her bathed in the orange neon of the Coors Light sign above our high-top table, I knew she'd never be more beautiful. I said, "Sure, but lemme do this first," and dropped to one knee. Our fellow alums' howling drowned out the music, even the bass, for a few seconds, and I couldn't hear her response. From her tears and the almost-frantic nodding, I didn't need to. I'd been carrying the ring around for the past month, waiting for the right moment, and this felt like the best we could ever have. *You better lose yourself in the music / the moment, you own it, you better never let it go.*

The music seemed to get louder, and my brain filled in the congratulations between the handshakes and pantomime. We'd joined together as a drunken, colorless mass where only joy and celebration mattered. To my mind, how I met Emma was the best story. I'd quit GM after wasting over a year at one of their auto plants, and Emma had just started at the college's student financial aid office. As I filled out entire forests' worth of forms, we talked about my immigrant father, my emotionally disabled brother, my net worth. She plucked liberally from this bounty of weakness, plugged the right surpluses with the right traumas, and the office somehow covered my tuition.

The strange thing about proposing is that—for a man, anyway— there's this extended pause after one's fiancée ducks outside to call everyone in her contacts list. Even though the cheer circling our table still hung in the air, I left it behind after spotting an open seat at the bar. Catching the bartender's eye would be more of a challenge. A new group, including a bachelorette party, shoved their way toward the back room, which held the promise of a pool table and jukebox. Sitting behind the speakers meant I was enveloped in a lesser riot of sound, so I exhaled and tried to quiet the ringing in my ears. Calling my family, especially this late, would have been weird. My younger brother and I were estranged, though this news was a good excuse to reach out. Something a woman might do.

"Where you from, young man?" the man sitting next to me said, wrapping his arm around my neck to pull me closer. He was a middle-aged white man with a scraggly gray beard that nearly reached the neck of his faded green T-shirt. Whoever he was, he sat on his corner stool with the authority of a regular.

I sat up straight, which tugged his arm up a little. He got the hint that I didn't want him touching me. Although I was happy enough with MGD, the occasion seemed to call for a more sophisticated libation. "Two Molson Ices," I told the bartender.

"Toledo," I told the man. He squeezed his hand into a friendly claw and pushed a knuckle into my chest. "No, *originally*."

I knew what he meant. Some people get coy about it, but not me. "I'm Korean."

"I had some friends in Korea."

"It's a big country," I said. He wanted to buy me a drink, and I didn't know how to decline politely. The bartender made a big show of producing and opening my beers. They sat on the bar, sweating. The man—Ted—was trying to guess my age when the bartender returned. "Rum and Cokes," he said. Ted took one and passed me the other.

We chatted about the Tigers game on the TV, but it seemed like he wanted something else. Emma told me once that if a man buys a girl a drink, she's supposed to chat with him until she finishes it. She rarely did, though. Maybe I was trying to balance things out when I decided I'd give him until my glass was empty. It was halfway there.

"Everyone wants replays," he said. I thought he was referring to my proposal. I'd acted so quickly no one thought to whip out a phone and record it. Then I realized he was talking about baseball. I decided conversations about baseball were easier to exit gracefully than conversations about weddings.

"I guess it's fine if the umpires aren't calling it right," I said.

"It's a beautiful game, the athleticism behind the stats. People make mistakes."

"That's true," I said. Ice clinked against my teeth as I swallowed the last of the drink.

"My friends were in Korea, in the army. During the war."

"Oh," I said. The alcohol was stronger at the bottom, and the dregs burned into my stomach lining.

"I was in the infantry, Seventh Infantry Division." He reached out for my neck, but I pulled away. "My machine gun heated up. You can't imagine. I remember it just like that. The casings, sometimes they fly and get stuck under your collar, just hot brass. Sizzling. And those boys kept coming. I didn't want to hurt anyone," he said, leaning back to take me in. He wasn't crying, but he had to shift his weight to keep balanced. He shook his head and stared up at the television. "They kept coming," he said, wiping his face with a sleeve. "I'm sorry. I really am."

The ringing in my ears had ceased, and I felt like someone standing and looking around after washing ashore. On the television, a young man slid into first base in a dirty plume of dust. A young woman wearing a sash and a tiara brushed past me. The sash had something handwritten on it, but I couldn't make it out. Other patrons were leaning against me as they waved money, but I couldn't feel anything. Ted's eyes bored into me, waiting.

"It's okay," I said, the words feeling wrong. I didn't know what else to say. He handed me his drink, which was half-full. I finished it quickly, tilting my head back, feeling the numb speed of the liquid as it poured down my throat.

"What are you doing?" Emma asked. She must have really pushed to get to us.

"I don't know," I said, grabbing the two Molson Ices from the bar. Ted looked at us and nodded sagely.

"Fancy," Emma said, glancing down at the bottles. I couldn't tell if she was kidding. She wanted to leave—either to drunkenly consummate our union or to drunkenly brag to her sorority sisters from our quiet hotel balcony. Even if I wanted to argue, she was already striding toward the exit. As we maneuvered through the crowd, I turned back—I knew there would be another Asian guy in the place. He'd be about my size, with something approximating my face. Like an alternate version of myself, or an earlier version. A siren pierced the music, or maybe he felt my gaze, and this lone Asian at the bar glanced toward the door. I held up a hand tentatively. He nodded thoughtfully, grabbed an empty glass from the bar and held it up in a toast. Emma didn't seem to notice. We passed into the humid night with traffic as our only soundtrack and moved deeper into the crowd on the sidewalk.

RUMORS OF MY DEMISE

Every time Steve hears the word "streamline," he pictures his Airstream, that uniquely American love child of a space shuttle and a beer can. His sleek aluminum dream. But it's not his anymore, he reminds himself. He had to sell it years ago.

"Start at the top when you streamline," his son says. "Everyone's objective nowadays is to be a goal-oriented team player, so maybe cut that line. Are you listening?"

"Yes sir," Steve says, and he is, as much as you can listen to anything you've heard dozens of times. His son Jason is a graphic designer for a startup that sells posters of vintage ties. He's worked there for six years, long enough to convince Steve it's a real job, stable enough to build a future on. Then again, everything seemed stable once.

Jason says, "Add that you're creative."

"I thought you said to be honest."

"It doesn't matter. That's the hot word this hiring season, so you need to include it as much as possible."

"And if they ask me to be creative during the inter—"

"It's just a buzzword. They want to see that you know it. They calibrate the software to search . . . so if your résumé has five buzzwords and the next guy's has four, the computer moves yours higher up the stack."

Steve tapped his ear with the old, corded phone. The thick plastic receiver was pleasantly cool. So people didn't actually read through the résumés? He'd never considered that. But it made sense. In the old days, they'd just hire more people to winnow the stacks. But again, those days were long gone.

Of all the adjectives Steve could use to describe himself, "creative" would be the last. "Korean" would be the first, simply because it was obvious. It must have been the brown Rockports, the pleated khakis, the stiff, near-formal posture, but everyone said he looked like a Steve. He'd picked his American name from a phone book shortly after arriving in the country—or that's what he told everyone. The truth was, he'd named himself after Steve McQueen and eventually adopted the close-cropped helmet of hair the *Bullitt* actor wore late in his career. No one knew the unpronounceable name he'd shelved. For all he knew, not even his sons remembered it.

In college, young Jason dressed in slacks and short-sleeved dress shirts, usually cinched together with a Looney Tunes tie. But a few years ago, when Steve flew down to Tucson to visit, Jason waited by the baggage claim in a plaid flannel shirt, cuffed skinny jeans, and a pair of ratty Nikes with the ironic, old-school air bubble in the heel.

"My uniform," Jason said, laughing, but there was a flatness to it.

"You're not at work," Steve said, but what he meant was, *You could change and we'd both be happier.* What he meant was, *That mustache looks ridiculous on you.*

His son pointed to the outline of a cell phone in his jeans pocket. "I'm always at work."

This was shortly after Steve sold the Airstream. After a surprise downsizing, he'd been out of work for months, and everyone hoped

Steve would cheer up after meeting his grandson Geoffrey. This expectation placed a new pressure on their interactions, even though everyone knew that newborn babies are basically blind, only able to detect changes in light. "Still, I'll remember," Steve said. Even if some details were lost in the chaos of their first meeting, there were gigabytes of data to remind him: a crystal-sharp video of his entrance into the hospital room, looking for a place to set the gift-store bouquet as Geoffrey screamed and the nurses parted, passing Grace some final advice before giving the family some privacy.

Of his two sons, Jason seemed most likely to marry white, but ever since college, he'd almost exclusively dated Korean American girls. It must have been a challenge at times in Arizona, but he found them with a rather grim determination, as if he were trying to make up for something. Steve's favorite had been Grace the baker, who'd grown up near Busan and could perfectly recreate some of Steve's childhood sweets. Grace the percussionist was lovely, though, and Steve knew she'd be an excellent mother.

The main excuse for Steve's visit was to help while Grace recovered from the C-section, but of course he still wanted to spend time with his grandson. Jason stood nervously, almost knocking over the chair beside the bed before trading places with Steve; Grace smiled and laid her head back on the pillow to watch as Steve's arms assumed just the right position to lift and cradle Geoffrey. The newborn's face was a grumpy swoon, mouth opened in a perfect O.

With the infant in his arms, Steve was transported back in time, to those long years as a new father in an invincible-looking tan high-rise in downtown Busan. He'd been happily married then, only a few years out of the university. He barely knew how to use an iron or balance a checkbook, and now he'd been thrown into this whirl-wind called parenthood. He thought about how capable a partner his ex-wife was, even entertained a thought of calling her before deciding the results would be disastrous and scarring. Watching Jason and Grace, Steve fussed at his own nostalgia, focusing only on the happy moments in his own marriage: the hikes, the dancing, the shared secrets and sacrifices.

The baby's newness and the rush of memories was intoxicating: more than once, Steve would stumble in the hall or brace himself before standing, sucking in air as he waited for the lightheadedness to subside. He decided the feeling was second-best to falling in love. Jason turned off his phone for the week and never seemed happier, more attentive to the world. Steve ferried his son to and from the hospital, rewired the hallway to add another light switch at the opposite end, ordered takeout, helped Jason dodge his boss's calls, and even cleaned out the litterbox of the cat who'd remained hidden throughout the visit.

He hadn't felt this good in decades—being needed and productive was almost as invigorating as cradling his grandson. On his return home, Steve gathered his strength and did his best not to slouch as he walked through the airport, toward the cramped, grimy 737 that would transport him to his studio apartment in Pittsburgh. As if in protest, his back throbbed and his arthritic hands swelled. He still hadn't gotten over the one-two punch of living alone and losing his job and likely never would. But what else could Steve do but accept who he was, hold tight to his memories, and bear the weight of his own decisions?

A couple years later, Steve listened intently to the static on the phone line and marveled at how Geoffrey was forming complete sentences, more or less. The boy must have stumbled into the room, so Jason handed him the phone and let him ramble. Steve happily let the child's nonsense wash away the talk of unemployment and computers.

"Oh, really?" Steve said to a sentence that sounded like "It kiss misses you. May day."

"Sing, sing, tattle."

"Are you sure?"

"It's all lies to the plane."

"My, my." Steve leaned forward in his office chair and rubbed his palm over the smooth surface of the desk.

"Essay sock," his grandson babbled. Maybe it was the purity of the little boy's voice, along with the hiss and crackle as his words traveled thousands of miles, but somehow even language was new. Each of Geoffrey's words was an offering in the purest sense: no judgment, no expectations. Steve cocked his head and hit the degauss button on his ancient computer monitor. The screen buzzed and the display flickered before returning in a slightly bluer tint. His degrees remained atop the résumé like a stubborn monument, but the objective stood alone, the tendons of attachment finally worn away. The cursor ate the objective—it was replaced by white space so quickly that its memory already felt distant.

After that, something untwisted in Steve brain. Why had he been so attached to that objective? A more honest one might have been *I would like a job because I struggle to find a reason to crawl out of bed in the morning. I need something to structure my days. I am the victim of a great purposelessness, like my bones and brain are dissolving from the inside out.* And now, *poof*. Steve nodded, as if he were surveying his yard after a good mow, taking in the scent of slightly wet grass and mulch and not a dandelion in sight.

There was a little yelp as Jason pried the phone from his son's hands. "Sorry about that. Grace needed—"

"No need to explain, believe you me."

"It's hard sometimes," Jason confessed. He meant raising a toddler. "I'm not sure how anyone does it. I'm not sure how anyone turns out okay."

"I did it. You turned out okay." Steve tried to hide the annoyance in his voice.

"You were good. A good father," Jason said. There was something in the tone that Steve didn't care for—a forced cheeriness, a little boy's voice seeking approval. Delete, delete.

In the silence that followed, Steve realized something his son wouldn't tell him, a truth Steve probably knew all along: companies didn't want to pay more money for more experienced workers. Younger workers were cheaper, malleable. It took them too long to figure out what they were really worth.

"I'm thinking of deleting my consulting work at Alcoa," Steve said. Not necessarily tied to the current job market.

"Good. A big mistake people make is trying to please everyone. Tailor things to your dream job or dream city." There was a crash and a high-pitched shriek from Jason's wife. "Oh geez. I think—"

"Understood. Love you, bye."

Life in Pittsburgh, Steve thought, was good enough. Decent weather, lots of excited, bearded young men. It was a good tech city, whatever that meant. Did Steve really want to stay here, though? He missed his grandson, and it would be nice if they were in the same time zone. Jason had his own life, though, his own identity, and having Dad around complicated things. Still, there were plenty of petroleum-related jobs in Arizona, but moving there was a possibility Steve didn't really want to consider. To get excited about something and then have it taken away—a man could only bear so much.

On his résumé, he deleted a line about volunteer work (handling logistics at Meals on Wheels for two years). He'd been inspired after both sons graduated from college. In his fifties, he started taking evening classes, eventually moving from Toledo to Pittsburgh to finish his engineering degree. Something about his age, moving, and living alone caused thoughts of suicide to froth up from his subconscious. Of course, he didn't put that on his résumé: *Volunteered as an excuse to talk to other people.* No one needed to know about that gray, foggy period and how he dragged himself from the soggy pleasures of self-pity and back into the blinding sunlight. With that line of text gone, he felt an odd sensation, a lightness not only in the head but through his chest. He had to look at the ground to make sure his feet were touching it. He deleted another section, then another. The cursor blinked as the résumé devoured itself.

The next section covered his experience as a petroleum engineer. He kept it. Keywords: sand, aptitude, energetic, perseverance. Maybe a company in Arizona would pick him up. He imagined a map of the state: vein-like rivers, rock-ribbed amber valleys in a streamlined landscape, windswept cacti. Nature worn down to its bones, as if awaiting renovation.

At the heart of this carving process was a memory Steve will eventually reach, the swirling desert sands leading him to it. At the beginning of his career as a petroleum engineer, Steve was late for his flight home from a consulting trip in Qatar. He'd never been to the Middle East before and would have stayed to sightsee, but his travel visa ended that day. He rushed off the bus, dragging his briefcase and laptop bag (laptops were considerably heavier then) and frantically sprinted, almost like someone in a cartoon, to the old Doha airport, a squat tan rectangle soaking up the desert heat.

Even as his flight accelerated wildly toward the clouds, Steve was still trying to catch his breath. He looked down at the tops of the white buses driving away and realized that nobody had helped him carry the rest of his luggage to the airport because he hadn't asked. Also, when he changed buses after the first one had broken down, he'd just assumed that someone transferred the rest of his suitcases.

From above, he followed the last bus until clouds obscured it. Optimistically, he assumed it was returning to the main terminal, where it would be washed, and where his luggage would be discovered, tagged, and shipped back to the United States. But the bus probably hadn't been washed in the Emir's lifetime, and the closest bus terminal might have been in Egypt. More likely, the driver had already discovered Steve's suitcases and was rifling through them, sorting his shirts by resale value. Steve had purchased several items while in the country, as gifts for his sons. There were wooden puzzle boxes with intricate mother-of-pearl inlays, slightly risqué calendars, a bag of mysterious spices, and some copper bracelets. As the plane steadied, Steve let himself exhale. It was shocking how free he felt. His shirt and slacks hung on him, paper-thin—it felt like this scene was a drawing and the artist had erased the outline around his body. The pilot mumbled something into the intercom, and Steve found himself stifling a giggle as he imagined all the different places his possessions were heading. With his nose pressed to a cold window twenty-five thousand feet up, he wished them well.

Somewhere in America

AN INTERLUDE

CLICK

'm sitting in my pickup truck minding my own business. What that looks like is a middle-aged man with a salt-and-pepper goatee trying to take a selfie. They're all coming out poorly—my smile looks more grimacing with each shot. My friend in the passenger seat is not cooperating. That's the thing: I guess nothing's photogenic once it's dead. I suppose I won't be, either. I'm leaning over to readjust him when the cruiser pulls behind me flashing its lights.

This situation is already precarious: we're on a barely paved country road, miles from civilization. And by "civilization," I mean Pittsburgh. I slide my phone onto the dash as the cop approaches, roll down the window, and set my hands ten and two on the steering wheel.

"Good evening, officer. What seems to be the problem?"

"Turn off your radio."

I'd been listening to Justin Bieber to get in the mood. My sons like him. He sounds better on the radio, especially when static from another station washes through. I turn the dial. Even though it's light out, the cop sweeps his flashlight over my face, then peeks in the driver's side window. He steps back, drops his hand on his service pistol, then hesitates and takes it away. His hand.

In this critical moment, I could be a good sport and say, "Yes, officer. It is strange that there's a dead deer in the passenger seat. Allow me to explain why." Just like he could be a good public servant, admit there's no crime here, and move along.

In a surprisingly calm voice, he says, "If you could hand me your license, registration, and proof of insurance, please."

I wasn't driving when he decided to oppress me, so this can't be a moving violation. I tell him so even as I dig into my jeans to retrieve my wallet. The glove compartment door drops down and I pass him the paperwork through the window.

He hesitates and takes it, then shines his light on the passenger seat again, as if in disbelief. Then the driver's-side door gets the spotlight of scrutiny. The cop is in his late twenties, about six foot, with a farmer's tan from his short-sleeved blue uniform. And his stainless steel chronograph. The academy weathered his face into a numb mask, but a pair of curious hazel eyes peeks out. He has the same haircut as Dave Kaczmerek, our high school anti-valedictorian: short hair in a jagged part to the side. Like that was the best he could do each and every morning. I've already decided to call him that when Officer Kaczmerek says, "Turn off the radio. This is the last time I'll ask."

I comply.

"Have you been drinking this evening?"

"No sir. Not a drop." I follow his gaze to the passenger seat. "I know it looks bad, but it's not open. You can see that, right? It's a prop." A six-pack of Natty Ice is six reasons to rethink your choices in life.

"There's a lot of blood on this door handle. That's—"

"Blood all over the driver's-side door, too. You should see the inside. It's not mine, though. Hey, do you know anything about Snapchat?" I start to explain that it's a mobile application popular with the youth of today, but Officer K takes a few steps back and taps his walkie-talkie, unsure of how to call this in. He's not going back to his car. Usually, they go back to the squad car and take forever doing something. I'm never quite sure what that is.

In the stern voice of an assistant principal, Officer K asks, "Sir, why is there a deceased deer in the passenger seat of your pickup truck? A very bloody one at that?"

It seems like the later you are, the more of a hurry you're in, the longer cops take to write out that speeding ticket. Today, I've got nothing but time. "Have I broken a law, officer? I can tell you I went hunting earlier. I loaded the game into my vehicle, which was parked by the side of the road. I had my flashers on, and I thank you for stopping, but I'm fi—"

"I am giving you a lawful order. Explain . . . to me—"

"And I'm giving you a lawful answer. I spent the day working as a whitetail population engineer"—I point to the hunting license clipped to my baseball cap—"exercising my second amendment rights"—my rifle is on the gun rack behind my head—"and now I'm exercising my first amendment rights. I understand the blood isn't tidy, but that's not a law-and-order issue." It's going to be a major cleaning issue, though. I bagged a respectable four-pointer, and the cab is filled with an earthy animal musk. Sort of like a herd of goats. Luckily, he wasn't in rut.

Officer K says nothing for a moment, just stares at me with his impassive, sick-of-your-BS cop-face. He draws an orange cylinder from his belt and lazily shakes it like it's spray paint.

"What's that? Mace? The constitution—okay." I return my hands to the steering wheel and stare through it at the long asphalt shoulder, the tall pines. The trilling birds just emphasize how thick the forest is, holding all the sound.

In the patient voice I should have used when I was lab partners with Dave Kaczmerek, I tell the cop, "I am cooperating, officer. If you just could tell me what law I've broken, please." A squawky message comes in over his walkie-talkie. He hands me back my license and paperwork. I set it all on my lap. His expression hasn't changed.

He asks, "Mind if I take a look around your truck?"

"You're more than welcome to search my truck after you produce a warrant." A slight frowning tic pulls at his mouth. "And with all due respect, officer, this is a pickup truck. It's an open book, really." I turn in my seat and gesture to the truck's bed. "You can see inside . . . there's a tarp and some bungees, and my cammies. Here's my rifle, which I have paperwork for, on the rack, and you saw inside the glove compartment when I got my papers. There's some gum wrappers in the wheel well and, of course, my friend here. He's pretty harmless, officer."

"You're alone in a secluded area, in a truck whose doors are covered with blood. The inside of your cab is covered with blood, and there's a hundred-and-twenty-pound dead animal jammed into your passenger seat. That is a textbook definition of probable cause."

"Do you have a cell phone? With the Snapchat?"

Officer K leans his head to speak into the walkie-talkie on his shoulder. "Calling to request an ambulance, I'm on Bonniebrook, near Chicora."

I ask who the ambulance is for. Then it dawns on me, and I can't hide the tremble in my voice. It feels like I'm winding up to something when I say, "You know why I hunt? To fill the freezer, feed my kids. I'm a family man. And you're going to what, mace and tase me for no reason? Put me in the hospital for no reason?"

He might as well be staring at me with his face half-hidden by sunglasses. A fly lands on his neck and spins around on the stubble. If I picked up my phone to record this, you'd think I was arguing with a statue. An angry statue. With a gun. "Okay, you want to know why there is a deer in the passenger seat of my truck. I get it. I really should have put the tarp down first. I didn't expect this much mess." Which is true. I might have to pick up new seats at the junkyard. "Do you have kids, officer? No? Well, that's probably for the best. But as far as I can tell, I haven't broken any laws here."

To the walkie-talkie, Officer K says, "Dispatch, requesting backup as well." To me, he says, "Animal cruelty, for one. Reckless driving. Poaching, and—"

"What animal cruelty? It was a clean enough shot and I am a licensed hunter. I know this isn't the recommended way to transport game, but—"

He reaches behind his belt to unclip something, and his voice rises to a slightly higher pitch—the animal parts of me clench. How long has my heart been drumming against my ribcage? "Get out of the truck," he says, but what he means is *I'm giving myself permission to hurt you.*

"Okay, you got me." I've had my hands raised in surrender, and I keep them that way. "You want to know why. You said you don't have kids, right?" I open the door slowly but stay in the cab. The cop's hand is hovering near his service pistol, and the other grips his Maglite, his fingers sort of drumming. "The thing is, when my Sean and Trapper—my sons—were four, they loved her." I point to the truck. As babies, it was how we got them to sleep, drive around the block with the old V-6 purring. When they were little, old red here was a spaceship, a sailboat, a rocket. We'd picnic out of the bed every summer night if my wife would let us. "But my kids get older, and someone points out their old man's oil-stained jeans, his dirty boots. They hear it when I say life's going good instead of going well, and suddenly it ain't nothin'.'"

Officer K hasn't changed his posture, but I can tell he's relaxing just a hair.

"My boys, they're in private school, you know where Saint—well, never mind. I don't know where they get their smarts, but it's not me. I don't like going inside that school, even for conferences. People like me stain the chairs. And Sean, about a month ago, he's thirteen, he says, 'Dad, can you wait around the block from school to pick me up?' And I should have asked why, but I don't, because we both know."

Here, I turn and face Officer K, who has returned his Maglite to its belt loop and sort of hitches up his belt. He's maintaining that poker face, but his eyes say he's willing to hear me out. "And I do it. Because I'm a rusty . . . river turd sailboat and that school is a spaceship. I mean, when you're a dad and your kids are ashamed of you . . . the way I was raised, when life hands you a problem, you dig deep and fix it. I buy this"—I flick the Pikachu bobblehead on the dash—"change my presets and put a spoiler on the back. When I hear them talking about this Snapchat, I add it on my phone. Didn't know how to use it, still don't. And then, this morning, I'm in a tree stand for nine hours, just turning all this over in my head. And along comes Bambi here, bang, you've got a deer, and a camera, and a truck. It all came together."

"What?"

"What I mean to say is . . . after shooting Bambi here, I drag him into the cab and sat him like this. Messed up my shoulder doing it. The plan was to take a selfie of the two of us chilling in the cab like bros and post it on the Snapchat with the caption "Road trip with my new, deer friend." And he'd be holding the six-pack. Well, between his hooves. Hashtag deerfriend. Like D-E-E-R . . . and I'd send it to my boys, prove the old man's still got it. And then you drove up."

For most of our exchange, he's been standing with his hands on his hips. He lets out a long exhale and gives the cab a once-over, then the truck bed. Then, he says, "Sir, you're free to go." Officer K isn't willing to give up a smile, but I can see him arranging this encounter into a story for the enjoyment of friends and family. To his shoulder, he says, "Cancel the request for the ambulance and the ten-ten."

More than anything, I wish my boys were here to see this. Dad fought the law—and Dad won. "Thank you, officer." I hope my story makes his greatest hits collection. You'd think he'd at least offer to help clean up. He's walking away, scratching his neck when I call out. "At the risk of . . . when I asked about kids, this look came on your face. You're either trying, or you got one on the way?"

He turns back to me in that territorial stance men take when an unfamiliar car pulls into their driveway. "Fiancée's in her second trimester," he says in a flat, neutral tone that's clearly a warning.

"You should know you get twelve or so good years, then your kids want nothing to do with you. We'll end up on the island of misfit toys together, you and me. But you don't give up on your kids, you work through the pain. I hope it doesn't happen, and I wouldn't wish it on you, but you'll see. So, I'm just saying, be sure to hold onto those years."

"Drive safely, sir," Officer K says, but he's bobbling his head like my words are pushing into his brain-folds. He takes his time returning to his car, and I wave as his cruiser rushes past me. I'm in a contemplative mood myself when I reach over to pull the seat belt around my passenger. I tell him, "You know what I should have said? Well, a number of things." What I should have told him is that being a dad is a journey that takes you to the strangest of places. What I should have said is, "Officer, buckle up."

DRESSED IN RED

My girlfriend dresses like a communist. She doesn't wear the hat, though. You know, squarish with a short bill. Castro wore one. That would be a dealbreaker, I think.

People living in this century shouldn't wear olive drab. The worst is her jacket, which looks suspiciously like the ones you see on homeless vets as they beg for change near the freeway. Except she's hemmed it so it falls just above her hips. My beautiful comrade is only five feet tall, and I can't help but wonder what kind of army makes uniforms that small. No one else seems to mind her cargo pants. Or, since it's summer now, cargo shorts. Sometimes, I'll ask what she needs all those pockets for, and she'll look down like she's noticing them for the first time.

"You never know," she replies. I tell her communism was a failure. If everyone's going to be rewarded equally, why bother? She has a round, girlish face and strangers assume she's still in college. The summer humidity has made her hair thicker and curlier than usual. Something about the way the wind catches it makes me want to pause, wrap some of it around my finger. "People don't work hard if they know it won't matter."

"What are you talking about? And what are *you* wearing?" she asks, as if I weren't sitting on the couch next to her.

"Banana Republic." Which, incidentally, sounds like a socialist paradise but is not. Their khakis and polo shirts are stylish and breathable, and it's hot in our apartment. If this were any other day, she'd say something about labor laws and basic human decency. She'd mention my financial troubles and tell me I can't afford to shop there anyway. And I'd say she looks like a cheerleader for the military industrial complex. But we both know it isn't an afternoon for arguing, especially over fashion. Things have been tense since she lost her job and I picked up the slack, but we have found a distraction.

In Shanghai, in the neighborhood where I grew up, there aren't many pet-friendly apartment buildings, so dog lovers go to little shops stocked with a variety of puppies you can frolic with. It's better than eating them, I suppose. Some of the stores even have indoor runs and endless racks of chew toys. But we live in a small town in Ohio, and the best we can do is to drive to the pet store at the strip mall.

"Are you seriously interested in buying a puppy?" the skeptical teenage clerk asks. They must be cleaning the cages, because all of the dogs are out, barking in the pens in the middle of the store.

"We are seriously interested," my girlfriend and I say, almost in unison. Except I'm lying and she sounds dangerously sincere. We are not ready for a puppy. We have discussed this. "This is Ming and I'm Beth," she tells the clerk, as if the introduction will instantly secure her trust.

Beth's chosen a small white terrier named Cookie. The clerk retreats to the register. In the little pen, the dog licks our hands and jumps. His fur sticks to her green shorts, and I know I'll be picking white hairs off my car seats and couch for weeks. The other dogs can hear us but can't see us, and it drives them crazy. We play with Brett, a little tan dog, then Lazer, a golden retriever puppy. Beth's red T-shirt has tattoo-style stars on it. I'd like to think she considered the symbolism of it. That she knew how pleased I'd be to see my childhood flag across her bosom. "Who loves you?" she asks each dog as if we're alone in the store. As we're leaving, we tell the clerk we have to think about it. "We'll be back," we say.

"I bet," the clerk says.

At a red light, I pluck stray hairs off her shirt. I know it's just something she grabbed out of her closet, and I don't know why this bothers me. It seems like most of her clothes are like fatigues, designed to endure. If her clothing could speak, it would say, *We stand in solidarity,* as if we're crouched in a trench, our backs and hearts aching toward some hopeless cause. The car behind me honks. "What's wrong?" she asks as I step a little too hard on the accelerator.

"I'm fine," I say again as we enter the apartment. I sit at the couch and she digs through her purse, which is more of a messenger bag. "Maybe you're allergic?" she suggests. She sits next to me and pulls her phone from one of those unnecessary pockets, begins looking something up online. I rest my hand on the rough cotton of her shorts. If she ever asks, I'll say I want to see her in a dress. Maybe it's sexist, but just once would be nice. I picture the two of us in a large ballroom filled with men in tuxes with real bow ties, women in crisp gowns. The one she's wearing is gauzy, the color of poppies. It rests on her figure perfectly, sways and clings like a magic spell when she moves. If this dress could talk, it would say, *You don't have a choice but to love me.* It's a strange fantasy, I know, because neither of us can dance, but here we are, moving swiftly in some eternal rhythm, the stars wheeling perfectly above. It's one of those roofless nighttime ballrooms. I'm sure they exist.

Back in the real world, with its dog hairs and credit-card debt, I move my hand up her thigh and she pulls away a little. The mood isn't right: it's too hot, and we both know it. I can imagine it happening later today, but not much beyond that. It's been like this for weeks, but I'm still a little high on my dress-fantasy and still picture the world as a big party, a black-tie event with potential partners everywhere. The wooden floor glows, smelling of fresh wax, cut flowers, and money. Some of the fine ladies actually have dance cards, but Beth doesn't. We're past the point where we can walk away unchanged, unhurt, but maybe not by far. I know it would be better for me to tell her I'm not allergic to dogs. But I need a quiet moment to think, and I press my hand so it's arched against the contour of her thigh. When she puts down her phone, I should lean in and tell her the truth: that I loved her once but can't remember when. But other men will have to wait for her. We have made our sacrifices, both of us, and I will not share.

SCENES FROM THE REVERSE METAMORPHOSIS

I

One morning, a beetle turned into a man. The setting: an observation room in the corner of a basement laboratory. Two unpainted concrete walls, one with a large circular window. The other two made of shatterproof glass, with a glass door.

Describing the former insect's emotional state requires translation. First, his sight no longer compounded. His panorama reduced, it became necessary to swivel and tilt his head, the range of motions dizzying. His antennae had shifted south, the segments reformed into joints and tendons. He had neither the language nor the desire to explain the oddness he felt. There was a new vulnerability that, if dwelled upon, would have wrung from him an intense sadness. Transforming from invertebrate to human meant his invincible shell had compressed to the elegant interior curve of bones. He received the heat of the world through an expanse of flesh.

This was the secret project that had drawn the researcher every night to the soundproof basement of the house he shared with Corrine, his daughter. His legacy. "I'm close, and I'm sorry," he told her in the hospital shortly before his death. Even during the funeral, God help her, she imagined herself finally walking down the unlocked stairway to his lab.

Later that day, Corrine stood outside the lab, watching. On hands and knees, this new man moved along the walls. He would circumnavigate the room forever if uninterrupted. The crawling wasn't out of confusion, she knew. She had read her father's notes, left for her on the lab table outside. "It is crucial to understand his mind, the collective nature of insects. He was once a tongue of flame in a great fire of consciousness. And now: a candle, truncated." Ultimately, what he sought in his rectangular path was a way to return. Knowing he never could, and the vastness of everything he would never understand, she felt godlike, a sensation that settled heavily in her chest and limbs. She was almost forty, had spent her life as her father's assistant.

And now, this discovery made her a caretaker. She watched the man pause and glance at her, raising slightly on his haunches to sniff the air. She noted the muscular line in his thighs. Something didn't register, and he returned to his travels. It was unsettling, the way his fingers undulated. She understood—antennae—but felt a wave of revulsion nonetheless. In a few minutes, she would have to open the door and face him. She stood with her hands clasped, as if in the position of a supplicant, her back perfectly straight. What held her back for a moment was his sheer physicality—the muscular, sinewy arms, his genitals, two rows of teeth. *How long has he been alone?* she wondered. Which of his hungers coalesced in that tiny glass room?

II

Corrine reminded herself it was a "him" and not an "it," but she felt the pressure of caring for him; gravity changed and came in waves, pushed new wrinkles around her eyes and mouth. She had a dancer's body that once moved gracefully down library aisles. Around it, she draped her white lab coat, which she paired with colorful skirts, her feet silent in leather oxford flats. Time and gravity had overlooked her, quiet as she was, but found her the day she discovered her father's terrible secret. She knew it wasn't a coincidence. There was no such thing.

It took weeks to teach the new man how to dress, how to eat—that his hands were not feelers but tools. Helping him stand, she realized it had been years since she had pressed against a stranger's flesh. She tried not to shudder at the smoothness of his skin, the fresh baby-scent of it. She had never been a mother, never dealt with issues of bodily waste. And urges: she knew that female zoologists who worked with male primates often drew unwanted attention. Even his gaze, through large, brown, long-lashed eyes, was unsettling because she could still sense the insect in him, the digital thought process, the reliance on instinct.

But he was human, technically, a fully formed adult man. Anyone watching them would have wondered why a Caucasian male in his midtwenties was sitting quietly on the observation room floor, his eyes darting a little as she ran blood tests through the machines at the in-house lab. He didn't have movie-star good looks, but he was handsome enough with his close-cropped blond hair. Corrine dressed him in teal scrubs—the less she saw of his sleek, muscular body, the better.

Why this particular experiment? What were her father's goals? The questions would have grown had she given them room to breathe. But there was so much to do. Simply feeding him took hours. When Corrine was young, her father would not permit her to name the lab mice or rabbits. Still, she saw them as rows of Elizas and Ogras and Kenneys, waiting quietly and blank-eyed, as if slowly processing the horrors that awaited them.

She named the beetle-man James and moved him upstairs to the guest bedroom, which was furnished with a bed and dresser. There was also a window, covered by a green gingham curtain. There was also an outside world, and knowledge he needed to grasp.

"I'm sorry, James," she said, and pulled aside the curtain.

In a previous life, his compound eyes saw color, but mostly in washes, like a black-and-white television—or, more precisely, a Technicolor film from a great distance. Now, he saw the garden in the inner courtyard, each flower its own color. Due to its wavelength, red had been invisible to him until this day.

It must have felt as if his soul were being pulled from his body through his optic nerves. Adding to the trauma was the fact that he recognized plants, remembered paths he used to wind through on six legs. Insects he'd never seen vibrated and zipped through the air. In the end, his own height overwhelmed him: imagine waking up five miles tall. Colors magnified and he backed away, hands cupped over his eyes. He was trying to unsee, Corrine knew. He made a giant wailing noise as he backed into the wall and fell to his hands and knees before sitting, pushing himself against the wall. He covered with his arms as much of his chest and face as possible.

She knew James needed sensory stimulation, and this was a first step. But still, she marveled at her power over this thing she never wanted. And the height, perhaps, of her resentment. What were her true motivations?

"Stand," she said. She hadn't meant for it to sound like a command. It had taken months to teach him how to walk on two legs. She walked over and gently lifted his elbow. He pulled away. "Stand," she said, louder, but now she was sobbing. She left the room quickly.

III

There was an adjacent observation room, in which she noticed another beetle brimming with possibility. She placed a petri dish over it, watched its awful potential curl into nothing.

IV

The salt was delightful, and he loved the heat of them. The way he cupped his hand around the thin red-and-yellow container, the warmth and smell blotching through the paper onto his fingers, washing over his face. But he ate them with a fork because she had taught him to. Chewing carefully before swallowing required self-control. Because there was no such thing as taste in his previous life. How surprising, this short fleshy proboscis. He tumbled the food one last time before swallowing. How could anyone not want to do this every single moment? He looked up and she paused before nodding. She said something, but he still couldn't understand. There was a gratitude in him that he couldn't express. He wasn't even that heartbroken when the container was empty and she didn't have any more.

V

Compared to teaching James how to stand, eat, and bathe, dressing was easy. On his first day outside, he wore a pair of jeans and a cable-knit sweater. Corrine walked next to him as they navigated the sidewalk. She was confident that passing neighbors would see two normal humans out for a stroll. James walked with a slight limp and was prone to stumbling—a side effect of evolution, she figured, less stability with two legs as opposed to six. Still, he was smart and eager to please. Cut off from the chorus of the hive, he fixated on following her commands, watching and reading her in a way that was eerily patient. She thought, *When they perfect artificial intelligence, it will act like James.* As they passed a white house with vinyl siding, she remembered that neither she nor her father had spoken with the neighbors in decades. It wasn't a feud—she couldn't remember the last time she'd gone for a walk, pursued the outdoors. Anyone seeing her with James, she realized, might assume they were mother and son. She pulled the fur-lined hood of her coat over her head but didn't change her stride or pace.

To James, the cold was a blessing. On his face, the soft skin of his neck, his fingers—it was a glorious sensation, the way it called attention to one's nerve endings, the slick layer of moisture over the eyes. The cold penetrated and spread itself evenly over all creation, holding it all together under its brief dominion. He pushed up his sleeves and breathed in as deeply as possible, feeling the air coat his lungs. There was a slight hiss as he exhaled, but he stopped when he noticed the woman frowning.

The snow—he'd seen it from the window but had never felt it. He swatted at the air and she didn't seem to mind. The snow, its particles like atoms shed from some great collective. They drifted and kissed the sidewalk. In the past, he would have simply frozen, let nature's grip hold him. Now, he kept moving. Maybe it was the warm coils inside him. Something in the cold made his joints click, but he knew he could walk forever.

VI

She watched his eyes widen as the buses pulled in. They were standing near the terminal and had gotten used to the cigarette smoke just as the diesel fumes clouded the air. Her hair was all gray now, the years spiriting away the color. Time had cut into her, but she'd withstood it until today. She said to James, "I'm sorry. Maybe that's all you've heard from me, but it's true." He nodded even though she knew he didn't understand. She gripped his shoulder and leaned in, but didn't press her head to his chest like she wanted to. Years later, even as she basked in her freedom, Corrine would regret not leaving that tiny impression on him. She'd wish she'd marked him somehow before sending him out into the world.

"You'd better go," she said. "The truth of the matter is that you'll never truly be alone. If you remember anything from me, remember that. Please remember that I tried." He handed the driver his ticket and walked up the stairs to the bus. He didn't look back at her because she hadn't asked. He wanted her to see how perfectly he obeyed.

The seats on the bus were soft and something about the wash of pastel rectangles pleased his eyes. He stepped carefully down the aisle, his hands occasionally grabbing headrests for support. The woman he sat next to had long hair, brown, that fell straight down her back. It didn't cascade, but rather hung stiffly, as if she'd just straightened it. He couldn't see her face until he leaned forward and craned his neck. He'd thought maybe it was the woman who taught him things, but it wasn't. This woman next to him had smaller bones. And she smelled different, a scent of rosewater and musk. James slid his hands so he was sitting on them, just like he'd been taught to. No one else on the bus would understand how much he'd learned, how far he'd come.

He was wearing a thick jacket with a large pocket in the chest. Inside were important papers and a paycard with yellow arches. He could point to it at any stop and people would direct him to the eating place.

. . .

Now, as he looked at the pattern on the bus—people scattered, sitting by themselves, tiny circle lights shining on some, some sitting alone on the outside seat—he understood what the woman who taught him things had wanted.

"Window," she once said, pointing to the glass he saw the garden through. Outside the bus, the landscape sped and blurred. He glimpsed a beautiful patch of color and mouthed a word to his neighbor, almost ready to breathe life into it. Everyone on the bus was once insect. But now, they were like him. He could teach them. And soon enough, they would collect.

LIVE FROM PLASTICVILLE

You would pity anyone living in my father's town. First, it isn't big. Oval railroad tracks cut the place off from the rest of the world, and trains often pass dangerously close to homes and businesses. There is a post office and a radio station but no grocery stores or restaurants. Families stroll stiffly down Main Street, heading somewhere they'll never reach.

When I say it isn't big, I mean the town itself is about forty square feet, on an elevated platform in my father's basement. No one in town has ever seen the sun, only a fluorescent lamp that reflects dully off their faces.

My father was an officer and a veteran. After he retired, he built this little plastic world. And he loved it. Or, I should say, he loved the trains. Lionel O-Gauges. My sons loved them when they were young. In the dark, you could see hundreds of pinpoint red and green signal lights, and the trains lit up. Silhouettes of cheery passengers steamed by. But as I grew older, I worried that my father spent all his time in the basement. I never resented it—every man deserves a hobby—but I didn't understand the hold these trains had over a grown man. I never asked. My father passed away last week, and much was left unsaid between us.

Tonight, I am not the unemployed middle-aged son whose best wasn't enough. Tonight, I'm the son who will catalog each train before returning it to its original box. I will gather the happy little families and place them in plastic baggies. Tonight, after a long day of settling his estate, I will walk upstairs and fold myself into bed. Everything will be perfect, in place, under a round glowing moon, so that my father, hopefully looking down from somewhere, might see us and be pleased.

Han

There's a Korean word, *han*. I looked it up. There is no literal English translation. It's a state of mind, of soul, really. A sadness. A sadness so deep no tears will come, and yet still, there's hope.

—**PRESIDENT BARTLET**, *The West Wing*

If every family has a memory palace, a shared repository of first kisses and lost pets and white-hot shame, the Moon family would remember Jennifer in a groundskeeper's house neatly hidden behind the palace walls. Except the house would be one long, circular hallway. At one end, Jennifer is eight years old, wearing a green velour dress, arms clutching a small Christmas tree, a handful of lights, and shoeboxes full of glitter. "I'm dropping everything," she calls to the nearest adult, who doesn't respond. Behind her, a few more boxes fall and tumble. "I need help."

At the far end of the hall, rounding the corner and nearly out of sight, Jennifer is an old woman in a pink bathrobe, her gray hair pulled into a crown plait. Her posture is that of someone who is about to start crawling. She's searching for everything she's lost over the years. Occasionally, she stumbles over toy horses and rolling pins—and her father, who never seems to share her surprise.

ALPHA

It was the only orange book. There was a metal clasp over the paper's deckle edges, but otherwise, it looked like a thin hardcover novel without a jacket. If Eric, her boyfriend, were here, she could ask about it, but then again, he'd probably frown at her snooping. As she returned the book to the shelf, she noticed the clasp was made of brass and shaped like a human hand. The keyhole was fitted for a miniature skeleton key.

Eric wasn't the type to keep a diary. She thought she knew him pretty well: after all, they'd been living together for a month. Years ago, they'd watched countless horror movies in his dorm room at Illinois State before she transferred to the Moda Institute of Fashion in Paris. He'd gone on to major in engineering: the bookshelf was mostly textbooks, organized chronologically by semester. The simple maple bookshelf was the highlight of the living room. Eric angled the ceiling's track lights so they bounced off the thick, glossy spines. He wanted to give the impression he didn't own a TV, although he finished each night with *SportsCenter* on the flatscreen in their bedroom. Still, the bookshelf deserved some of that light—a few times a month, Eric plopped down on the loveseat and reread a textbook such as *Strengths of Materials* or *Introduction to Infrastructure*. Once,

Jennifer would have felt a sympathetic shame for anyone displaying this level of earnest dorkiness. However, on the turbulent thirteen-hour flight from Paris to Indianapolis, she'd squeezed the armrest as she watched the jet's wing flex and curl like a cheap kitchen knife. Miraculously, it remained intact. Complex traffic signals, the level and plumb walls of their apartment—even the meticulously tongue-and-groove wooden siding in their living room gave her a newfound respect for engineers. It was a well-paying career, too, which was nice. Jennifer grew up rich, but she was poor now that she was estranged from her family.

She'd been rearranging his books by the color of their spines, ROYGBIV, when she discovered the orange book. Whatever it was, reading it might make for a nice indoor diversion. The weather had been pleasantly bland the week she moved in, but as the summer wore on and newscasters warned of "heat domes" and "corn sweat," it felt like someone had twisted Indiana's thermostat to max before ripping it off the wall.

The building quivered as a fleet of tractor trailers rushed by. There was a Walmart distribution center outside the city. That was one surprising aspect of rural Indiana—she'd never imagined eighteen-wheelers could drive so fast down residential streets. When they passed, the floor didn't just shake—it was like standing on the back of a shuddering giant. Her phone rattled on the counter—Eric texting that he was stuck in traffic.

She pried at the clasp with her fingernail, but it didn't budge. Jamming paper clips into the keyhole accomplished nothing. The junk drawer in the kitchen held only Allen wrenches, batteries, and a blue dry-erase marker. *U hav toolbox?* she texted back.

U want red/white 4 dinner? he responded. The Kroger was on the way home, and they needed wine. She slid the locked book into its place on the shelf's rainbow.

That evening, Eric heaped corn salad onto his plate. Even though he was originally from the Philly suburbs, he could have easily played a farmer's son in a Hallmark Channel movie: blond hair parted in the middle and feathered—a haircut gloriously out of style that somehow suited him. At five foot eleven, he was the tallest man she'd ever dated. He'd been a walk-on at Illinois State, had "clawed his way" (his phrasing) to earn a football scholarship his junior year. Removed from the buzz of the campus, though, he had the placid air of someone who didn't expect surprises but was delighted enough when they parachuted into his life. "It's funny," he said.

"What's funny?" she said. Jennifer wondered if he'd finally gotten the joke. The day she arrived in town, they'd dined at the fanciest restaurant in town, which had a Bible verse stenciled above the entrance. When Jennifer, bemused, asked their waiter about it, he said it was an "affirmation of *traditional values*." She feigned ignorance and the waiter's mouth split into a dazzling paternal smile. "Man protects, woman provides," he declared. Jennifer and Eric laughed about it on the way home, but the next evening, Eric trudged into the apartment after work and glanced at the empty kitchen table. "Oh, I thought you'd make dinner. Since you're just hanging out here all day," he didn't say. His fridge was barren, filled mostly with condiments. She plunked a jar of olives at his place at the table and he forced a laugh.

The next day, she decided to put her own spin on the "traditional" role she'd been nudged toward and prepared the most Caucasoid Midwestern dinner imaginable: pork chops, Jell-O casserole, red potato salad with chives. The tradition persisted: tonight's offering consisted of creamed corn soup as appetizer, corn salad with black beans and bacon, and sweet grits as dessert. He'd wolfed it down without comment until now.

He gestured at his plate. "Obviously, this food came from somewhere, but I can never picture you cooking."

Jennifer shrugged. "If you want, you can stay home and watch." His eyes lit up a little, set off by an oversensitive innuendo meter. "All my friends in Paris were foodies. They were really into dinner parties, and you can only attend so many before you're obligated to host one."

"I like American, but do you ever make Chinese food?"

Jennifer's grin faded a little, then she tried on a more quizzical version. Didn't they know each other pretty well? For example, he knew she wasn't Chinese and was actually Korean, right? Korean American. She tried to recall whether they'd discussed it. Of course, Korean Americans could still make Chinese food. Even if he didn't know her ethnicity, the truth was, she didn't know everything about him. In the weeks since she'd moved in, he'd complained more about his boss, the job site, and "damage ratios," but she couldn't picture exactly what he did as a civil engineer. At this point, it seemed weird to ask. There was an orange INDOT vest in the backseat of his Civic Hybrid. Maybe he was responsible for maintaining the traffic grid? Was that a thing?

"You okay, babe?"

"No, it's cool. I can make Chinese if you want."

"I'm not picky."

In this chapter of her life, Jennifer Moon thought of herself as a fugitive. After all, she'd fled her domineering Korean American family, which had its own set of "traditional" demands. She pictured her father hanging Wanted posters bearing her face in career centers, singles bars, family gatherings. She had a narrow face that bordered on plain, but a good sketch artist would accentuate her high, near-Mongolian cheekbones and meticulously threaded eyebrows. A good painter would emphasize the way she took in a room or landscape, perhaps by suggesting the broad sweep of her scrutiny with an unconscious clenching of the jaw, or the faint squint when a color or shape drew her interest.

Locals probably assumed she was a college student. To blend in, she should have donned a hoodie and yoga pants. Still, she accessorized like a fugitive, with scarves and a gray bucket hat. She wanted the option to obscure her face—in a small town, someone was always watching.

Her mission for the day was to find ingredients for pork lo mein. The heat dome still shimmered above Indiana, and she regretted sleeping until noon. It was a long, toasty walk to the grocery store, since she didn't own a car and Eric needed his for work. She would have cooked more Asian food if Eric owned a wok. Moving in, she was stunned by how little he owned: aside from the basic hand towels and wooden spoons, his apartment contained an IKEA wardrobe, a modest flatscreen TV, a loveseat, and a crowded bookshelf. It was a one-bedroom apartment, so the sparseness seemed fitting until she focused on it. She couldn't help but suspect he rented a storage locker stacked high with mildewing sports equipment, family photo albums, lawn chairs, and a vacuum cleaner.

Jennifer doubted the local grocery store carried fresh bamboo shoots, but sometimes this town surprised her. Treading down the apartment building's staircase, she decided the stain on the gray industrial carpet was from an exploded two-liter of Pepsi. It had the right color and scent. A fixture with a motion sensor and bulbs hung from the ceiling, but it wasn't connected to anything. With some effort, she shoved open the tall wooden door and braced herself for the weather.

On the sidewalk, children had abandoned their chalk next to half-finished cats and mermaids. Wilted shreds of water balloons baked into the cement. As she followed the shade cast by the building's awning, she felt a tap on her shoulder. She turned, but no one was behind her. She glanced up just in time to dodge a thin arc of liquid. "Hey," she yelped, stumbling back. With a hand shielding her eyes, she glared up at the building's second-story windows. One was open, the bottom portion occupied by an ancient air conditioner. "What the fuck was that?" she yelled up. A man's face appeared in the window, followed by a few more arcs of liquid that landed wide to her left. It was hard to make out his features, but she was clearly in his line of sight. A focused squint revealed long brown hair that fell around the man's shoulders. A long goateed face sporting a pair of oval wire-framed spectacles.

"Hi," she called up in a perky cheerleader voice. The man's placid expression didn't change, and he remained motionless. Another spurt of liquid arced from the window. "Okay, well, nice to meet you. Guess that's the Midwestern niceness everyone talks about." She muttered the second sentence to herself. Spending all day in Eric's apartment hadn't made her lonely yet, but it would have been nice to befriend a neighbor. After she'd crossed the yard, she checked over her shoulder: both the face and the air conditioner were gone.

As the heat evaporated the stain from her sundress, she crossed into downtown and passed the county courthouse, a tan three-story affair whose Corinthian columns and limestone exterior lent it the proper amount of gravitas. The week she'd arrived, each window was festooned with patriotic bunting, but today they stood bare. She was tempted to call a cab but decided against it.

She'd sworn off cabs after the harrowing ride from the airport to Eric's apartment. After loading her suitcases, the cab driver had started with innocuous questions, smiling back at her through the partition. Where had she flown in from? Mentioning Paris opened up any conversation. The driver knew about the catacombs, and she recommended them, although the weirdest thing about seeing mosaics made of skulls and femurs was how quickly you got used to it. She hadn't conversed with anyone in over thirteen hours, and talking felt like a long exhale. He asked what she was doing in America, and she said she was visiting her boyfriend. "A mutual friend from college said we should go on a date. Before, Eric and I were just friends."

They started texting, then Skypeing, then Skypeing nude, her leather office chair surprisingly cool on her butt and back. "I was impressed he'd rearranged his schedule to cover the time-zone difference. Seven hours. That's when I knew he was different." She admitted that she was a little nervous about seeing him in person for the first time in years. The cabbie nodded and didn't mention the four large suitcases in the trunk.

After watching the sum on the fare meter increase alarmingly, she consulted her phone and the GPS said Eric's apartment was still twenty miles away. He'd claimed to live on the outskirts of Indianapolis, not in an entirely different city. As she tossed her phone into her purse, she frowned at the cracks in the vinyl backseat. From the outside, the cab, a scuffed yellow Crown Vic, seemed charming. Upon further inspection, the acrylic partition looked like someone had stabbed at it with a screwdriver. The door to slide money through had been epoxied shut. Either security cameras were new in American cabs or she'd never noticed them before. This camera was brand-new, with a greenish tint to the spider-eye lens. With a grinding noise, it followed her as she leaned from its field of view. A vague panic slid into the back of the cab like a gray mist. Her heartbeat felt muted, the air pressure suddenly thick in her ears. She regretted giving him Eric's address.

She loved Paris so much that she hadn't planned on returning to America, but her father suddenly stopped paying her tuition at Moda. She found out when she tried to register for classes. She surmised her father's decision was due to her grades. Had he deigned to ask, she would have explained that long hours at an internship plus a case of mono had tanked her GPA. Either her mother and sister didn't know—or, most likely, they approved his decision. Her older sister, who had never left Illinois, certainly wouldn't protest some tough love for the Paris Party Girl. By that point, Jennifer had been chatting online with Eric for a few months, and when she raised the possibility of moving back to the States, he invited her to his place.

The security camera in that cab was manufactured by Moon Electronics, her father's company. Just like the chipsets in most Android phones, or the sound systems in most movie theaters. She waved her hand in front of the lens and pictured her dad sitting in their living room, toggling a joystick to zoom in on her face. Maybe with her mother leaning on him with a hand around his waist, blowing on a mug of green tea and shaking her head slowly.

"Miss? Are you okay?" the cab driver asked.

Later that afternoon, condensation beaded on the plastic milk jug sitting on the kitchen floor. Sweating eggs darkened the cups of the papier-mâché carton. The plastic grocery bags balled up in a corner slowly uncrinkled. Eric would be home in an hour, meaning she should have been preparing the marinade and slicing the pork.

Instead, she sat cross-legged on the living room floor, the locked book on her lap. At her feet was an aluminum tenderizing mallet, which was the closest thing to a hammer she could find at the grocery store. It would be hard to hide the damage, she thought as she squeezed the book between her feet and aimed the mallet at the lock.

The first page was blank, with a seven-digit number scrawled across it. Since there wasn't a title, dedication, or chapter heading, reading the second page felt like skidding down a rabbit hole:

> Sigmund Freud (ya know, that old psychologist egghead) once said there are two mysteries in the world, and one of them is "What Do Women Want?" The truth, gentle reader, is that every problem has a solution. It doesn't matter if it's a Rubik's Cube, a Chinese finger trap, or a quadratic equation. Women are no different. Thinking otherwise is a Regressive Step.

She skimmed the next few pages and realized she was holding a seduction manual—she'd heard about these on the news, had seen them advertised in the back of magazines. *Unlock the secrets of the female mind! 100% guaranteed results!* There were a few typos and the phrase "according to Wikipedia" appeared often, but otherwise, the text in this manual was formatted like any book available at the library. Except it didn't have a title, and the publisher wasn't listed. As for the author, it obviously wasn't Eric. Only a certain type of male could write something like "Picture a sleek dog that always heels, faces forward with her tail down, always reliable as she trots alongside you. If you want the girlfriend equivalent, consider the training it took to achieve that. If you're not willing to commit, you're too young for this book, bro." She imagined the author as a twenty-year-old man-child clad in denim short shorts and a pink crop top. He was the type of guy who stumbles into the party and knocks over the TV because he's wearing a lampshade over his head. The type of guy who whips off his sunglasses to reveal a pair of sunglasses underneath.

You may have heard the phrase "Communication is key." Everything from your clothes to your posture tells your Target Woman something. Notice I didn't include "words" in that list. Words are important, but body language is just as important. According to Wikipedia, body language conveys more info than speech or tone. The good news is that women communicate, often unintentionally. The main way a woman communicates her attraction is by playing with her hair.

Jennifer paused—she'd been absentmindedly twirling a strand of hair around her index finger. According to the book, though, every gesture she made was charged with meaning. However, if her actions were truly rooted in her subconscious, she thought, she'd be rolling her eyes and winding the hair around her *middle* finger.

The book's cover was scratched and battered. Eric might not notice the damage if he were in a hurry or not paying close attention, but it was only a matter of time. Confronting him about the seduction manual was tricky now that she'd snooped and ceded the moral high ground. As she mixed together rice wine and soy sauce for the pork marinade, an odd grin pulled at the corners of her mouth. She couldn't explain this new giddiness, but according to the book, women apparently couldn't help being unpredictable. And difficult. Eric didn't comment on the pair of chopsticks she laid next to his bowl. He handled them clumsily, occasionally stabbing at the pork.

As a joke, she'd given him traditional Korean chopsticks, thin and made of slick steel. It was funny at first, since of course he didn't notice the difference, but he was patiently scooping at the bowl long after she'd finished eating. Occasionally, he glanced up for approval. After an hour, she found herself heartened by his resolve. As a little girl learning to use chopsticks, she'd smashed more than one bowl and cursed her parents while her older sister primly lifted a black grain of rice and dropped it onto her plate. Eric simply frowned at the metal sticks, considered his finger placement, and began again.

Presenting dessert, her grin shifted from forced to genuine. "The Chinese serve oranges for wishes of a sweet life," she declared, passing him a saucer of immaculately sliced orange wedges. He pulled the flesh from the rind and chewed slowly.

His mouth half-full, he replied, "You're Korean, though, right?"

A carefully constructed latticework of jokes and assumptions collapsed around her. Turns out, she wasn't dating a guy who thought she was Chinese, or who assumed all Asian cultures were interchangeable. "Yeah. I guess I don't talk a lot about Asian stuff," she said carefully, casting out a line. She tried to recall when they'd discussed her ethnicity. "We, uh, have desserts in Korea, but usually not orange slices. Koreans don't have illusions about the sweet life." She meant to say it sardonically, with a bitter laugh, but here was that silly grin again, and her laughter sounded surprisingly genuine.

The next morning, the fridge was packed with glistening pork. The dishes held their poses on the drying rack. Native Hoosiers swear you can hear corn grow—it's a staticky sound as cells in the stalks rip open, but as Jennifer slid the seduction manual from the shelf, all she heard was the faint hum of the air conditioner and, through the window, chirping birds. In the distance, an eighteen-wheeler's brakes shrieked as it entered downtown. She whistled to the birds as she plopped down on the pleather loveseat. There was something classic about the scent of dry paper. A used book has a comforting feel, like entering a familiar garden path.

Another way women communicate their desire is by crossing and recrossing their legs. Eye contact is an obvious-but-overlooked indicator. If you're the type who can do more than one thing at a time, count the seconds she makes eye contact and compare the duration to chart 2A.

Jennifer scanned the book for highlighting, but any notes Eric took were mental. Thinking back to their Skypes, she never crossed or recrossed her legs—she didn't sit that way. Or did she? The thing about unconscious gestures is that you're not quite in control.

The next page listed "gambits" for chatting, which included several dad jokes: "What do you call a bear with no teeth? A gummy bear." Eric had actually used that one. She'd been draped across the couch in her underwear, and since the book only listed the jokes, it must have been Eric's idea to use a sock puppet to deliver the joke. After that day, her image of him as a stodgy engineer wavered a little before melting away.

As effective as these tactics might have been, it was hard to imagine Eric poring through these chapters. Her first week in Indiana, he'd taken her on a "gastro-tour" (his phrase) through the city's three decent restaurants, then the KFC buffet. He'd been thrilled to buy her jars of organic honey at the farmer's market, along with kitchen magnets made from braided corn leaves. She couldn't remember him playing a single mind game throughout their courtship, online or IRL.

She reclined a bit on the couch, turned the page, and looked down at the bookmark she'd been using. It was a small square school photo—Jennifer recognized her sixteen-year-old face instantly. In the photo, she was wearing the blue plaid skirt and white dress shirt of her high school uniform. She was sitting primly on a stool in the gym, but the photo only showed from the waist up. Her father's company made the camera, the film, and the machine that processed the film. Everyone thought it was sweet that he'd ordered so many photosets of her—bookmarks, wallet-sized prints, key-chains—and she'd responded with a flat smile, unable to explain her ambivalence. And now, this old photo was stuck between the pages of this unpleasant book. Had she absentmindedly grabbed the photo from her wallet or whatever? Unlikely, although she some-times used checks or her driver's license as bookmarks. Had she gifted Eric the photo? No.

The next chapter contained topics such as "Negative Thinking," "Beta Male Habits," and "Asserting Your Domain." There were two types of males: a beta passively accepts his circumstances and refuses to challenge any situation he's placed in. Jennifer couldn't help but note that she'd rejected both her circumstances in Paris and her father's need to control her. Leaving his orbit had hopefully been a body blow to the old man. While she wasn't sure she had the confidence and "wolf-dick charisma" of an Alpha Male, a wave of relief accompanied the knowledge that at least she wasn't a beta.

She checked the back of the book for citations or acknowledg-ments but couldn't even locate the author's name. Eric presumably knew. When he caught on, he was amused by her dinner perfor-mances, but she wasn't sure how to ask about the manual. Maybe snatching the cover off a silver platter to reveal the book? Except

Eric didn't own a platter, silver or otherwise. She should have started prepping dinner, but that seemed like something a beta might do.

She was beyond the point where she could serve anything but leftovers, and the pork lo mein had turned out so well that she wanted to save most of it for herself. She called a local chain and ordered a pizza for delivery. The next chapter on penetration was decidedly unsexy. She skipped ahead a few pages.

more you can control the variables, the greater the likelihood of success. A number of Casanovas (including yours truly) have surveilled restaurants for weeks, charting waiters' schedules and tipping the right folks the right amounts. One time, I'd secured a date with a redhead lass from Ireland, and I needed to seal the deal before she flew back to Dublin. After making friends with the whole waitstaff at a Michelin Star–caliber restaurant, I rented a good suit and met with the restaurant's Executive Manager. I casually mentioned a few investment firms I was "affiliated with," along with the phrases "angel investor" and "maximizing market share." When I'd rang the right bells to make the right dogs drool, I made a reservation for two. The manager himself walked my date and I to our table. Imagine the service I received that night, from the waitress and my date. But that's another story!

Jennifer tossed the book onto the coffee table and slid the window open. The air rushing in had the intensity of a jet engine's wash. Tractor trailers were probably driving past the building all day, but as rush hour approached, their gentle rumbling grew more insistent. Jennifer was bracing herself for the next chapter, "Yellow Fever," when the doorbell rang. The pizza delivery man was her father's age, with a salt-and-pepper beard and the gaunt face of a chronic plasma donor. He seemed annoyed that she didn't tip him but left without comment.

She snapped a fresh tablecloth in the air and draped it over the table, then placed the pizza box in the middle, on a trivet. Well, a salad bowl, since Eric didn't own a trivet. She'd left the box closed, and the crust was soggy.

"It's fine, I don't eat the crusts," Eric said. Jennifer could have sworn she'd seen him eat crusts before. This evening, Eric had plodded to the table right after entering the apartment, stepping over Jennifer's shoes, which were laid out as always on a bamboo mat. In nearly a month, he hadn't taken the hint. She couldn't help but recall a sentence from the orange book: "Make sure to assert your domain in small ways: clothing draped over chairs and seats, silverware spread out across the table. Her unconscious cave-babe brain needs to recognize that wherever she is, *she is in your cave.*"

"Honestly, you cook every day," he said. "I'm thinking of taking that pork for lunch, but my coworkers hate it when people microwave stuff like that."

"*Stuff like that?* It's food. Millions of people eat it every day."

"It's like a policy, no microwaving exotic food, fish."

"*Fish* is exotic in Indiana?" She almost shrieked the whole sentence.

He laughed, eager to defuse this new weird tension. "Well, think of how far we are from the ocean."

"Oh, I have."

"What do you miss most about France?" he asked. Another snippet from the seduction manual popped into her head: "Much like a sheepdog, you must always nudge the convo in a self-beneficial direction." What she missed most about France was, honestly, public transportation. Indianapolis was only fifty miles away, but without a car, it might as well be on the moon. The cornfields and gravel roads had a way of stretching out, making her feel tiny and stranded. "Where I lived in France, there weren't any carpets and everyone took off their shoes in the house," she said finally.

"Babe, believe me, you don't want me taking off my shoes right now." He scooped up a slice of pizza, which was topped with red onions, green peppers, and sausage. The sausage was in bite-sized pellets that had, Jennifer thought, the same texture as cat turds.

"And in Paris, they chew with their mouths closed," she said.

"Mmm." It seemed like he was about to make a joke—maybe open his mouth to reveal a mashed pulp of dough and meat. Instead, he bobbled his head in apology and chewed quietly. Something about the gentle deference nudged her irritation toward rage, but she squeezed and flattened her feelings as she drew and exhaled measured breaths. Eric had a pensive look on his face, as if trying to recall why he was eating so carefully.

"Well, it is your house, after all. Or should I say, your *cave*," Jennifer said. She knew the best course would be to push the argument away from the white heat of her rage. Because although she had the moral upper hand, there was no way she'd be able to articulate why she was so upset.

"Man-cave," he said flatly, pinching a blob of congealed cheese. "But I will say, it's a lot cleaner—"

Was she more upset over the book's content or the fact that he'd kept it hidden? She pictured him smiling and signing off Skype after their first date, closing the laptop with a sharp click and a wistful smile. In her mind, his smile receded and the emotion drained from his face as he opened the laptop to access the Skype archives. He reviewed the video, measuring her eye contact with a stopwatch.

Bathed in the monitor's pale light, his face looked even blanker. Only his eyes moved. Across the table from her, Eric eyed the pizza box. He'd been debating aloud whether it was okay to use the term "man-cave." "I know it's a new era and people are touchy, but I never questioned the term before."

She leaned her chair back a little. "That's because you're the kind who swings his dick and doesn't care who he hits. Your"—a laugh bubbled unbidden from her throat—"swinging wolf-dick."

Eric, who was clearing his plate, began to sit, then stood back up. "I don't get it. Why is—what is happening here?" He placed his plate in the sink, and, noticing hers was clean, returned it to the cabinet. "I usually understand your antics, but—"

Jennifer imagined the inevitable fight—her, struggling to maintain composure while explaining her feelings. How would he react if she retrieved the book and hurled it at him? He might say she was overreacting, or feign offense that she'd invaded his privacy. He might claim that the seduction manual was satire. The possibilities branched out into a decision tree that grew heavier with each possibility. Suddenly exhausted, she rose so they were eye to eye. "I'm calling a peace treaty for now. A détente."

"Well, in a détente, there's further—okay, okay. That's fine." Her plan was to storm out of the room, but he was standing there wide-eyed. As if he were in a museum, realizing his favorite painting was much bigger in real life, the swirls of the paint more textured. Before she could ask, he declared, "I think we just had our first fight."

The next day, Jennifer woke early and headed downtown. She stopped at the ice cream shop, then a couple boutiques stocked with expensive scarves and paperweights. She chatted with the clerks about Paris and Chicago. They seemed to like her. Maybe being Korean

American helped—in a state where fish was exotic, her clear skin and tailored outfits created a metropolitan impression. She frowned when Lampshade-Head, author of the orange book, popped into her mind, jabbing his index finger at her shopping bags and nodding. *You bought just enough to be memorable, and you did a decent job mirroring their speech. Any indications on whether they'll hire you?*

They were vague. I forgot to measure the eye contact, Jennifer replied.

Mention that your dad's CEO of Moon Electronics and you'd be hired in a flash, he stage-whispered. She shooed him from her mind but couldn't help sifting through her memories for clues. The clerk at the upscale boutique was wearing a silver Cuban-link chain that she kept tugging at, like she was trying to saw through her own neck. There were two young women behind the register at the ice cream shop, and their eyes widened perceptibly when Jennifer mentioned the Moda Institute. Presumably, the seduction manual had a chapter that interpreted gestures and expressions, but the book sat untouched on the shelf. When she passed through the living room, she avoided looking in its direction.

Two days later, Eric cooked spaghetti with meatballs that were still a little frozen, but Jennifer buried them with noodles in the hopes they'd thaw. Men Jennifer dated in the past would have treated cooking dinner as a heroic act and expected a stream of compliments. With Eric, there was only a hopeful, vaguely canine expression as he watched her take the first bite. As she crunched through the last of the meatballs, he retrieved a blindfold from his pocket. Unfolding it on the table, he said, "I have a surprise. Let's go for a drive."

Jennifer raised an eyebrow. "Are you wearing the blindfold? If so, there's going to be lots of surprises."

He laughed but got the hint. He wasn't out of the doghouse, so she wasn't going anywhere blindfolded. She followed him down the stairs of the apartment building, noting that their upstairs neighbor's door was slightly ajar. The apartment was dark inside, with the occasional flicker of a blue light, presumably a muted television. Eric held the building's door for her. Parked in front of the building was a red Mini Cooper convertible, its top already down. Eric unlocked it and hopped in. "Stole it from my boss," he said, laughing. The interior was surprisingly roomy, with beige leather seats and a round display monitor in the dash.

They'd eaten late, and the sun was setting. The buildings on Jackson Street were prettier in the gloaming: gone was the corrugated metal siding of unromantic shops like the HVAC repair center. Instead, one's eye was drawn to the solid lines of brick buildings and the stone facades' historic silhouettes. As they exited downtown, the Mini's icy blue headlights slid across the broad glass storefront of the abandoned furniture shop. Jennifer scanned past the country music stations on the car radio, then the Christian talk shows, then the mariachi station. By the time she'd settled for a staticky Top 40 station, they were cruising down a rural highway.

They passed cornfields, the sun skimming through the tassels at the top of the stalks, the leaves broad and healthy. Having grown up in Chicago and driven across Illinois, Jennifer had witnessed pastoral sprawl, but now that she'd lived in rural Indiana, she could better imagine the reality of living someplace where one might not see a car all day, with an endless cornfield as a backyard. Eric pointed out the window to a white two-story Victorian house that seemed to mark the edge of town.

"One time, I was driving this highway and that house was on fire. There was a blue pickup truck in the driveway, and it was on fire, too."

"Oh my God. What did you do?"

"Kept driving. It was like five a.m. and I was coming home from a job site. It was one of those moments where you don't know if you're awake or dreaming. But I remember the smell of it. Burned plastic and rubber. The next time I ventured out here, it was six months later, and the exact same house was back. Looked just like before— same style, color, everything. Same blue truck in the driveway."

An old man in denim overalls jogged across the street to his mailbox. Eric waved, and the man waved back joyfully. Really put his shoulder into it.

"Do you know him?" Jennifer said, changing the station and then turning the radio off.

"What?"

To fill the silence, Jennifer marveled at the almost toxic green of the corn leaves, especially when the stalks were short. She'd honestly never seen that color before. One might expect it in a rainforest, but not on a gravel road in Indiana, lined on both sides by tall cornstalks and trees choked with vines. She said, "I always thought of Indiana with a cream-and-aluminum color scheme. Like Wite-Out on a feed trough. But those corn leaves . . . I could live in a house that color." Eric nodded sagely, then bobbed his head to a song only he could hear.

Ahead, a utility truck was a tiny speck in the distance, but the plume of dust it kicked up stained the air. Eric pushed a button and the soft top unfolded around them, sealing them from the dust and road noise. Gravel pinged off the wheel wells. Beyond the acres of soybean crops, the sky was near indigo. They drove for a few more miles before he checked the rearview mirror and slowed.

"Finally!" he said with mock exasperation, pulling the car onto the shoulder. "I was waiting for the dark, that's what took so long."

"I didn't mind."

A white barn loomed proudly on the opposite side of the road, its loft doors opened to release fluorescent light so intense they could hear the transformer's hum inside the car. The barn sat on a gravel lot facing a small metropolis of grain silos and corn bins. Under cover of night, which hid distant cornfields and elm groves, seeing this cluster of buildings felt like discovering a perfectly preserved ruin in the middle of nowhere. The dark gravel road, the clear night sky, the corn crackling as it grew—it felt like Indiana and perhaps time itself had folded around them.

Gesturing at the structures, Eric said, "Bins are vented . . . they're the fatter ones, with cylindrical roofs. Last year, two of these collapsed and sent ten thousand tons of corn onto this road. Just picture these steaming golden mountains spilled across, with steam rising off them. Well, corn dust, but you get the picture. INDOT supervised the cleanup. I was always out here late, and—I don't know, I thought it was scenic."

Through her window, she followed a pasture as it sloped down gently. There was a patch of grass that resembled a dark sheet weighed down by cylindrical bales of hay. Beyond that were infinite rows of cornfields, and among the rows floated a Milky Way of fireflies, flashing to each other in frenzied constellations.

"Oh. Here," Eric said, following her gaze. He pressed a button and retracted the roof. There was the faint sound of cars whizzing down a faraway interstate. Their road was uninterrupted by headlights. Above them were stable constellations, the stars clear and bright. There was something about the silent car, their pocket of air conditioning meeting the humid night air. Jennifer's heartbeat slowed until she simply wasn't aware of it. The flatness, being enveloped by the quiet dark, unclenched something. "It didn't really feel like I'd lived in Indiana until I'd seen this. So I just wanted to—"

She rested her hand gently on his leg, and he got the hint. Eventually, she said, "You hear stories about people who immigrated to this country and had never seen fireflies before. Or snow. But this . . ."

"I know." The sheer scope of it. And the idea that every day while she slept, this beauty persisted, with no one to witness it. "I think Indiana likes you," he offered.

Without a second thought, she replied, "It's growing on me."

A few days later, as she retrieved the last oatmeal packet from the pantry, she was still making excuses for her boyfriend. At Illinois, she'd owned a few textbooks she never read. The orange book was probably a gag gift that had remained locked the entire time Eric owned it. Any connections she'd made between its techniques and Eric's behavior were merely coincidences. She approached the bookshelf for confirmation and, opening the book, recalled the title of the next chapter. She brewed a mug of mint tea and settled herself warily on the loveseat.

Chapter 9: Yellow Fever
Asian women aren't hard to date if you're White, but luck favors the prepared. That's the difference between rejection and success. If you've been reading and taking notes diligently, you're almost ready for that fortune cookie nookie. Otherwise, get ready to watch her pretend not to speak English and then giggle to her friends as she slurps down the drink you just bought her.

If reading the book made her feel like a dirty vacant lot, the largest billboard on the horizon now shouted "fortune cookie nookie." Beneath the billboard, a crowd of mannequins posed, planted in a patch of crabgrass. Each mannequin had bright yellow skin and the same vacant expression, and Jennifer found herself among them. Blinking, she skipped to chapter ten, titled "Over the Moon."

In 500 BC, Confucius say "*hyo-do*," meaning mother good, father best. I cannot overstate how hard this concept of "Filial Piety" was drilled into every generation so that respect for their elders became almost an instinct. In Confucianism (which had the same effect on Korea as Jesus did America), men were the undisputed head of the household, with children raised to respect elders and care for the elderly. In the man's house, everything had a proper place and order. Women were firmly at the bottom. To disrupt that order was a big no-no, since it basically made the chaos dragon descend from the heavens.

The book hit the opposite wall with a surprisingly loud thud. Hurling it was a fleeting pleasure at best, though. "This is outrageous," Jennifer wanted to shout. She pictured herself growing like a giant with each word. What. The. Fuck. Was a chaos dragon? Maybe it was a magic creature that fed on casual racism. She rinsed the drying oats from her bowl, then paced the apartment, delivering a point-by-point rebuttal to the wall, the microwave, the refrigerator. There were a million better ways to appeal to Asian women, and none of them involved mind games or dragons. Jennifer ticked them off on her fingers—don't be boring. Flirt without being an asshole. Read her cues. Back when they were dating, Eric had . . . Eric had. Those words tumbled in her mind, then settled like dice in the middle of a sentence: their relationship was so smooth, you never would have thought Eric followed a playbook. After what felt like miles of pacing, she returned to the book, if only to fuel her rebuttal.

Just as Whites no longer wear powdered wigs and breeches, Korean Americans don't wear *hanboks* or sacrifice goats to ancestors. However, some concepts still apply:

I. *Han.* Korea is located between China (the original chaos dragon) and Imperial Japan. As a result, Korea was invaded and defeated and colonized countlessly. Then, the Korean War split the country into North and South. By the war's end, each half was ruled by squinty, bloodthirsty dictators.

Imagine if the Civil War didn't end and Americans just built a wall between the Confederate and Union states. That wall keeps the pig-fuckers in Tennessee at bay, but it also keeps you from your family members south of the Mason-Dixon. Same deal with the Koreas, except the North Koreans are starving because their leaders are filthy communists.

South Korea isn't poor anymore, but they'll never forget the humiliations and defeats. They can't unify their country. American military bases act as babysitters. This results in a unique mélange of spite and sadness that echoes in the blood of all Koreans. On the plus side, han is responsible for great Korean songs, paintings, pottery.

Jennifer paused to listen for echoes of sadness in her blood. Maybe she'd ask Eric to buy a stethoscope so they could listen together. She was fairly confident the author didn't know many Asian

Americans, period. In order to finish the book, it was best to com-
partmentalize. Chapters one through nine were wrapped in thick
sheets of plastic and rolled to the deep-storage section of her brain.
She needed to make room if she wanted to learn what a sizeable
portion of this country actually thought of women like her.

> II. Education: grueling civil servant exams were a big part of
> the Korean Confucian system, and this tradition led to a big
> respect for education. Also, while children are supposed to sac-
> rifice for their parents, immigrants who give up everything to
> come to America have flipped the script. This leads to a one-two
> punch: like Jews, Koreans see education as the path to success.
> In America, immigrant parents expect even more, academically
> speaking, from their children.

Even if she'd noticed, Jennifer would have never admitted to
nodding along as she read this passage. She'd never been to Korea
and hadn't given much thought to the life her parents left behind in
Busan. They rarely mentioned it. She'd seen a few photographs from
that time, but they were all portraits, and no one was smiling. The
reds and yellows had faded in a way that didn't flatter the subjects.
Had Jennifer been the photographer, she would have opted for black-
and-white film.

As a teenager, Jennifer developed an obsession where she
couldn't help mentally reinventing the world, reorganizing the color
schemes in hotel lobbies, curating new wardrobes for political candidates, rearranging the racks in department stores for more efficient
traffic. This particular vision earned her a paid internship at Jalou
Media Group in Paris, but people like her father couldn't help but
wonder what she could accomplish in a boardroom.

She skipped the "Harmony" section after the sentence "Sexual energy must be balanced with an opposing force." Otherwise, presumably, the chaos dragon would appear. The next chapter was titled "Family."

Her father has money and influence, which makes him extremely dangerous. If you haven't already, scrub all social media accounts. No doubt, this tech CEO has a team combing through your Twitter for evidence that he'll present TO HER as signs of your racism or inadequacy. He already hates you because you're White, which means you're established in a world he's working hard to infiltrate.

Your best hope is appealing to the mother, Myeongja "Diana" Moon, whose occupation is listed as "homemaker." You'll need to convince her that you're a different type of boyfriend, which won't be hard. You'll need a soft touch regarding confidence: convince Mom that you have options, which means if Mom doesn't play nice, maybe she'll end up with the deep han-shame of an unmarried daughter.

Jennifer also admires her older sister, Laura, who is the eldest and most loved. Laura is the ideal Jennifer constantly falls short of: Laura attended a local college to stay close to her parents, graduated with honors, and currently utilizes her math brain to advance her career at Moon Electronics.

Jennifer wandered dazed through the chapter—what else did the author know about Laura? Jennifer learned that her sister was briefly on Twitter and had volunteered for an NGO in El Salvador. It felt like there were tiny points of light in her blood, dancing, and they were heating up her face. She held still, the book on her lap, afraid of what it might vomit up next. The book contained appendices listing Jennifer's height, weight, date of birth. There was a chart of her menstrual cycle and a list of comforting techniques. On the book's last page was a short benediction:

Remember: our girl is at a stage where she's trying to break free of family expectations. Jennifer is tired of her family using her own potential to smack her around, but she still wants the warm blankie of shared history and love. Being so far from her family has opened a ragged hole in her soul, and you can't close it by yourself.

Aside from indulging her outbursts of han, listening to her, and taking her seriously, the best way to handle her is to give her intellect a purpose. That's the primary absence in her life.

Jennifer finished her tea without noticing it had grown cold. She returned the book to the shelf. As the child of a tech CEO, one of her favorite activities had been peeling off the plastic film from appliances and gadgets. That fresh chemical smell underneath. Reading the orange book was like peeling a sheet of plastic from reality's surface, except underneath was this pulsing rot, and part of her was peeling away, too. Eric had clearly commissioned this book somehow, then internalized its lessons. What's the appropriate reaction to learning your entire relationship is based on surveillance and traps? At dinner, she played the girlfriend role, even though her lips were numb and rubbery when she smiled. He must have talked for a while, since it was well after eight when they cleared the dishes.

Though she lay on her side and tried not to touch him that

night, her back sometimes pressed against his. He was turned away, and though she knew he hadn't written the book, she couldn't help but picture a lampshade over his head, radiating a soft amber glow. Beneath was a face that never slept. Its eyes might have been lit by a drunken, celebratory glow, but the face itself was a dull symbol for everything unloved and predatory. Wasn't there a curse in the Bible, something like *May you fall in love with the devouring and never be full?*

There were four apartments in the building; most of their neighbors worked the midnight shift at a local Subaru plant. Even so, no one had a regular schedule: sometimes, the murmur of a party would rise through the floor at noon on a Tuesday. Someone occasionally practiced jazz saxophone in the morning. Jennifer slipped out the building's front door dressed in her long pajama T-shirt and leggings. As she wandered down the sidewalk, most of the building's lights were still blazing. It was two a.m. She wondered what their upstairs neighbor, the long-haired weirdo who'd squirted water onto her dress, was up to. The night air cleared her head a little.

On the opposite side of the street, a man stepped from a white Chevy pickup and turned her way. She couldn't discern his face, especially after the truck's dome light winked out. Moonlight gleamed off the cars parked along the street. For all she knew, there was someone seated in each one, watching. She jammed her key between her fingers so the serrated part stuck out like a claw. The man spread his arms in a *What, bitch?* gesture and jabbed his index finger toward her apartment. The pulsing in her temples matched her heartbeat, but she couldn't quite force herself to run. The man opened the driver's-side door and swung himself inside, the dome light illuminating a curly quiff of dark hair. She wanted to yell,

I'm not afraid, asshole! but knew her voice would shake. A firefly pulsed above a strip of grass near the roadside. Another landed on a branch, like a green cinder. The man sat without moving in the dark cab. Later, as she lay perfectly still in bed, she thought Pickup Man was pointing at the moon, or the building itself. For all she knew, he was standing outside the building at that very moment, pointing at her.

She skipped dinner the next day and piled the refrigerator's contents—a packet of hot dogs, a squeeze bottle of expired mustard, and a Tupperware full of pork lo mein—at Eric's spot at the table. He wasn't thrilled but didn't complain. That evening, as he lay in bed watching *SportsCenter*, Jennifer watched through the window as a white pickup truck drove past their apartment building again. A silver sedan honked and sped around it. She regretted not getting the truck's license plate when she had the chance, but its driver would have noticed and things might have taken a darker turn. Finishing the seduction manual meant crossing into a chapter of her life where anything was possible: maybe her father hired the man in the white truck to spy on her. Or, recalling how he'd pointed at the apartment, Jennifer thought maybe Pickup Man was guarding her.

The next afternoon, she woke around two p.m. and the books on the shelf were back in chronological order. The orange book was gone. Eric had finally figured it out—he knew Jennifer had seen his true face, the one that whispered its mantra of *Manipulate, Dominate, Penetrate.* What would the scene look like when Eric arrived home? She pictured a quick bulge in his jaw muscles as he steeled his resolve, his eyes the last thing to deaden as he quietly pulled the door shut behind him. Crying and packing didn't go well together. At one point, she was shaken from a stupor by a passing car's bass—she realized she was holding a bra and wondered where the past thirty minutes had gone. What did her time with Eric mean? When she recalled their relationship, a figure with a lampshade on his head now danced in the background, a dim orange light seeping from his head. The horizon in those memories dipped and swung as they revised themselves, and she fled the nausea to focus on the present. She was stuffing shirts into garbage bags when Eric arrived home.

"You're early," she said. Her words stuck a little from unexpected mucus in the back of her throat.

"Look," he said, unzipping his messenger bag and holding the seduction manual out like a confession, or a shield, before tossing it on the floor. "I'm sorry. I messed up." There was that earnest, plain face she'd loved, but there was something disarming about the new stubble around his mouth and his harried, pleading eyes. She'd never seen him beg before—not really. "There's no excuse."

She resisted the instinct to comfort him, although this sudden outpouring of apologies felt contagious. "*But . . .*"

"I'm not making excuses. I skipped work and drove to the library just to reread this . . . thing. When we started dating online, things were different. We weren't in college anymore. You'd moved to Paris, and I was—school kept me busy and I hadn't dated in years. I was afraid I wasn't interesting enough." He dropped his hands to his hips, then crossed them like he was hugging himself.

"You could have—"

"I mean, I found advice online, but about dating, I didn't know what I didn't know. And you're not on social media, so there were these gaps. Look, I wanted things to work out. At the job site, there was this guy who used to be a cop. He did contracting work for INDOT but claimed to be a private investigator. I told him I was nervous about dating you, and he started emailing me dating tips. Then he started researching you. I guess he printed out this book online or something. I don't think he ever stopped writing, I just stopped paying him."

"I won't ask what it cost," she said, pointing to the book, which he kicked. It slid along the carpet into the living room.

"Not you, I hope. I really like you. Look, people stalk each other now. Online. It's weird, but it's normal? You only learn so much by talking, and no one's themselves when you start dating. Plus, I know I'm a white guy." He lowered his voice. "Everyone hates us now. I didn't want to say the wrong thing and lose you."

His eyes were huge and damp. *Don't cry*, she thought. She was building a metaphor to explain how she felt, but she could only locate easy phrases: "betrayed trust," "built on a lie," "violation." Whatever she was thinking, it came through clearly on her face. Eric's face scrunched like he was biting down on an ancient, bitter truth, and he started bawling in earnest. His lip quivered even as he tried to steady his breathing. Nothing could prepare her for this moment, but there was something about the way he cast about for a prop—glasses to remove and wipe, a cell phone to hold. Despite his fidgeting, he seemed to know there was nothing to hide behind. There was only him, and her. He wiped at the tears with his palms, but his frustration wasn't directed at her. He was used to being in control, and he hated airing his shame, even as penance. A few tractor trailers rumbled down the street.

Finally, he leaned against the wall and blew out a long exhale. "Okay, just think about your options. I'll drive you to your parents' if you want."

In the quiet that followed, she compared her family to the book's grotesque sketches. Being exiled to a quiet town emphasized how much she missed them. They hadn't spoken much since she'd moved overseas—old resentments, her discovery of wine, and the time zone difference hadn't helped. Eric was still talking, a little panicked by her silence. "Or—I'll get you a cab. If you can't stand to be near me. I'd understand."

"It's a three-hour drive to Chicago," she said, then realized he meant a cab to the airport. "That investigator, the guy who wrote the book. Does he drive a—"

"Silverado 1500. It's a stick shift, actually." He confirmed it was a white Chevy.

"That man knows things *my doctor* doesn't."

"He's good. I mean, he's a thorough creep, but that's what I wanted. *Was* what I wanted. I don't know, he goes through your trash and interviews your friends. Poses as a journalist or a cop, whatever it takes. But that's all that happened: he gave me the book. I skimmed it when we were dating, forgot about it, and never saw him again. I don't know how to get ahold of him. I'm just—if you believe in forgiveness . . . someday. And if you think people can change."

She called for another détente. Her suitcases and trash bags of clothes remained near the door. The book rested on the floor, open to a chapter titled "Kino 101." They carefully stepped around it. At some point, she had packed food in a suitcase; mustard and hot-dog water leaked into her blouses.

"The stuff he wrote about my family was really fucked up," she said, meaning it was invasive and terrible, as opposed to inaccurate. It was late and her face was obscured by shadow as she leaned against the bedroom doorway. He was lying on the love seat, his pillow tossed on the floor because there was barely room for him.

"I'm sorry," he said, sitting up to face her. "I didn't know he was going to do that."

Around midnight, she left for a walk, except this time she packed pepper spray, a pocketknife, and her cell phone. Her plan was to photograph Pickup Man's license plate if he showed. There was a window outside Eric's door that allowed in some moonlight, but otherwise the hallway was dark. The door to their upstairs neighbor's apartment stood wide open, a cave-dark expanse behind it. She'd have to pass within a few feet of it. Once she started down the stairs, the railing's spindles would protect her, though something determined could grab her, pull her through. Outside, the street sweeper was grinding its way across the parking lot, its headlights casting out a weak yellow.

"Hello?" she whispered, her heartbeat warning her that any sound was a risk. The unmoving dark in the neighbor's apartment took in the sound, returning nothing.

The next afternoon, she wedged the orange book back onto the shelf and threw away the food in her suitcase. "This doesn't mean anything," she said. Eric nodded, then passed her on the way to the bathroom. He'd taken the day off of work and was slightly stooped from the cramped loveseat. To distract herself, she lay in bed and watched a documentary about Moon Electronics, which included several shots of her dad standing on a pier, hands clasped behind his back in a vaguely martial pose. The screen slowly zoomed in on his expression, which he'd carefully assembled into that of a benevolent visionary as he nodded thoughtfully and answered softball questions. The narrator called him a "transcendent figure" more than once. Who could believe this kind-faced, pensive man was just as insecure and controlling as a bad boyfriend? What made him that way?

Later that evening, the pickup truck returned. According to Eric, the private investigator's name was Dustin. Jennifer wondered if Dustin was writing a new edition of the seduction manual, updated since the estrangement. Alone in her bed, she'd thought about her father, about the concept of filial piety. It was true he'd cut her off by not paying tuition, but why? She'd assumed it was a power move meant to control her, but what if it wasn't? She knew people could change—she barely recognized the young woman who arrived at the Indianapolis airport with a hopeful smile, whose sound decision making led her to shack up with a man she hardly knew. In a sinister town hidden between cornfields. Her father had to know she was back in the States, practically in his backyard. Why hadn't he reached out? She mulled over the numerous ways she could find out. "You're sure you don't know how to contact Dustin?" she called from the living room.

"I've tried. He keeps sending bills, but there's no return address," Eric said. He was cleaning the kitchen.

She retrieved the book and flipped to the first page, which contained those handwritten seven numbers. "What's the area code here?"

He told her. She punched the digits into her cell phone and waited for the truck to reappear before pressing Send. The pickup truck slowed to a stop and Dustin held a glowing rectangle to his ear.

"Edward Moon. My father," Jennifer said, picturing a thick

hardbound volume, one that was exhaustively researched, one that could finally explain her father in a way that made him forgivable.

Dustin stared forward through the windshield. She'd expected him to at least glance up toward their apartment, but he just nodded. In a soft Kentucky accent, as if he'd been expecting her call, he replied, "What about him?"

BETA

360

For the third time this week, my father appears on television. This evening, he seems at ease in Anderson Cooper's studio, with its electric blue background and glass tabletops. Dad's fingers drum lightly and the threads in his linen sports jacket shimmer in the bright lights. Cooper begins with a list of my father's accomplishments as founder and CEO of Moon Electronics, "a company that's giving South Korean rivals LG and Samsung a run for their money." Dad stares humbly at his lap, and the veteran journalist transitions into his opening question. "Everyone's so concerned about the future. As someone who's practically an oracle in the tech industry, can you provide us with any hope?" Cooper punctuates the last sentence with a slight tilt of the head, a perfectly timed raised eyebrow.

My father chuckles. "Well, I'm not an oracle. I don't wear a robe and carry a torch. But it's a good question." He folds his hands and pauses. "In the tech field, companies keep using the term 'ecosystem,' but I think that's wrong. At my company, we use the word 'family' to describe our product lines. Our smartphones and fridges and security cameras all communicate seamlessly. We don't view one as better than the others, they just have different tasks. In Asia, we think a lot about harmony."

Cooper nods before seeming to realize that Edward's answer is more of an advertisement than a revelation.

He rephrases his question, but my dad is a step ahead. "The term 'ecosystem' suggests companies like Apple and Microsoft are trying to create their own worlds, terrariums to trap the consumer in. The problem is that most tech companies view technology as a tool. And that's why every other company will ultimately fail."

Reeling a little from the jargon and bluster, Cooper pivots. "What would you say to people who might be skeptical of your grand vision? Just last week, Tesla Motors—"

"Technology is merely a reflection of who we are. With every step—every iteration of product development—I consider who we are as a species and then imagine the best version of ourselves. As a CEO, I find there's nothing more resilient or beautiful than my family."

He delivers this last line so earnestly I can picture his company's stock price rising on the spiced-vanilla breeze of his charisma. Somewhere, his shareholders are swooning. The truth is, the man hasn't spoken to me, his youngest daughter, in over two years. Aiming the remote at his face and hitting the Mute button feels satisfying. I'm recording the interview, and it's weirdly comforting to know I'll be able to rewind and replay the best scenes. The screen flickers, and the silence enhances the mastery of his performance—he's nearly lost himself in the role of a family man moonlighting as a CEO.

I pause the interview to take in Dad's hollow smile. He's never sought the spotlight—it must have taken a team of media coaches to sand his personality down to this wise, serene persona. A line of text is frozen midcrawl at the bottom of the screen: "Changes on the horizon for Moon Electronics." Truthfully, it's a bit sad seeing him reduced to a spokesman, with all his weapons left behind.

What would happen if I called in and set the record straight, live on TV? It would be worth breaking the two-year silence just to see Dad's mask slip a little. Onscreen, his black hair is neatly combed and severely parted to the side. His most distinguishing feature is a pair of low-set jug-handle ears that should be disarming but somehow contribute to his natural resting expression, which is a broad ray of paternal disappointment. It's mostly in the eyes: looking enough, one senses a welling sadness, but the gaze clearly says, *You'd never guess where I'd rather be.* And sometimes, *I'm documenting your mistakes.*

I hit the Live TV button on the remote to see if there's a number to call in. The screen judders before the pixels reassemble into the unexpected shape of my sister, Laura. This must be a prerecorded clip because she's on a living room set, perched a little too straight on the edge of a leather wingback recliner. Light glints off her silver pendant earrings, and from the look on her face, she's repeating to herself, *Don't screw this up, don't forget to smile.* Cooper sits opposite her on a couch. "Laura Moon started her career as a marketing intern at her father's company when she was still in college. She rose to the rank of senior project manager by twenty-two. When she isn't crafting viral videos or helming ad campaigns, Moon volunteers her skills for water-rights NGOs in Honduras. Did I miss anything?"

She shakes her head. I wish she'd announce that she's much more than a senior manager. I want viewers to know that as a six-year-old, she only drew horses. She's the girl who boycotted the grade school spelling bee because, as she announced to the teacher, it was "i-m-p-r-a-c-t-i-c-a-l." She believed everyone's time could be more wisely spent elsewhere. Those flashes of rebellion became rarer in seventh grade, when she decided she wanted to be class valedictorian. Laura still has some fire left in her: I wish Anderson Cooper would tell viewers Laura's origin story. When she started at Moon Electronics, Dad didn't have much faith in her and locked her away in the grimy tower of the Innovative PR division. They were in charge of regional social media, and this—plus her family name—gave her just enough leverage. Behind the scenes, she pushed for the industry's first e-waste recycling initiative, which saved the company millions and netted millions in free airtime when the media picked up the story. Months later, Moon Electronics was back in the news when she started a campaign to move the company's supply chain out of countries that use child soldiers. That year, Laura also graduated high school, where she'd been crowned covaledictorian.

The white-haired journalist asks what it was like being raised by a visionary. I turn the volume up, loud enough to hear the tremble in her voice. "In a lot of ways, it was a traditional Korean house-hold," she says, smoothing her dress against her thighs. Translation: *I was passed from the jaws of a tiger mom to a tiger dad for eighteen years.* She offers a quick smile before composing herself. "But I'm not just the CEO's daughter anymore. I'm looking forward to taking an active role in the company as we begin our next phase." Her delivery reminds me of a hostage forced to read a list of demands, and I make a mental note to investigate what my father's company is up to. But I forget it, because when the camera zooms in, it's clear Laura's been crying. Her eyes are bloodshot, and when the camera zooms in, I can see her forcing herself to return its gaze.

I've been living with my boyfriend for the past couple years in a small town outside Indianapolis. If he were home, he'd wrap his arms around me and then distract me by taking me out to dinner, or for a long drive. He certainly wouldn't let me finish watching the interview, which features a cameo by my mother, who holds hands with Dad in the living room of their Chicago house and leans her head against his before lovingly scolding him for forgetting her birthday. His eyes widen in genuine panic before she says, "Just kidding." To Cooper, she says, "See, this is how busy he's been with his project. Beta testing. Committee meetings." In a chair next to them, Laura forces a smile.

The show concludes with Cooper remarking how "complete and full" Edward Moon's life is, how his family is the embodiment of the American dream, and how his company "seems poised to reshape not only how we live in the future, but what we believe to be possible." I watch it again just to make sure, but no one—not even Laura—mentions me. Alone on the couch, I can't help but feel misplaced, or like a glistening appendix that's been excised and plopped in a jar. I tell myself that there's no way my family is really this happy. They might have tricked everyone watching *Anderson Cooper 360°*, but I know they're covering for something. Most people probably skipped over Laura's segment, but watching her stumble through the interview felt startlingly intimate—I've never seen that raw, plucked version of her.

I call my boyfriend, Eric, but he doesn't answer. He's traveling for work and won't be home for a few days. If he were here, he'd remind me why I stopped talking to my family in the first place. He'd say that I should just call Laura to see if she's okay. He'd explain that returning home unannounced is a bad idea. Online, red-eye flights from IND to MDW are surprisingly affordable.

MILES

The cab I hailed at Midway drops me off in Edgewood. My parents' house, a white Victorian with a prominent bay window, looks the

same as when I left. Nobody's home, so I let myself in and head to
my old room upstairs. The decor hasn't changed since I escaped
to college. Unchanged are the cream-white walls and the empty
clear-plastic shoe organizer clinging to the closet door. Years ago,
my mother rubbed the bottoms of the dresser drawers with green-tea
soap ("To grease the sliding") and left an extra bar in the sock drawer
for fragrance. I'm grateful for the gentle maternal scent as I open the
dresser to survey the clothes seventeen-year-old Jennifer left behind.
Except those drawers are empty now. There's only a bar of soap.

A car pulls up the driveway, and I jog down the stairs and fling
open the door. No one appears for a long time, and as I circle around
to the backyard, my sister rises from a crouch, alarmed by my footsteps on the gravel. There's a waist-high hedge between us.

"Oh," she says, with more relief than surprise.

"You're smoking now?" I ask.

She shrugs and ashes on the lawn. "Don't tell Mom. Dad probably knows, but don't tell him, either."

It's October, too early for the thick coat she's wearing. Without
makeup, she looks especially sleep-deprived and wary. The skin
around her eyes is red, as if she's been rubbing at it. I let her observe
me in silence as she finishes the cigarette. Her expression changes to
something more neutral, but the way she crushes the cigarette butt
with her heel feels a little sinister.

Once inside the house, she ducks into the bathroom as I head to
the bedroom we shared as teenagers. A minute later, she strides in
and sheds the coat, revealing a white Akris blouse and black slacks.
Surveying her silver necklace and earrings, I realize she's returning
from a business meeting, or a power lunch. Or a date. During the
television interview, her hair was parted in the middle so she looked
like a tour guide in a pottery museum. Now, she's stylishly parted

it to the side, with gentle feathering and a few strands of premature gray. It's hard to tell whether she's grown into or grown beyond her big-sister role now that she's in her midtwenties.

"You're not going to ask why I'm back?" I ask. She sits on her bed and stares at the lone poster on the wall, which depicts Miles Davis exhaling a rainbow-colored cloud.

"I guess it doesn't really matter. You're here at the worst possible time, though," she replies.

"Look, I'm sorry," I tell her. Three years ago, when I started studying in Paris, I thought fashion school would be like the movies—an electric metropolitan zeal, classrooms full of witty, capable women wearing scarves. I sit up so I can look her in the eye. "I thought the Moda Institute would solve all my problems. So prestigious, something I could be proud of, even if Mom and Dad disapproved. But the truth is, Moda thins the herd by keeping only the most devoted. I'm talking sleep deprivation to break you, elitism, emotional highs and lows, cutting off family and friends. Guilt. If you're not pinning fabric through a nervous breakdown, you don't really want to be there."

She barely skips a beat. "And you want a cookie for surviving two years, then fleeing to Indiana to shack up with some white dude."

I shoot back, "I didn't realize you're running low on cookies. Jesus Christ." In less than ten minutes, we've reverted to the familiar groove we'd carved throughout our cohabitation. As she removes earrings, it dawns on me—the formal event was last night, and she's only now returning home, worn out with puffy eyes. From the smell of the jacket and hair, she spent most of last night filling up an ashtray between bouts of crying. I know those tears weren't for me. "You slept in those clothes," I say, studying the wrinkles on her blouse. "Where were you last night?"

"Minding my business," she replies. "Some of us can't run away when we want to." That last sentence has a stinger, and I let its venom pump into me. I want to fill the silence with apologies—for not being here, most of all. How many other times has she cried alone? Only the perfect apology, words in the perfect order, delivered in the right tone, can fix two years of absence. Another car pulls up the driveway. I peek out the window—it's Mom, carrying a bag of groceries. "Welcome home," Laura says as she slides off the bed and pads from the room. My apology, a ribbon of neon-blue words, floats silently and breaks against the creases in her expensive blouse.

SILK DAMASK

With Laura gone, the tension in the room recedes, leaving me stranded with chunks of debris wobbling around me: a half-finished pier of regret, a clot of weed-strangled guilt. I don't realize I've fled until I'm in the hallway, breathing Lamaze style as I fight back tears. Despite my mother's best attempts, I'm not a crier. It feels like accepting defeat. Maybe I'm trying to overcompensate for my disastrous meeting with Laura when I head to Mom's room.

From the look on our mother's face, Laura must have warned her that I'm home. Our mom is short but proportional at five foot, five inches. Up top, she's still rocking the *ajumma* curly-helmet perm. In her arms is a traditional hanbok, neatly folded so the cavernous white collar opens atop the folded silk pieces, the wide pink sleeves folded in traditional-style disapproval. Her stoic expression remains unchanged as she places the hanbok next to me on the bed. Our eyes meet, and she almost imperceptibly lifts an immaculately plucked eyebrow. "Every wedding our family attended, every gathering, people ask, 'Where is Jennifer?' I tell them you're busy in Paris. My brother calls during Christmas and New Year—'Where's Jenny?'

My father dies, and at the funeral, I make the typical excuses—Paris, fashion school, internship. Cousin Min says you're in Indiana, living with a boy. That's how I find out."

"He's white, too," I say, because I'm cornered and need to push her back a little. Also, it's true and she'll find out eventually. My parents are first-generation immigrants and have a deeply ingrained mistrust of white people. "I still would have been in Paris, except Dad stopped paying tuition at Moda. I found out when I tried to register for classes."

"Your grades—"

"I had mono, and I was slaving away at that internship. Dad didn't bother to ask before cutting me off. Neither did you, or Laura."

"Well, you're here now. What did you learn?"

I run a finger over the neck of the garment. It dawns on me that mothers and daughters have been fighting and healing for centuries. Language contains culture, but looking over the garment's deceptively complex layers and textures, I think fashion makes tradition and conflict just as visible.

None of the women in our family were fighting when we took the special trip to Albany Park to buy hanboks. I was eight, Laura was ten. This was before we had a driver, an accountant, or a stylist, my mother dutifully performing each task as required. The store itself was a few blocks removed from the main drag. The entryway made it seem tiny from the street, but it revealed itself to be warehouse-sized once we passed through the door. Every style of hanbok hung over our heads, stiffly folded and pinned to the walls like butterflies. Inside that shop, Korea owned every color, from the lemon-yellow jackets to royal-blue sashes to milk-colored tops whose embroidery cataloged infinite varieties of flowers and birds.

A pair of wizened Korean women stood behind a table piled with silk damask. The smell of dust and peach-scented fabric somehow emphasized that these women were the wisest, most capable people in the world.

Over a decade later, my mother holds the jacket up to my neck, checking it against my skin tone. I tell her, "You bought Laura a hanbok, too." To this, Mom just grunts.

"Always together, you two. Now she's busy, busy, busy. Stand up," she says. Hanboks are complicated—even families in Korea hire consultants to assemble them properly. But my mother expertly wraps the skirt around my waist. "Turn." I feel exposed somehow, the silk bright against my jeans.

"When we looked at them, I thought these were the fanciest things I'd ever seen. Laura and I wanted to wear ours everywhere, but you never let us touch them. Remember how we'd beg just to see them?"

"It was never just *see*. Then touch, then try on. One of you would start, then both of you." She smooths out the jacket on the bed. "You can tell," she says. What she means is that after a year of fashion school, I know from the fabric and stitching that they're well constructed but modest, the kind of garment a middle-class family might aspire to.

"Everybody wants fancy, but at the time, this was all we had. And two daughters." What she means is, *Once upon a time, this was the best we could do. Even now, all I can do is offer everything I have.* We'd both imagined the person who would someday wear this complicated outfit to the most formal of occasions, and she's hoping I can still measure up.

I'm extending a thin and spindly olive branch when I ask if she wants me to try the whole thing on. Her face brightens, as if this wasn't her goal all along.

THE EXECUTIVE STUDY

Downstairs, it's a little cooler, and since I have the floor to myself, I start snooping. In place of a couch and television, our living room features an oak desk sagging under the weight of engineering manuals, stacks of fan-folded computer paper, and an ancient CRT monitor. Under a canvas drop cloth is an old synthesizer, a precursor to Moon Electronics' ubiquitous studio model.

He—I mean they—are up to something. I can detect Laura's presence in the stacks of paper placed in stations around the room. Nothing's labeled, but it doesn't take long to find two file cabinets packed with financial documents. I cock my head and listen to my mother's footsteps upstairs. She's putting the hanbok away, perhaps taking out Laura's to examine. From the rhythm of her footsteps, she's dancing.

This particular cabinet was raided by someone who closed it in a hurry—a manila envelope is caught in the door. There are five battered hanging folders inside, and I photograph their contents with my phone, feeling like the star of my own spy film. A black Town Car pulls up to the curb—through the window, I watch my dad exit, buttoning his suit coat before striding toward the house with the grim determination of someone called to testify before Congress. I quickly replace the files and slink upstairs.

The truth is, I barely know my father. It's been so long since we've spoken—and even before that, I'm hard-pressed to find a strong moment of connection. I'm not sure what these financial documents will reveal about him, but maybe the best way to understand a family is through their secrets. In the corner of my room, through the stereo, Freddie Hubbard's trumpet makes neon-red scribbles of notes in the air. My father's voice passes by my door. Sensing me, he pauses in the doorway. His powder-blue tie is loose around his neck. He's on an important call, assembling himself into a salaryman as he preps for a meeting, but he's not busy enough to express annoyance that I'm lying in bed at two p.m., staring at my phone. If he were monitoring my screen, he'd be surprised to see me poring over his financial disclosures and internal memos. He'd be shocked to realize I understand them, but he's always underestimated the fashion industry. "Art and commerce are fraternal twins," my advisor loved to say, and I took every business course Moda Institute offered. Some of Dad's financial documents are murky (I didn't say I *passed* every business course), but I can still weave the numbers and tables and memories into a narrative. I wish it were a happier one.

LONESOME TONIGHT

The year is 1978 and his name is Moon Jeong-hun. I wasn't there, but if I know my father, he wasn't surprised to learn about the bounty on his head. Picture him standing proud in his charcoal Western suit, his oxford wingtips gleaming and a fat silk tie around his neck as he receives the news from a distant relative nicknamed "Rabbit Ears," who works at the marketplace newsstand. He steps away a little unsteadily.

Back then, South Korea was a backwater third-world country where parents held their pooping children out over the street. When Dad was born, they were spraying the blood of student protestors off the sidewalks in Busan. The blood of protestors and political opponents and incorruptible businessmen fertilized the nation's economic miracle to the point where even a self-made man like Dad could be successful enough to wear a price on his head. As he exits the marketplace, he recovers enough from the shock to find himself upset that the sum is so low. ₩2,000,000 is only about $50,000 in today's dollars.

By this point, he'd studied in America and earned degrees in electrical engineering and business from Seoul National University. Picture him muttering, "If I sold my heart and liver and kidneys on the black market, I'd net about two million." It seemed his enemies were only interested in his brain. Then, as now, South Korea was ruled by five chaebol families who basically owned the country, and they didn't particularly welcome competition. The trouble started when Edward returned from California with a notebook full of foreign ideas.

Packed in his luggage were measurements and blueprints. He started a business in his living room, crouched in front of an upright piano, stacks of magnetic tape reels scattered on the carpet. This was an early analog synthesizer: pressing a key would trigger a sound preserved in a length of magnetic tape. My father hadn't invented this: he'd played a Mellotron at an electronics trade show while studying at Caltech. He simply reverse engineered the technology and stream-lined the manufacturing process. At the time, South Korea's postwar economy was booming, and pianos were popular: imagine a status symbol that doubles as an educational tool for children. The export market was heating up, and Edward waded fearlessly into the fray carrying his sexy electronic piano.

As he wades out of the fray, Edward wonders if he thanked Rabbit Ears for the warning. He scrutinizes the neighborhood, the alleyways. As for the pedestrians, each is a potential assassin. My dad imagines his death: the likeliest method is poison. He sees himself at a round table in a restaurant, surrounded by close friends, when the waiter holds out a cup of soju, cupped between both palms.

By the year's end, my father had settled in Chicago and taken the name Edward Moon, although the name didn't quite suit him yet, since Edward Moon is a multinational entity. As my mother arranged furniture, he paced in this office, his neck cocked against the phone's warm plastic receiver. Edward has never heard my grandfather sing and is surprised by the man's warm baritone as Elvis lyrics soar through the crackle and hiss of the long-distance line. *Hal-abeoji*, my grandfather, worked in the music field and had the foresight to purchase the Korean distribution rights for RCA and other American record companies. As rock and roll waned, he succumbed to dementia. Though he regularly forgot names and dates, some trick of the brain allowed him perfect recall of old song lyrics. There was an urgency to the way he sang, as if to say, *This is the last thing I do well,* so my father listened, tapping and swinging the phone cord to the rhythm.

In 1978, in Chicago, the Moon family was tethered firmly to Korea: Edward paced and worried at the phone cord while he consulted with his engineering teams in Seoul, their ideas hurtling back from fourteen hours in the future. That year, Soviets launched satellites and cosmonauts into the heavens. Over a thousand people had settled in Jonestown. South Korean actress Choi Eun-hee was kidnapped and spirited away to North Korea. In this age of extreme displacement, Edward Moon listens to his father falter in the middle of "Blue River," filling in the frustrated silence with humming. In the silence that precedes another attempt, Edward wants to respond by singing the first song that pops into his head, "Arirang." Instead, he gently places the receiver onto its cradle and wipes his eyes with a sleeve. As the phone rings, he sits at the piano bench and sucks in a rattling breath, but under this pressure, he can no longer hold himself together. He fractures into the helpless firstborn son, the wary immigrant, the sturdy husband, the anxious inventor, the thwarted entrepreneur. In that moment, one that he'll never quite escape, he stumbles to gather these shards of himself as the phone rings, and rings again, and then stops.

CLOUDS

The phone keeps buzzing in my pocket as we prepare a late lunch in the kitchen. I know it's my boyfriend, Eric, texting me, but my hands are full right now. Laura's posted in front of a silver bowl, mixing pork, kimchi, and ginger. When the batch is finished, she passes it to Mom, who scoops the filling into gyoza wrappers and pinches the dumplings into perfect crescents before passing them off to me. My job has the highest stakes: add the right amount of water, cook to the correct shade of brown, remove to a baking tray to cool.

"It's ironic, since Mom retired from cooking when I was ten," I say. She scoffs and waves the idea away. "Remember?" I ask Laura. "She actually used the word 'retire,' announced it at the dinner table in this very house."

"I don't remember anyone volunteering to help her cook," Laura pipes in to score an easy point.

Mentally, I compose a text message to Eric: *Relations w/ Mom & Laura thawing. Dad TBD.* "Where is the patriarch?" I ask. Downtown, Laura reports, meeting with clients. Before he left this afternoon, he mumbled something about "the merger" as she helped him into his coat. Mergers happen all the time, but this one feels different—he's been on the phone nonstop since I arrived. I've heard him turning down meetings with celebrity VCs. If will.i.am can't get a meeting with him, it's not looking good for me.

"Save room for the family dinner," Mom says. If necessary, I'll reconcile with him publically tonight, but right now I'm more concerned with the Moon women. I mentioned before that my cooking station has the highest stakes, but it also has the best reward: there's a special alchemy when the dumplings, soaked with rice-vinegar tang, hit the skillet. The crisp sizzle. The steam whirling through the kitchen carries a blend of pork, garlic, fermented cabbage—in short, it smells like my childhood. Cooking was Laura's idea, her own olive branch. She knew I could handle this station, and a comfortable peace settled as we assumed familiar roles. We have a tall stack of wrappers left—and I can't help but start humming. *Let's get it started. Let's get it started in here.*

THE EXECUTIVE BOARD

Moon Jeong-hun is a family man in his sixties who is most comfortable in a white cotton dress shirt, gray slacks, and a red tie. Baek Soo-min, CEO of Ppalgancheol Heavy Industries, is wearing a three-piece charcoal suit in his only existing photograph. Mun Young-soo, the CEO of Nakdong Life, an insurance company, is thirty-five years old and owns no clothing. Kim Sang-chul, CEO of the Hongcheon Tech Incubator, has technically been dead for over a decade.

Imitating the fracture he experienced during his nervous breakdown, Edward Moon split his Korean corporation into a several non-threatening small businesses. Imagine a lizard shedding its tail to avoid predators. To keep control over this new empire, he created several fake CEOs—paper golems—and legitimized them with stolen family registries and diplomas. Behind the scenes, trusted executives from my father's old company ran day-to-day operations. Edward started his own company, Moon Electronics, but its market share was so microscopic that the chaebol cartels must have written it off as a hobby.

In a collision of displacement and time travel, Laura's sitting cross-legged on her bed, reading the same paperwork I'd looked over a few hours ago. She's tossed some receipts and memos on the floor, confident that I don't understand them. She frowns, retrieves her laptop, and researches something online. Back in high school, Laura was the student who would revise a paper so she could turn it in early to impress her teachers. Then, she'd ask for it back so she could edit it some more. From her intense concentration, whatever she's working on with Dad must have no room for error.

Intentionally or not, each alias is a funhouse mirror reflection of my father: the CEO he created for his shipbuilding company is a master of persuasion. From what I read in acquisitions contracts, he always walks away with more than he requested. In a telephone interview published in a local newspaper, the reporter fawns over the CEO's history of success even though the CEO never directly mentions it. Reading the transcript, one almost misses the hints and allusions, and of course these personality traits are evident in the man's parenting.

Here is Laura at seven years old, sitting next to Dad at the piano in his study. Her back is impossibly straight, perhaps reinforced with pride after she's finally been allowed to sit next to him on the stool, which is covered with a cream-colored lambskin rug. Mostly I notice the bench has legs that end in clawfoot talons, each clutching a clear marble. Five-year-old me wants to gnaw on them.

"We'll start with the Bach prelude," he says, and she beams up at him like she understands. She's so overcome that it takes a few minutes before she recognizes the pattern: two notes with the left hand, then the right completing the melody. Slight variations repeat in a pleasant-enough fashion, but it feels like a continuation of the scales she mastered during piano time in preschool.

Playing the showman, he demonstrates the features of his new piano, which is actually a synthesizer. "You choose the instrument sounds," he says, playing a minor-key trill as he cycles through them:

a tinny trumpet, a harpsichord, a celestial choir. She hesitates, then pushes the Piano button, glancing up to receive a subtle nod.

"The best way to hear classical," he begins, but even as she's committing the sheet music to memory, she wishes he'd pick a different song. She can't name it yet, but she wants the music she hears drifting through the floorboards late at night: the staggering notes of Miles Davis's muted trumpet, like an elegant dancer on a rooftop, bathed in moonlight and pretending to be drunk. Although there's a Trumpet button on the keyboard, it's not the same. She'd even settle for the frisky piano propping up John Coltrane's soprano sax in his version of "My Favorite Things," which my father plays on repeat late at night. It's that or Elvis's early *Sun Sessions*.

Back then, those names were foreign to us. Laura stumbles through the first few measures and Dad is silent as she tries again, correcting her mistakes on the fly. In the shadow of his silence, she plays the whole song, but hesitating, at the speed of a dirge, a soundtrack to a film where the pallbearers keep dropping the coffin. After a few more tries, he pushes the bench away from the synthesizer and without a word exits the room. Laura folds her hands on her lap, concentrates, and begins again, almost pounding the keys in the hopes he'll notice.

SUMMA CUM LAUDE

Laura could have sabotaged our father's happiness by announcing the truth: she really wanted to play the violin. There was something hypnotic about the sawing motion of the bow, not to mention the shape of the instrument and its plaintive vibrato. If she noticed the frown on Dad's face, she might have connected it to the fact that the violin was one of the few instruments Dad's synthesizers couldn't replicate. One might imagine her cataloging this particular weakness for use in the future. That's of course the path I took, and if my sister knew I was projecting it on her, she'd shake it off like a horse twitching its haunches to shoo a fly. As engrossed as she is in assessment paperwork and shareholder memos, she knows I'm thinking about her. It's hard to explain—our relationship is like a magnetic field, one that causes iron shavings to shiver and dance before standing on end. In accordance with our parents' wishes, Laura studied business at the University of Chicago before graduating SCL in three years. In accordance with my parents' secret wishes, I left the country and put seven hours' worth of time zones between us. Today, though, we're basically back to where we started.

The unofficial truce we held while cooking has steamed away— she subtly turns so I can't reread the papers she's holding. A second later, she shuts her eyes hard, eyelids pulling her eyeballs toward her brain. I've seen this before. She's warding off a migraine. I should rush off the bed, close the curtains, and bring her a steaming mug of jasmine tea. Instead, go for the throat: "What exactly are you and Dad working on?"

She rubs the spot between her eyes, which are still screwed shut. "It's complicated," she responds, which could mean:

a) Your nimrod brain could not possibly comprehend this business deal
b) It's complex and difficult, "it" referring to Laura's relationship with our dad
c) Its complexity is excruciating, "it" referring to her impending migraine

I don't know why this sets me off. Maybe it's the shit sandwich of options "a" and "c." I should take the high road, but I can't help myself. Laura's worked so hard over the past decade for one simple reason. "It's the stress . . . you're so afraid of becoming me."

"That's not true," she says, pinching the bridge of her nose and releasing a steady, controlled breath.

"Really? Name one way you're proud of me. One." She opens her eyes, wincing a little. Maybe she's trying to stall. All her life, she's let the spotlight shine hot on Jennifer the family burden, the fashion school dropout who sleeps in till noon. The family shame generator who skipped cram school, wore makeup, and napped during school assemblies.

"I could name lots of things." I'm demanding specifics when she says, "You got out."

My mouth hangs open as the retort I'd prepared falls silent. Before my eyes, my sister shimmers a little in her transformation from a high-functioning praise addict into a familiar stranger. This new Laura's gaze is almost too painful to return. In a panic, I throw out something to change the subject. "I know about the fake CEOs. Dad's multiple business personalities. You two left the paperwork out. I can still read Korean, you know."

She's good at hiding her surprise, but mentally, she's walking it back. How hard is it, really, to read an invoice and piece together a narrative? "If you already know, why ask?" she says, flopping backward as she retreats into her migraine. A thin orange paper floats to the ground.

"This big merger that's killing you . . . mergers happen all the time. What's the urgency?"

"It's an issue of magnitude. Nobody's ever tried anything this big. But nothing's happening if I can't attend dinner. Right now, this light feels like broken glass stabbing into my eyes. Like, through them, into . . ."

"Gotcha," I say, and the mattress squeaks a little as I hop off. It's overcast out, and the few birds patiently sitting on the power lines turn to watch me draw the curtains. I would describe my demeanor as quietly contemplative as I leave the room to brew a pot of jasmine tea.

UNEXPECTED GUESTS

Our family dinner takes place in Avondale, which in my absence has finished gentrifying. The Korean restaurant we're dining in has a weathered brick facade and barely any signage. Our private room in the back radiates order and serenity. Gone are the music and laughter from the main dining area. The tables here are cut from a darker, more endangered wood. The point of this evening's dinner is allegedly to celebrate my homecoming. Laura, to my left, hasn't recovered from her migraine, but the room is dimly lit and she manages to flash a convincing-enough smile when necessary. It took effort to coax her into that striped knit top—she complained it was too formfitting—but it pairs nicely with the white skirt. To my right, my mother folds her hands as she exchanges pleasantries with the strangers across the table. On the drive here, I asked if she knew what this "family dinner" was really about, or if she knew anything about the merger, and she just quirked her mouth into a half smile before remarking, "It's almost over." She's dressed conservatively in a navy blazer and wool skirt, but over it all she wears a cloak of aloofness. Her expression is that of an unimpressed poker player sizing up the competition.

The men across the table talk quietly among themselves, but a jolt of energy crosses their faces when my father steps into the room. False alarm: he apologetically gestures to his phone before ducking away. While the men we're dining with seem unperturbed, they exchange glances like this dinner is already deviating from the script. I gesture to the youngest one, who sits across from Laura. His name is Min-soo, "but just call me Kevin." He's my age, early twenties, dressed in a suit that's slightly too big, like his mother bought it for him and left some room to grow. He's Korean, with a flattering Ivy League haircut. On his face are a pair of designer spectacles with clear plastic frames—they're angled to give him an incredulous, vaguely flirty expression.

"So, Kevin, how do you know my father?"

"I'm the CPO of his tech incubator," he brags, earning an elbow nudge from the older man beside him. "The *acting* CPO. Chief privacy officer." The man next to him is his uncle, who does consulting work for Moon Electronics.

Kevin says, "My other uncle was the former CPO. He died of *gwarosa*, and I'm decrypting his files."

"Gwarosa?" I say.

Kevin's uncle provides a definition. "Death from overwork. *Karoshi* in Japanese."

A giggle escapes me, followed by an apologetic gesture. "The French don't have a word for that."

Kevin's uncle forges ahead, stone-faced, with his explanation. "With the last CPO dead, heart attack, we can't access accounts. Can't regulate the cooling in the server farms. Two already burned. Kevin has degrees in computer science. For the past two weeks, he's recovering the files and working with Laura so everything else with the incubator is ready to go." Laura nods, widens her eyes a little as if to say, *And what a wild ride it's been.*

It's hard to gauge where the silence is coming from, but it goes on for too long. I grab the first anecdote that comes to mind. "When I was in Paris, my Textile Sciences prof emailed me this article 'Five

Habits of Successful Millionaires.'" At the word "millionaire," Kevin perks up.

"She likes starting sentences like that. 'When I was in Paris,'" my mother says.

"Ever since I came back from Paris. It was my first term abroad, and that listicle reminded me of home. Before that, I'd only felt homesick in grocery stores. The French have a strange aversion to peanut butter."

"What were the habits? Of millionaires?" Kevin asks.

I do my best to remember. "Habits separating millionaires from the rest of us are: They cultivate knowledge in their field, daily. Maintain social networks (mostly in-person visits or phone calls), and spend no more than sixty minutes on personal delights each day."

"And what do you do for personal delights?" he asks. I can't tell if he's flirting. His uncle studies the menu with practiced inattention.

I say, "I have to admit, I'm impressed by how Dad combined all three with this meal. Cultivating knowledge and maintaining relationships with your family, plus family time with his own." That's only part of his agenda, though.

"And how did you improve after reading this article?" my mother asks, her Asian tongue stumbling a little over the last syllable.

I reply, "Well, I'm not a millionaire. Mostly, I thought the advice was obvious. Even if someone formed all those habits, even if they made everyone millionaires, they'd still be light years behind someone like my dad. Infrastructure repair."

"What?" Kevin says.

"You asked about personal delights," I say. "Well, today, I spent more than sixty minutes rebuilding my 'social network,' but I want you to know about my progress with infrastructure repair."

So far, Kevin's been conducting himself with the wary politeness
of a young Midwestern Republican, but now he's willing to flirt back.
"And what—"

"Sorry," my father announces with an apologetic smile. No one
saw him approaching. He grabs a glass, which he holds up in a toast.
As he says, "To my daughter," I'm trying to remember the last time
I heard the man apologize.

"And to Lee Sang-chul," Kevin mutters to his uncle, whose face
hardens a little. Everyone else pretends not to have heard. Mentally,
I'm Googling the name: picture a thought bubble where a cell phone
screen glows a dim blue. Our brains might be supercomputers, but
mine yields zero results.

"Lee Sang-chul's in good company. Lots of friends to share a cell
with," my father says, breaking the tension. The men laugh. After
the waitress takes our orders, Kevin shifts his focus to Laura, even
making her laugh a few times. I reaffirm my mission for tonight,
which is to figure out what Dad's up to with this merger. Maybe I
can find a way to pull Laura from its stressful vortex. And I need
to start fixing my relationship with my dad. We've been stuck in a
pattern where we fight and separate, and if we can't break that pattern
soon, I doubt our relationship will survive. In the meantime, I wait
for an opening. Phrases I overhear my father say as my chopsticks
lift slices of pickled daikon from the banchan dishes:

"Without Laura, there is no merger. Honestly."

"I haven't been back since 1978, but I still wake up to the KBS
news broadcast every morning." To Kevin, warmly: "What year
were you born?"

"Sometimes, when I say I'm from Korea, Americans still ask—
completely straight-faced—'North or South?'"

Our main courses arrive, and Kevin's ordered the spicy pork

belly, which sulks and hisses on his plate, threatening to spray red bean paste onto his tie. The scent of the pork is so thick I'll be washing it out of my hair this evening. I don't mind at all. Laura's jealous because if we were sitting in the main dining room, and it was just our family, we'd be parrying each other's chopsticks to snatch the perfect fatty piece of maroon pork. Laura picks at a conservative fried-rice dish, something she doesn't risk wearing on her shirt.

SONG ROOM

As we finish eating, Mom feigns a stomachache, dialing our driver and exiting on a wave of envy: everyone knows that Korean business dinners end with several hours of liver torment. The word "noraebang" gets tossed around like a beach ball at a concert, my father flinching each time he hears it. Moon Electronics owns a music subsidiary, so everyone assumes its CEO must love singing in front of strangers. It wasn't solely my idea to change venues, but how could Dad turn down a public request from his homecoming daughter? Our private karaoke room looks like a dorm study lounge, with IKEA chairs arranged around a pair of round tables. There's a loveseat near the back, but the room's focal point is the giant flatscreen.

My father's company made the TV, the karaoke software loaded onto it, the microphone, the remote we use to call up songs, and the lighting system that casts disco neon on Laura and me as we launch into "Steal My Sunshine." It was our go-to song during high school, and since we memorized both parts of the duet, we can prompt each other instead of turning to the screen for the lyrics. Some magic combination of absence and soju is propping Laura and me up as we bounce along to the slightly deranged piano. She's hugging me around the waist, really digging in, but it's what we both need. I make sure she's the first to pull away. "I love you," I shout to her over the music. I don't care that we have an audience and I'm tipsy: I'm going to remember tonight as the moment dancing with my sister revealed the truth: relations with my parents will always be fraught, but I'll always have my sister. I vow she'll never shed another tear of loneliness or sorrow. Everyone thinks they're clapping at our singing. The television flashes our score: 79/100.

Dad has the same expression you see sometimes on animals at the zoo. *Please, we won't tell anyone if you just unlatch that gate.* He's surprised to learn that anyone can sign their companions up for songs, and that I've assigned him the Red Hot Chili Peppers' "Give It Away." It feels good to know more about his software than he does, and he dutifully faces the screen as the slightly off-brand music starts. He's a good enough sport—doesn't want to embarrass himself in front of his subordinates. Two verses in, he finds his groove and slides out of his suit jacket, his tie swinging as he jabs at the air with his free hand. Somehow, this makes his singing sound worse. The chorus ends, then ends again, and when he scores a 60, we make a big show of protesting. "Meaning I should sing it again?" he says, a kamikaze gleam in his eyes. We protest in earnest. I grab the remote and sign Kevin up for "Where Have All the Cowboys Gone?"

EIGHT LIVES

Long after midnight, the five of us have relocated to the private dining room of a different restaurant my father owns. This one is in Bridgeport. My dad pats Laura's hand as Kevin makes a long pronouncement about supply-side economics. I'm not sure if Dad's conveying sympathy or encouragement. Our faces are bathed in the green light of at least five empty soju bottles in the middle of the table, meaning we've consumed enough rice liquor to wipe out a preschool. As Kevin sermonizes, my father nods along. It occurs to me that for most of the dinner, my father's stories have been aimed at Kevin, even when Dad wasn't directly speaking to him. Laura's expression is neutral, hooded.

Kevin's uncle has mastered the art of flirting without actually flirting and is practicing his craft on the middle-aged waitress. It's all I can do to stay upright. I am proud of my finishing-school posture. At the far end of the table, Laura has her phone out, and she's puzzling over the screen with Kevin.

"Growing up, that never would have been allowed at the table," I tell my father.

"Cell phones didn't exist."

"Still, any kind of distraction. We couldn't even watch TV while we ate."

"You lived." He tells me Laura and Kevin are always collaborating. She knows the corporate structure and he knows the tech infrastructure. If Kevin can decrypt the accounts, he'll "win the kingdom." Dad mentions something about personal and professional spheres.

Intentionally or not, he's given me an opening. "They say every politician has two selves: the tactical self and the private self. Each with its own face."

"I'm not a politician. And who says that?"

"My poli-sci professor. And I do think you know what I'm talking about. Except you have maybe more than two faces? Maybe five?" I relish the pause and let the number roll off my tongue. Something in my father's brain wakes and waves away the soju fumes as he swings the full weight of his attention toward me. While he's trying to figure out how much I know, he glances over at Laura and Kevin, who are still leaning over the cell phone.

"You've traveled only for vacation. You can't imagine leaving everything behind. It's hard to leave family, so much behind."

I say nothing.

"Splitting up my company and hiding behind a shell corporation saved my empire, but it scattered me. I never got over it. Running with tail between legs to America. Licking boots of the people who destroyed my country. You know five companies?"

I list the CEOs for him, making sure to do so with perfect Korean intonation, and in alphabetical order.

"You know partly, as usual. I created seven companies plus Moon Electronics, which means eight different lives. Eight lies. Every morning, I remake myself. You have no idea how exhausting that is." The next part he explains with the flourish of a weary magician: "What we're technically doing is a mass acquisition, but the paperwork's as complicated as merging eight companies at once. But when it's over, I step from the shadows. Complete. No more hiding." No doubt he's picturing himself as a reassembled colossus, the Pacific up to his waist as he wades toward the southern coast of Korea, his home city of Busan, his enormous moss-covered fingers straining toward the curve of sand. One CEO, reunified and fearless.

"Everything was on track. Then the CPO of the Hongcheon Tech Incubator died from gwarosa. Your sister wasted seventy-four hours trying to reconstruct his files before we called Kevin."

Kevin's uncle shuffles from the room, probably for a dignified bout of vomiting in the bathroom. Kevin and Laura conspire quietly. The cell phone has returned to Kevin's pocket, but neither have moved from each other. He sneaks a quick kiss on her ear and she stiffens—just for a second—before relaxing her posture and sipping her soju like nothing happened. Only I saw it. In the moment that follows, I become aware of the acrid smell of tabletop disinfectant. The waitress complains into her cell phone as she paces the kitchen.

When she returns, a calm half-smile on her face, Kevin orders another bottle of soju.

I turn back to my dad. "You know, if you're having trouble cracking a hard drive, I know people who can help." His smirk fades when I say he'd be surprised by the number of smart people I know.

"Kevin has things covered with Laura. This merger needs to happen soon. Lee Sang-chul"—a small ding goes off in my brain— "was arrested in an anti-corruption sting and is waiting sentencing this week." Experts predict a life sentence. My father explains that his company needs to file its paperwork before the National Assembly passes new regulations in the wake of the scandal. "If we don't complete the merger in the next few weeks, I'll lose Korea." *Again*, he doesn't say. It hits me: Lee Sang-chul was the chaebol boss who tried to assassinate my dad in the late seventies.

"We're headed to the office," Kevin says, standing to pass the fresh bottle of soju to his uncle, who accepts it stoically. It is around three a.m. Laura has the same defeated expression she wore this morning as she returned to her own bed at noon. In the world I've returned to, everyone has an agenda and nothing's free. My father wants those files decrypted, but what he really wants is to unify his companies so he can feel whole. Laura, who understands that her father's love is conditional, has retrieved her coat and folds it over her chest. She won't look at me.

"Wait." Standing so quickly was a mistake—the liquor has soaked through my stomach and into my veins, and the lozenge-shaped light fixtures on the ceiling tilt grotesquely. Somehow, I maneuver myself between Kevin and my father. I drop my voice to the most threatening hiss I can muster and whisper in Dad's ear, "You can't seriously—"

"We're on a deadline," my father says, but it sounds like a warning.

The evening has worn him down to his capitalist war-face. His gaze has sharpened into the kind that carves meat from bone, bundles and weighs the wet mass before calculating a value. This kind of gaze can look past a lot of things to justify a result. "Funny, you're not dressed like a pimp" is what I should have said.

He's still seated, but five thousand years of culture means his presence towers over us as he studies his warm, half-full glass of soju. *This matter is settled*, his demeanor says. Before I left for Paris, I would have backed down with an apology. But I'm remembering the Anderson Cooper interview, and the quiver in Laura's voice, and I'm not willing to look past the trade that's happening here. My father's presence is nearly blinding from the corner of my eye as I turn back to Laura.

She's donned her coat, gathering and flipping her hair so it falls over the collar. As if we're alone, I tell her, "I thought we could spend some sister time together," adding a hopeful lilt at the end.

Kevin frowns. "We're on a deadline. The merger."

"Merger merger merger murder," Laura intones flatly, resting a hand heavily on my shoulder. "But I'll . . . spring back to life once it's over. We can have sister time then."

Before I can stop myself, I pluck the glass from my father's hand, somehow managing not to spill a drop. "Are you seriously letting this happen? This is your *daughter*." Kevin's uncle is deep enough in his glassy-eyed stupor that he only now turns to us. "Do you really think this will fix you? Nothing is worth this."

"I'm standing right here," Kevin says, jamming his hands in his pants pockets, then taking them out once he realizes how pouty he looks. "Seriously, we're signing paperwork. Reviewing balance sheets one last time—"

"Organizing audited financial statements. Maybe you can help," my sister says, her eyes broadcasting innocence, but there's a patina of acid etched into her tone. Her attitude toward me has returned to its natural condescending state as she makes her decision and returns to our father's orbit. Maybe she really believes that she and Kevin are just going to review paperwork this time.

Earlier today, I started to understand my father—he wants to recapture the joy he felt when he was poor and desperate, frantically dialing his own father in Korea to hide assets while he budgeted his meager resources in America. During that era, he was drunk on faith—in his wife, in his own wits. My faith in my sister, and the future, withers in the fury she radiates as she adjusts her collar and gently nudges Kevin with her shoulder. I should have stepped forward and taken her hand, but the fight was already over. That feeling as Laura led Kevin from the room and toward his bed—I finally understood my father's quest to reassemble himself. I'd give anything just to step back from the threshold of that moment, to pause and rest my hand against the cold glass of my life before learning how easily everything could shatter, and how sharp the fragments would be.

For Laura, the family's memory palace is a brick firehouse nestled between Pullman's historic warehouses. The firehouse, whose windows have been bricked over, isn't marked with a street number. Entry to the lobby requires a comically large steel key. She trudges up the cobwebbed staircase to the storage unit her father owns and, after popping the lock with another key, slides up the steel garage-style door.

In the pause before entering, Laura recalls a story about a man who pantomimed hanging his troubles on the dwarf maple in his front yard before entering his house light and happy. There's only a metal folding chair in the firehouse hallway, but if she could, Laura would peel off her unhappiness and hang it on the chair like a soggy sweater, watch it drip onto the stone floor. Sometimes, she regrets working for her father. Interviewing a CEO to replace him would be stressful even if he weren't part of the search team. Her dad's top candidates are all unmarried men, and he wants his eldest, single daughter to spend an unreasonable amount of time getting to know each of them. She returns to this storage locker more and more often, partly for the thrill of invading her father's private sanctum. Also, he's long forgotten this place, the payments debiting automatically from an unmarked business account. Within these walls, there's a peaceful, temporary obliteration.

The far end of the room is filled with boxes stacked nearly twenty feet high. Against the far wall, her parents slid wooden trunks filled with artifacts from their travels together. Laura can smell the dry wood and rope, with a hint of garlic and musty spices. Her shadow falls over a living room–sized expanse littered with Berber rugs wrapped in clear plastic sleeves, art objects—a small onyx owl, a hardwood bust of a young man wearing a kaffiyeh. The metal rack pushed against the side wall contains outrageous turquoise blouses made of windbreaker fabric, leopard-fur coats, disco-era sequined dresses she can't imagine her mother wearing. Hidden behind the modern clothes are the more exotic treasures: a pink kaftan; a dazzling, vaguely martial Algerian karakou jacket embroidered in gold, complete with a jeweled headscarf. In the very front row, only three boxes are placed front and center, and Laura can't help but think they resemble a beige throne. An invitation. The room's stillness isn't enough. She wants to escape. She enters the room knowing exactly where she'll sit, which life she'll try on first.

THE IMPOSSIBLE DAUGHTER

We hold ourselves so still in this heat that one could imagine us as a tableau on a tapestry, woven so tightly that the fabric might split with the slightest change in air pressure. Our royal court, depicted in a vaguely Orientalist style, opens itself to the viewer in a panorama of Moorish arches, damasked curtains the color of tangerines, Turkish lanterns with flames nodding at the tan limestone walls. In the foreground—always in the foreground—my father the emperor faces the entryway. He leans slightly forward in anticipation. Out of fear and respect, someone weaving a tapestry of this scene might merely suggest the dark bags under his eyes. One sees his long, curly beard and thinks of moss covering a ruin. Still, even in his weariness, he is as imposing as a monument.

Arranged next to the throne are his advisors: four men who, in the style of the period, would be depicted as either comically thin or rotund. Each has narrow eyes and a wispy beard. My back is to the viewer, so the first thing one notices is my thick black mane, which my attendants valiantly brushed this morning until it was briefly presentable. In our empire, we do not apologize for the colour of our skin, and mine is the shade of ancient copper. I alone inherited my mother's hazel eyes—for their sheer beauty and rareness, I've always felt obliged to document the world around me. I call this chair my perch, as it is clearly not a throne but still rises above the head of every man save my father. Peering carefully through the stiles, one might notice creases in my dress from a long day of sitting, although the tapestry's weavers would omit the slowly drying sweat stains. I'm so far in the foreground that I may as well be in the background: one peers over my shoulder to watch the action. Fortunately, our visitor has finally entered the court. A hushed current of protest ripples through the room as he strolls past the emperor to approach me.

The visitor announces that his name is Samad. My father's advisors appraise his thick brow and meticulously groomed beard. He wears an indigo robe accented with gold embroidery along the hems, and a gold belt with a heavy buckle strains against his belly. The buckle's surface is oddly cratered: he catches my glance, making a curtsy-like gesture I assume is customary where he's from.

"I see you admiring my belt, Farah the Beautiful," he calls out as he dares to assess my face. At the opposite end of the room, the guards stir, but my father stills them with a wave of his hand.

"It's an honorary title at best," I say.

His hands dive into his pockets and surface with heaps of jewels. Cupping them in his palms, he pours them on the bottom step before me. "My porters lifted chests of pelts and spices and dyestuffs in your honor, heaved treasure after treasure onto ships and even shouldered them over the thousand stairs to your palace, but the guards bade me to leave them all behind. As I entered this room, I had only my clothes and my wits. In here, I only have what they let me."

I say nothing.

"And so," he continues, "in the courtyard on my walk here, I wondered what to offer. From my belt, I plucked what jewels I could—as a token of my admiration." They're lovely: fat rubies and amethysts so purple they're nearly black. Sunstone is difficult to cut, but each jewel is a geometric marvel. Today is overcast, but the stones catch and reflect the weak light in their orange bellies. I nod again—hoping to indicate that I am pleased with this offering and not that I am finished with them now that they've served their purpose, which is how I really feel. Samad backs away from me, oblivious of the guards and his close brush with death. The last suitor who strode up the stairs, presumably to kiss my hand, was promptly unmade by the guards into four pieces. Drops of blood flew into my mouth—I must have been screaming.

Because Samad so deftly navigated the line between courage and insolence, my father's advisors watch with the rapt attention usually reserved for falconry competitions or wrestling matches upon which they've wagered. Samad paces sternly, hands clasped behind his back, an index finger silently tapping as he bends to examine the task laid before him: on a wooden table rests Farah's Coil, an intricate knot the size of a human head. It's made from thick brown cord. From some angles, it looks more like a brain than a coil. From afar, its mazy lines remind me of a spherical labyrinth. Samad is competing in a contest whose rules are known far and wide: he who untangles this knot wins my hand in marriage.

If only it were just my hand. I imagine him sealing it in a crystal polyhedron for display in the throne room. At this late point of the day, I do not wish to consider how long I've endured these tribulations—I'm more disturbed by the notion that even in my daydreams, I cannot fully escape this competition. Still, especially on days like these, I barely exaggerate when I say I'd sacrifice a hand, left or right, for my freedom.

. . .

Samad was doomed the moment he entered the palace—men wearing belts of gold rarely possess the fortitude to complete such a difficult task, which was inspired by puzzles such as Luoyang's cryptogram, older than the Silk Road and unsolved to this day. Samad's task is harder than solving the Sphinx's riddle, freeing the Gordian knot, counting the Bisran needles.

As evening's shadows slide toward us, over vermillion Kirmans and hardstone sculptures of cranes, Samad's glances toward the door become more frequent. Hands folded, each advisor stares at his lap and considers the future, knowing as well as I that this room steals the present. Their thoughts fly to the steaming tajines waiting at home, the smell of almonds and coriander and fresh rice, the shrieks of their children. After giving up with an epic spasm of frustration, Samad approaches my father to explain. With a quick signal—the emperor's eyes hardening with a slight dip of the chin—the guards drag Samad from the room. He's imagining a future that cannot exist as he changes his mind and pleads for more time. The only thing he should plead for is a quick death. But when the emperor decides a suitor cannot complete the task, the suitor is killed. I don't know how.

Five. The suitor who tried to kiss my hand was cut into five pieces. Arms, legs, and the rest. It happened so quickly, I swear the guards' swords were back in their sheaths by the time the man slid apart. One arm hung by a tendon near the shoulder before the weight of the torso, sliding down the stairs to my perch, peeled itself from the rest.

It occurs to me that I should have deigned to rise, descended the stairs, and scooped up Samad's jewels. It might have heartened the man to see a princess, eyes downcast demurely, admiring his final gift. Once, when there was still light in my father's eyes, he leapt from the dinner table and commanded his daughters to bathe in jewels. Even in those days, the pheasant was dry and the wine slightly turned. He was likely bored, and, as we giggled in our trendy new pantaloons, annoyed that we were not conducting ourselves according to our station. We didn't view this "punishment" as a gentle nudge toward comportment as we sashayed from the room.

The truth is, bathing in jewels is as comfortable as it is practical: imagine lying naked on a cold bed of gravel. As my sister and I learned, it's best to have a tub carried into a forest at noontide, when the quality of light is at its most interesting. Lie in the tub first, then have the jewels poured over one's body. While one is being dazzled by facets of pain and coloured brilliance, try not to consider the cost. One has certainly read about sheaves of grain and bandages and fishing skiffs—how many of these could a single bright stone buy? Gravel, grovel. Had I conjured that special excitement reserved for sapphires beneath the forest canopy, Samad may have felt his death was not wholly in vain.

Back in the court, the emperor signals that the day has ended. Sending royal exhaustion through his nostrils, he stands. His attendants rush to steady him as always, and as always he waves them away. His exit diminishes the room somehow. The hem of my dress scatters Samad's jewels as I follow the men. Some days, it's hard being a prize.

Our palace looms over an ancient plateau, hidden by minor deserts and scrub forests. We are bordered by pale green rivers that overflow their banks every year. The palace was built over a stray tributary that dampens every room and carries our waste past the villages outside the city. Our exports of phosphorus and textiles are overshadowed by those from kingdoms along the coast, and we claim no renowned warriors nor poets. From our vassal states to the south, tributes of fennec pelts and eagle talons and coloured salt arrive late, in worm-eaten trunks. Father is rarely present to receive them, and the treasures are hauled with much ceremony, as in the early days of the empire, to fulfill their destiny as stately ruins in royal storerooms.

Visitors are rare, but a few years ago, a physician was summoned to help my father, who was suffering from a mysterious ailment. What transpired between them happened in the world of men and came to the rest of us through whispers in the servants' quarters, charged glances during conversations. All news carried into the world of women has the quality of a tale or myth.

The first myths explained how life came to be, so here is how Farah, the emperor's eldest daughter, came to sit on a mock-throne littered with jewels of the dead: Long ago and not so far away, my father the emperor stepped from his clothes like any other patient, and the physician, a urologist, impassively examined the problem. No one spoke of the ailment, so it remains nameless. Because this urologist was responsible for restoring my father to health, and because the recovery period was long, the urologist was allowed to send for his family to keep him company. No one knows what prevented his wife from completing the journey. Regardless, his son arrived alone. Reeve was ten years old and unusually pale, even for a foreigner, with dark hair the colour of acacia bark. My attendants and I were all taken by his eyes, which were pale blue, like the sky. His stiff posture made us conscious of our own, and the cautious manner with which he surveyed his surroundings made us wonder if we'd missed some danger only he could sense. He stood in front of the gate, sweating through his linen shirt and pulling a wagon, a souvenir from an island port the ship visited during its voyage. He abandoned this toy as he crossed through the gate.

In a fateful moment, I insisted on dragging it to his chambers in an attempt to coax from him a smile. The whole time, the wagon skidding and rumbling its complaints behind me. By the time I reached the palace, my fingers were numb. He had so little, though, and my heart broke to see him leaving this one nod to childhood behind. Reeve's wagon was simple and wooden, large enough to transport an adult goat. In the middle, attached to a pin near the hitch, my fateful knot sat like a giant tumor. The royal seamstress speculated the knot was never meant to be a puzzle—rather, it prevented livestock from lying down during milking. Some believed the knot was merely the work of a bored and brilliant islander, an architect who built a maze but couldn't find the way out.

Perhaps lonely himself, the urologist sat pondering the knot one evening when the emperor paid him a visit—in that moment, my fate was sealed. The cart was brought to the court, and after none of the royal advisors could untie the knot, they trawled their heavy books searching for similar puzzles. In the end, they found nothing that matched the elegant frustration of Reeve's toy. To make them feel better, my father asked, "What is a lyre, after all, but four strings and a tortoise shell? Yet it takes a lifetime to master."

A discussion about impossible tasks must have followed: it once seemed impossible to marry off the emperor's second daughter Nour, a stout beauty with hair black and glossy as a starling. Nour lived among the wreckage of her half-formed ambitions and was paralyzed by inner conflict: usually, her epic laziness overcame her penchant for pointless rebellion. Still, despite her ample shortcomings, she'd met a foreign nobleman and secured his hand.

As her wedding was imminent, my father allotted a modest amount of extravagance for the ceremony, his enthusiasm tempered by our family's ambivalence to Nour's fiancé. Though Nour's marriage was a minor miracle, it was still impossible to continue a royal line without male heirs. It's easy to imagine how these problems combined in the angry whirlpool of the emperor's thoughts. He wouldn't leave anything to chance when it came to his eldest daughter's wedding, or the royal succession. Shortly thereafter, the decree was issued that he who unties Reeve's knot will be awarded the empire, as well as my hand, and body, and seething resentment, in marriage.

I am summoned as morning breaks, and so I ascend the stairs to my perch. The early morning heat rises through the river coursing beneath the palace, and though we hold ourselves as still as possible, the humidity wrings from us its tribute of sweat. The finest layer of dust has gathered on the curtains, and my father's advisors appear more forlorn as the day uncurls. Sitting in this room gives one an eternity to think, and my thoughts settle again on the question, *Why me?* I was not raised to challenge and must have inherited this trait from my mother. Given her fate, I'm compelled to swallow my questions, though in the afternoon heat, I feel like I'm suffocating as they wriggle up my throat, inching toward my lips.

In the shadow of the palace, young men gather, agitated by the evening's possibilities. The night market will open soon, carrying faint wisps of incense on the breeze. A group of stablehands stare as I pass. I've pulled back my hair and donned a shapeless cotton dress over a pair of riding breeches, but these men aren't deterred. They would lower the magnitude of their leering if they knew my father would burn them alive for it, along with their horses. Inside the stalls, hidden among the heavy odors of manure and sweat, is my favorite secret: a Marwari stallion smuggled from India. I have named him Grapeshot.

His coat is brown, his muzzle long and white, and he's nearly impossible to control—as he bursts through the stable gates, I'm gripping the reins so hard my fingernails dig into my palms, slickening the leather with blood. Grapeshot doesn't care that I'm a princess—all he cares about is momentum, and I'm doing my best to steer him toward the northern border, where the rivers are shallowest. I can't savor the notion of escape as I cling to this sleek force of nature. My thoughts only extend to the next curve ahead, though there is a thrill in the rush.

At the banks of the river, I dismount and collapse to my knees, grateful that, once again, I managed to keep hold long enough. The birds are silent in the trees, and the water at this bend passes swiftly. Listening hard to the river, my world expands from the tannish delta of this empire to a vast topography of farms and kingdoms. My mind floats high above the globe as I imagine searching for my exiled mother. At this moment, she's perhaps returning home from the market, a basket of steaming flatbread on her arm, covered by a white cloth. Or perhaps she's crouched beside a fire at an inn, embroidering a pair of scarves.

Grapeshot stamps at the ground. He's facing the water, ready to barrel through it. He would gallop straight to India, crossing the Thar Desert to rest only once we reach the sandy plains of his foalhood. He tosses his head in impatience and dares a few steps into the shallows, but he won't leave. He's smart enough to associate me with these temporary freedoms, and so he'll permit me to gaze across the river. From here, I can imagine the world as an aquamarine dream, an infinite feathering of paths—anything but a descending order of cages. Exhaling and draining my mind of royal thoughts, I grab the reins and steel myself for the plunge into the cold water. Across the river, a pair of masked riders emerge from the forest, swiping at weeds with their longbows. Their armor is spotless, as polished as the palace guards. Their reddish mares sniff the air, and I curse at them until I realize I'm not quite out of range. I draw a red line through this site on the map in my head, and Grapeshot obliges a swift return to his hot stable.

Had I tossed Reeve's wagon in the river, all these problems would have floated away with it—but how could I have known? I've absolved myself for the tiny part I played in my own fate. On clear days, when the light in the court is warm and perfect, I believe this competition is my father's way of celebrating me. *See here, daughter,* he means to say, *only the smartest, most courageous man in the world will be good enough for you, and then you shall be queen as well.*

The torches on the walls are mostly ornamental—one assumes they're symbolic somehow. The maidservants must have used dirty pitch, as the flames are sputtering. In a different age, my father would have ordered them changed, announcing to the trembling servants that his empress and children deserved better. Today, he says nothing and grips his throne as if steadying himself. A new suitor named Farhad enters. He is my father's age, although to appear younger, this suitor shaved off his beard, revealing half a face that hasn't seen sunlight in decades. Some men, like this one, pay me only rote courtesy before turning their attention to the knot. The way this man grimaces and pries its cords makes me think of a clinical, shudder-filled wedding night, and I'm relieved when, after four days, my father loses patience and the guards advance on this pale-mouthed bore. The guards are faceless to me, but every time they seize a suitor, I'm reminded of my mother's last day in the palace.

. . .

Shortly before my sister Nour's wedding, my mother learned about the contest for my hand and decided to convey her displeasure during the wedding feast. Illustrations in the court records depict her scowling above an empty plate, one hand palm down in a protesting chop. Her necklace is discs of hammered silver, with matching earrings. Stationed next to her, I could measure her indifference or amusement simply by the metallic clatter. By all accounts, my father didn't notice her jewelry or her hunger strike until she fainted with an uproar worthy of an aggrieved empress: an anguished moan that rose above chatting diners, the harmonies from the twin musicians cheerfully plucking their canuns, the trills of the caged nightjars. That sound turned every head her way just as she collapsed in sections like a columned temple: first the ankles and knees, then the brocaded waist, and finally her ink-dark hair whipped into my face as she grabbed the tablecloth and pulled.

It took five servants to whisk her to her chambers. When she returned, my father attempted a rhythmic breathing exercise, his fingers tented. He couldn't see the rice and curry splattered on his slippers, but, steeped in the rules of decorum, he sensed disaster hovering slightly past his reach: his guests' feigned concern and suppressed laughter, the practiced indifference of his enemies scattered amongst the banquet tables. Behind those blank gazes, though, each foe was carefully tallying his vulnerabilities.

Ignoring his wife, the emperor declared to the whole table that while he was pleased to have Nour married off, this new contest ensured his empire's future. "The Berbers on the coast can keep their turmeric and copper, but in time, my eldest daughter will attract the wisest and bravest man in the world. Or, judging by the suitors' success, only our men will remain to repopulate the continent!"

This quip earned half the laughter it received, but guests were eager to break the tension. Before the joy had even cleared the air, my mother's earrings clacked as she leaned over the emperor's shoulder to whisper that she was blameless in the manner—even in the harem, no woman had borne him a son. "Farah is blameless as well," she declared.

Of course, the crowd didn't hear the first part, but they didn't need to. Guests, unsure whether they could return to their food or conversations, watched the face of their ruler redden, his mouth twitching beneath his mighty beard. "Empires need sacrifice," he said, his eyes imploring me to understand.

Feigning an innocent, girlish expression, my mother asked, "Why then, could you not sacrifice tradition and let a woman rule?" The next thing I knew, my mother was on the floor, holding her face. I was kneeling to help her stand when the palace guards dragged her from the room, then the palace.

New landscapes opened themselves to me after my mother's banishment—or, since I avoided the palace when possible, I was more open to sights, such as soldiers shyly lining up outside brothels. Sunbaked farmers, thin as their oxen, slapping rags on the river to wash them. The waves were stained with filth as they passed children splashing on the banks. Horses waded and pissed in the water. Upstream, downstream—no one noticed or cared. I described to my tutors the tiny gravestones in the children's cemetery outside the city. My well-fed tutors remained unmoved.

A wizened professor in the palace library told me to consider our social order as a tall, elegant tower—and then to imagine it crumbling. He said, "Sit among the rubble and consider each life after the collapse." The brawny guards with their swords—what would they use them for now? Could the milkmaids, released from their obligations to fill palace creameries, survive on milk alone? I was told not to think too hard, lest I end up like my mother, who had swung mightily at the foundation of our social order with one simple question.

In my dreams are many things, but behind them looms a mountain of bones: mostly ribs, a skull here and there. Thigh bones—really, a disproportionate ratio of thigh bones to skulls. A breeze whistles through the bleached eye sockets, accompanied by a vibration in a minor key. This odd note must correspond to something in the real world. Searching my chambers and memory in the morning, I still can't place it.

Days pass, and a new season begins, although the temperature and light in the royal court remain the same. Perhaps this is why my father loves his contest—he can pretend nothing in his lands has changed or ever will, no matter how many men attempt to claim his daughter and crown. Samad's jewels still lie on the bottom step, casting a pastel rainbow. Yesterday, a light-skinned suitor with wild, deep-set brown eyes let out a cry of frustration and yanked the knot, hard, tipping the cart. The guards made short work of him, as they do with others who try using their teeth, knives, or other trickery.

Sometimes I sneak into the court at night to fondle the knot. Whoever spun the brown cord was experienced, since the strands are perfectly uniform and smooth. Blood wipes away leaving barely a stain. Despite being poked and spread and pulled tight, by morning the knot has restored itself. This is a metaphor for why I don't simply burn or slash it: the men would simply dream up a new contest. But the knot's resilience must dishearten the suitors who last more than a day and the next morning find their loops and separations reclaimed. Some believe this is magic or trickery, but there's no magic in the way a building settles and sighs, or the way grasslands rise after being crushed by a storm. It's the kind of magic few witness, and yet the world always changes outside of our attention.

Nothing seems special about the final suitor until he approaches my perch. He holds his gaze downwards. I sense it's out of politeness. Something about his posture suggests he longs to look at me but perhaps doesn't feel worthy—or doesn't want to disturb me. He's wearing a pair of undyed linen trousers and a kurta-style shirt the colour of a robin's egg. As he approaches, the guards' hands inch toward their sword handles, but this man simply gathers the jewels and piles them to the side. He was worried I might slip. Even though he's facing away, I can picture his disarming smile as he flashes the guards his empty hands. He's only here to steal my heart, apparently. Turning toward me, his shyness returns. He smells vaguely of cinnamon and dried orange peels. "My name is Hassain," he says to my feet. I wiggle my toes in response.

He's young. I try not to become attached to these men, though some hold my attention longer than others. For better or worse, this contest reveals their true natures, and it dawns on me that perhaps *this* is why my father lets it continue. The knot is simply an opportunity to reveal a noble heart. And yet, the day runs its course. Hassain circles the knot, appraising it from different angles. At noon, he lays it on its side and systematically peels back the cords on the outer layer. He's focused on the lower hemisphere, figuring it's part of the primary tangle, which means he's already three steps ahead.

He glances at the advisors to gauge their response, but their faces reveal nothing.

That night, to postpone my dreams, I pace the length of my chambers. My attendants have retreated, and I am as alone as my father. In happier times, one of his hobbies was collecting lanterns. They are piled against the corners of his great room and hang on the walls in neat columns. The lanterns aren't organized by nation or size. As children, we were startled to see a Chinese-style paper lantern hanging next to a teak mask-lamp, the flames dancing behind its human teeth. Regardless, his chamber walls are so high that their exotic light never reaches the ceiling. I picture my father lying sleepless on his ornate bed, half of which lies empty. No matter how many territories he conquers or how many wise men he sacrifices in my name, this bed will forever be absent his first true love, mother of his first-born children.

She had so much to teach us of politics, modern geography, spices, and trade routes that her instruction often crowded out warmth or comfort. Scolding may have been her way of showing love—regardless, her daughters accepted it. I wonder if my father remembers her lying in bed, young and excited by the enormous task of safeguarding an empire, switching from Persian to Arabic to Latin to playfully bicker about music, irrigation, law. Were he not the emperor, he could simply leave behind his moldy storehouses and armories to pursue her. An exiled empress would surely be easy enough to find.

It brings me no comfort to consider my father a fellow hostage of this empire, but at least these walls block it from sight. I call for an attendant, who helps me from my clothes without touching me. I step from the dress and watch it slump over. My posture indicates I want to be alone, and so I am. Letting my undergarments fall to the ground, I stand inside the night air, which is thick and heavy even in the palace's upper chambers. It startles me a little to catch my reflection in a mirror and see myself so pared down. How simple we all are, I think as my reflection appraises this hair, these hips, this chest. How shadows fall the same over all of us.

From my window, I hope to see distant herds of cattle kneel as the stars emerge, but instead I catch Hassain setting up camp beneath a marula tree. Out of habit, I retreat and cover myself with the dress. Even if he somehow sensed my presence, the light has faded. A frizzy-haired silhouette, I let the dress fall and approach the window.

Usually, suitors repair to the palace courtyard, where their stewards and wise men wait with practice knots and kettles of strong tea. Under the tree with Hassain is a small dappled horse. Its bridle isn't tied to anything. Hassain stretches, checks a small rucksack, and retrieves a yellow apple, absentmindedly tossing and catching it as he ambles to the tree and sits, resting his back against the trunk.

Rattled by how I'm spying on this innocent moment, I turn back to the palace. It's been ages since I've scrutinized my own chambers: after my mother's banishment, I slashed the tapestries and family portraits. In my absence during the day, the light streams through the windows and reflects nothing, is absorbed by nothing. In my mind, I commission a long silk banner with silver filigree at the borders. In the center is the silhouette of a lone man beneath a tree. In the banner, the world calms itself: the high grasses in the fields, slightly browning at the end of a long summer, do not move. No rats poke their heads from the stone wall that surrounds the palace. The guards on the battlements exhale, but no one sees them shifting inside their heavy armor, only their eyes moving to survey the horizon. The apple rises and falls, a red horse's tail flicks, and I don't understand why I can't hold them still even in my mind.

I collapse on my bed and fold my arms over my chest, but sleep doesn't come. After an eternity, I return to the window and light a small candle. No one else can see it, but this tiny point of light means something, even if I can't explain it.

When the contest demands our presence the next day, Hassain seems amused that the knot has swallowed his hard-won progress. He dares a glance at me, then shrugs, and a laugh escapes my throat. Though I've learned to keep my heart clear and cold, I can admit he's handsome enough—there's something about the way his eyes convey a boyish curiosity. Surprisingly long lashes divert one's attention from a slim aquiline nose that's been broken more than once. Some elation stirs in me when he finds a small stone on the ground next to the steps. It's one of Samad's. He gestures toward me with it, asking permission, and I grant it with a nod, as does my father. Hassain begins sketching on the ground around the wagon. Although this strategy is obvious to a princess trained in cartography and portraiture, few suitors try it. Notes and diagrams bloom on the ground. Watching him work, it dawns on me that he's a fisherman: tanned, with the lithe movements of a swimmer. How many fishing lines or nets has he untangled even at his young age? Had he been born in the city, a teacher would have recognized his skills in drawing and mathematics and recommended him for an apprenticeship. Now that *he's* tangled in this royal net, what becomes of his cleverness if he fails?

He holds his breath and closes his eyes in prayer. Perhaps to stave off hopelessness, he surveys his arena, a small raised platform the width and length of an oxcart. Servants avoid this room as they would a charnel house. An attentive spectator would notice a stray fleck of blood on the wall, a patch of scalp beneath the table next to the platform. During the early days of the competition, my father let suitors eat while they worked. A servant must have forgotten a metal cookpot and brazier beneath the table. Hassain considers them briefly before wiping his brow and returning to his task.

Most suitors would work twice as quickly, racing against the tide of night. Hassain's pace remains unchanged. He asks the advisors to hold the cart upside down so the knot can dangle like a hornet's nest. They agree with a good-natured chuckle. It's a novel approach but ultimately futile. If only exhaling could expel my frustration. I arch my back and tell my muscles to relax. This man is young, with no experience in politics, but he clearly possesses the wisdom to respect and fear a queen. A solution surfaces in the snarl of my thoughts and I begin my own untangling.

You see, I know what Hassain's silent god knows, what the knot-maker himself (or herself) knows, what any woman from this damp empire would have figured out by now. Everything Hassain needs is in this room: he should first fill the cookpot with water and hold it over the brazier. Once the water boils, prop up the wagon over the steam and wait for the cord's fibers to swell, the knot unraveling enough for him to search its southern hemisphere for the simplest of Djebel knots. One tug and everything collapses in a beautiful, world-changing heap.

With my father's blessing, Hassain is climbing the stairs to my perch, and honestly, it doesn't matter what he says. It doesn't matter if telling Hassain how to untie the knot defies or defines my father's motive behind this long, bloody spectacle. Long ago and far away, a songbird named Farah was held against her will in a hot stone cage. Season after season, she wrapped herself in grief and refused to sing. Write your poems, sing your brightest songs, weave a new tapestry celebrating this, the moment she opens her mouth and seizes an empire.

On his last day in Atlanta, Edward Moon visits the civil rights museum, then the World of Coke, mostly to buy a keychain for his granddaughter Kacey. The purpose of his visit was to find a new Chief Transformation Officer for his company, but a cloud of dissatisfaction hung over each interview. It didn't help that he was trying to replace his eldest daughter—when she left, it felt like she'd taken half his brain with her.

On the souvenir keychain is a glass bottle, complete with a little metal cap, a pea-sized amount of brown liquid inside. There is also a clear glass charm in the shape of a hot dog. Edward wishes he'd chosen something less fragile, but as he holds the bottle up to the Town Car window, he thinks of the joy a child might find in the small details. He'll ask the question his own father loved to pose: What would this particular object look like inside out?

As they slide past through Piedmont Park, Edward commands his driver to stop. He pops open the door and walks to the lake, saying he needs to clear his head. His security team follows at a discrete distance. In the past, he viewed land and buildings through the hungry gaze of an emperor—this storied park, with the Atlanta skyline lined up in the background like a mirage, would be the perfect location to debut his company's new hologram rigs. But he already has a site reserved in Williamsburg. An emperor whose belly is filled to bursting would view food in a more abstract sense. As a souvenir keychain, perhaps.

Edward is startled to see a Korean woman his age stroll past him, a young Korean boy chattering beside her. He can tell from their postures, their faces, that they're not related. He smiles and gives a half wave as they pass.

On the flight home, both the Korean woman and boy materialize in Edward's memory palace. They don't seem to know why they've appeared, either. Maybe it's because their stories are hidden, are something he can never own. Grass and wildflowers sprout around them, a stone foundation spreads beneath their feet. Edward closes his eyes as the plane begins its descent. The Korean woman takes off her baseball cap and rubs her forehead, wondering whether the sidewalks have always sloped down like that.

EVERYTHING THAT RISES

"Beyond the mountains are more mountains."
—KOREAN PROVERB

It was likely a symptom of aging, but lately Auntie found herself waking in the middle of the day. She wasn't sleepwalking, exactly, but today she woke during an afternoon stroll, nearly tripping on the uneven sidewalk. Tree roots were slowly heaving up the concrete slabs, and she had to spread her arms for balance. She couldn't recall the minute—or hour—before. The neighborhood was familiar, though, which meant she was near her apartment complex outside of Marietta. She was also clothed, which was a relief. It was only a matter of time, she told herself, before she emerged nude, in public, from a fugue state.

In her hand was an index card with a name and address written neatly in Hangul: her destination was a nearby bus stop. The occasion was a doctor's appointment. She tucked the card into her pocket, embarrassed. As a child, she was so forgetful that her mother would safety pin homework and other important documents to the back of her shirts. Of course, no one who spotted her could have known that—and besides, she was alone. It was 7:14 a.m. according to her watch, and people in this neighborhood were only starting to stir in their squat brick houses. Each had a fussily maintained lawn; this put Auntie slightly at ease. She rarely walked outside anymore, and even in a neighborhood like this one, where houses sported eggshell-colored siding and Accords radiated aspirational blandness, she suspected people were drawn to their windows by the ripples of disharmony she sent out. It was clear from her face, from her age and uncertain stride, that she did not belong here. "This wasn't my idea," she wanted to yell—though to be honest, if it wasn't her idea to cross through this all-white suburban paradise, whose was it?

Near the edge of the neighborhood was a small park. She was five foot even, the green hedge beside her tall enough that she couldn't see over it. Somewhere a chain-link fence rattled—then a chuffing noise erupted as the hedge bulged toward her. Through the bushes came a musky animal smell. It reminded her of horses she'd cared for in Korea as a child, but this smell was wilder, more acrid. As she quickened her pace, she glanced over her shoulder but couldn't make out anything except this dark mass on the opposite side of the hedge, trailing her. Whatever it was, given her age, she wouldn't outrun it once it broke through.

Someone brushed past her, shoving her forward, her heart churning so hard that her vision dimmed. Of course it was a kid—his neon-green backpack bounced as he ran the few yards to the end of the street. He faced the hedge and yelled "Hey!" so loud that Auntie imagined windows rattling, birds scattering from tree branches. After peering through the hedge for a long moment, he nodded and turned to her.

"Auntie!" he said in Korean. From his voice alone—the American accent, amplified by boyish energy—she knew it was Lee, a boy who lived in her apartment building. He wasn't her nephew, but she was pleased he'd retained enough of the culture to use the familiar term. She'd first met him with his mother a couple years before in the grimy basement laundromat. By that point, seeing another Korean in Georgia wasn't rare, though it still felt like the blacks and whites took up most of the city's light and air, everyone else wheezing as they scrambled for what was left. Lee's mother, Hae-won, was young, early thirties. Auntie didn't know what the woman did for a living, or whether she was a single mother (a charity case to be pitied from a mountaintop of moral superiority) or a widow (a charity case to be pitied, with the knowledge that misfortune is inescapable). After introducing herself, Hae-won asked to borrow seven dollars from Auntie, who would recognize the tactic later in panhandlers—the specificity of the amount was supposed to catch passersby off guard. Lee was nine at the time, and Auntie took in his wide, innocent face, his budget haircut and hand-me-down overalls, and fished the entire amount from her change purse. Lee often played alone in the lobby, though he'd always offer to help Auntie carry groceries or laundry up to her apartment. Hae-won never paid her back.

"Boy, that thing really wanted out," Lee said in halting, bouncy Korean. It was clear he didn't speak the language even at home. She felt heartened by the effort he was making on her behalf, charmed by his clumsiness with the language. "I thought we were together walking to the stop."

Had she invited him on this trip? She dismissed the notion with a wave of her hand. She avoided Hae-won—Auntie had a vision of the young mother inviting herself over for dinner, the evening ending with the single mother crying on Auntie's couch, spilling her troubles into the air, where they'd hang like the smell of rancid oil. However, Auntie always checked for Lee when crossing the lobby. Occasionally, she'd bring him a box of Botan Rice Candy, which he'd snatch from her hand but would never eat in front of her. When Auntie was tired, the world fell away: chipped teacups and fraying towels and garlic bulbs sprouting in her cupboard—everything tumbled off the edge of her exhaustion except herself and Lee. She wanted to buy him clothes that fit better and scrape the rust off his Korean. In those moments of exhaustion, a long-lost maternal warmth welled up—even though he was way too young, she allowed herself to imagine him as the American son she might have had.

As Lee took slow, measured steps beside her, the aches in her knees receded and her heartbeat settled. Lee announced it was the last week of school. "All the teachers do is show movies." Auntie had trouble believing such a thing. By the time they reached the bus stop, she still felt rattled. Her mind was calm but her body was still catching up. The muscles in her calves twitched and quivered, and her stomach spasmed. Fortunately, they didn't have to wait long. The bus arrived on schedule.

As she gripped the railing and pulled herself up the steps, a cluster of teens sitting at the front stood to move a few rows back. There were six of them, mostly Korean American—from their dark uniforms, they were students at a private high school. They leaned toward each other conspiratorially, continuing their conversation and ignoring their surroundings as they walked. The seats at the front faced each other and were reserved for the elderly and handicapped. Auntie didn't consider herself either. It seemed rude for the teens to flee from an elder without even glancing at her, but it also seemed rude if Auntie didn't fill the seat they'd vacated.

She turned to see Lee settling himself next to her. "Oh, I thought you were just walking me to the stop. You don't have to come with me," she said.

"Oh, Auntie," he replied. Checking the index card, she realized she would arrive an hour early for the appointment. Her doctor in Atlanta was from Daegu. She liked him even though he stressed punctuality and his receptionist glowered at latecomers. Today, Auntie wouldn't be among them, though she hated to take so much time out of Lee's day.

She wanted nothing more than to close her eyes but knew she'd miss her stop and wake to discover the bus on a dilapidated stretch of MLK Drive, the engine silent, the driver gone, the door flung open. Luckily, Lee was there to bring her back to reality. He calmly watched the beige sound walls and pine forests speed by. Even though they were a few rows back, the teens' conversation grew louder, occasionally cutting through the engine noise. They switched back and forth between Korean and English, though Auntie noted the Korean phrases were always quieter. By the time she'd translated shards of their conversation, they'd changed topics from their least favorite teacher to the fragility of sunglasses to something called a "slam book." Auntie rubbed her eyes: when she was their age, she'd just immigrated to greater Atlanta from Busan, and the ability to speak English so effortlessly, without the stain of an accent, was every immigrant's dream. And yet, there were unspoken rules about exposing one's mother tongue in public: back then, even a quick Korean phrase would have drawn glares from whites and blacks alike. One quickly learned that Hanguk-mal was acceptable only at home, at Korean grocery stores, and church.

Before immigrating, she'd never thought so much about her mouth. She still remembers her first cheeseburger: the spongy texture of the bun and the unexpected pop of tomatoes and lettuce. Beef was an art form in Korean, but after the armistice, it was scarcer than fresh vegetables or clean clothes. In the aftermath of the war, there weren't many qualified teachers, either, so instead of continuing her education, she lived with her parents and assisted with housework until she turned seventeen. She never fully believed the stories about America's boundless prosperity, but she figured the country had to be less corrupt than Korea, which anyway felt more like a construction site than a country. One could barely move, barely breathe. Her decision to leave was hastened by her parents' relentless campaign to marry her off.

In 1973, the last stamp kissed her paperwork: moving was easier since Auntie's sister had recently relocated to Georgia. Auntie decided she liked the name: the way the soft vowel sounds dropped and bounced, "Jeaw-ja" like a nostalgic sigh. Or a pickup's gate lowering, overripe peaches bouncing into a basket. Much like a peach pit, English felt strange in her mouth. Four decades later, Georgia would boast the largest surge of Korean immigrants, but in the seventies, Asians were a rarity. When Auntie left her apartment, her exoticness was displayed for public judgment and comment. It often felt like keeping her mouth closed was the only power she had, so she used it.

After she'd been in the States for a month, her parents passed away—since Auntie had already spent so much on airfare, her sister returned to Busan to handle the estate. Auntie felt doubly stranded, but what could she do? Learning English quickly was her only option.

As the bus crossed into Fulton County, Auntie tried to determine whether the teens had learned Korean or English first. *How far have we come—enough to pass as American?* Lee had clearly allowed English vowels to crowd out the Korean ones. It would be easy to blame his mother, but were there other Koreans at school he could talk to? Come to think of it, he always seemed alone—there was a separateness about him even when he accompanied his mother.

At least Auntie had the local Korean Presbyterian Church, which offered free English lessons. She purchased a pair of elegant-looking glasses with gold-colored rims, starched her shirts, and pulled her hair into a modest bun. She wore her usual long pleated skirts and polyester blouses. During conversation exercises, her classmates always complimented her. This continued after she graduated and started a career as a nursing assistant, even though her coworkers, often black and rarely praised, were equally capable.

Auntie's sister remained in Korea for six more months to help "reduce the family's sorrow," then extended her stay another six months. In the end, she never returned to America, though her name was still on the apartment's lease.

Due to her impeccable appearance and serviceable language skills, Auntie started a new career in patient intake and spent most of her days directing phone calls and filling out forms instead of changing diapers and spooning oatmeal into elderly mouths. She'd always known the value of education, but some knowledge is instinctual: you feel in your finger bones. Following that instinct, she ruthlessly sharpened her English. ESL class was a public affair: students repeated words and phrases as a group and traded partners for conversation drills. Stationed by herself in a back office with only an ugly gray word processor and an office phone to keep her company, Auntie could better focus on pronunciation. Here, she didn't have to worry about spitting or drooling. She could obsess over the position of her tongue, how it moved, what it was or wasn't touching. Between calls, she warped the patients' words, growling and swelling them so she could bend them back to normal: "ArrRe you A rrresident of DeKalb County?" "MediCAY-tion." "ImPARErrments." "Nor-MULL." When she ran out of work-related phrases, she repeated sentences from the ESL workbook: "I think the smooth red ball is for the party."

Doctors passing her office were shocked to hear the pleasant "American" voice from the phone coming from an "Oriental" face. In a matter of months, her voice was free of the friction and stutter of any accent. The teens on the bus would no doubt scowl and cry racism, but Auntie basked in her colleagues' compliments and praise. It was a big step toward fitting in, toward counting as normal.

It was increasingly hard to listen to the teens and keep track of Lee, who kept glancing, wide-eyed, down the aisle, which drew a few friendly waves. The teens, though, were immune to his cuteness. He wasn't the type to wander off, but Auntie still kept an eye on him. Did she have her insurance card? The doctor would no doubt ask how long she'd been having these fugues. Even as she scolded herself for not knowing—and not returning Lee to his mother the minute she saw him walking alone down the street—her energy dwindled. At least she took some pride in remembering to schedule this appointment, even if this was just a routine checkup. *It is just a routine checkup, right?* she asked herself.

Auntie pictured the teens' words as a string of gems rising into the clouds, or a trail of breadcrumbs out of a forest. Being American-born and fluent inspired confidence, which showed in their attitudes and movements. The result was that no one, save Auntie, seemed to even notice them.

To keep herself awake and to distract Lee, she taught him how to play I Spy. It was clear he knew it was a little kids' game and played along just to humor her. She thought of word games she could play, especially Korean ones. Even after all these years, English wore on Auntie with its immense vocabulary and slippery articles and the verbs forever stuck in the wrong place. On long days like today, she imagined herself as a thick earthen dam holding back a sea of broken English. Every possible mistake churned on the other side and heaved itself against her, and it was all she could do to keep ugly, malformed words from leaking out.

She woke with a snort and a wild flutter in her chest. She was still on the bus, but how many stops had she missed? She half expected Lee to be gone, replaced by her own handbag or a homeless man with leaves in his beard. Instead, the boy was staring out the window, gripping its edge as if trying to push himself through the frame. His shoulder blades strained against his white T-shirt. Auntie noticed a dime-sized hole in a sleeve. The highway broadened: she was always a little stunned by the number of lanes on 75. More often now, rising above the forest was a new hotel complex or crane. The bus sped past T-shaped supports for a future overpass. She only visited Atlanta a few times a year, but it seemed like a new city each time. It was hard to reconcile the expensive parks and fountains downtown with the gravel-strewn maze of warehouses her sister had nervously sped through all those years ago after she picked up Auntie from the airport.

The bus stopped. Its doors opened and a stout African American woman heaved herself up the steps, her son in tow. She nodded at the driver but, Auntie noticed, didn't seem to pay. The woman was middle-aged and wore a floral-print jumper dress. On her head was a Braves cap—although Auntie was wearing the same hat, she wouldn't have recognized it as such. She had no idea who the Braves were, had bought the hat at a flea market because she liked the color scheme (red bill, black crown) and price. The plan was to turn it into a visor, but she found she liked the mesh back panel and suspected the airflow somehow prevented her hair from thinning further. Auntie had dressed up for the doctor, donning a pink polyester blouse with a rolled collar and wide-leg slacks. The African American woman lowered herself into the seat across from Auntie, who became aware that she'd been staring and looked away. The woman's son sat facing Lee. The door closed and the bus engine made a grinding rumble as they inched uphill.

"Joyce Peterson," the woman said. Auntie looked up: Joyce held her cell phone like a microphone and repeated her name, then mashed the phone against her ear. She repeated her name a few times, then overenunciated her date of birth and passcode ("Freckles") into the phone. Although Auntie was done eavesdropping on the teenagers, she noted with irritation that she couldn't hear them now.

Either Joyce lost reception or, Auntie thought with a tinge of victory, this uncouth woman felt Auntie's micro-waves of disapproval and decided to make such a call in private. Into her gigantic denim purse went the phone. "They can put a man on the moon, but you can't get a signal," Joyce muttered.

Her son had a primitive cigarette in his mouth—or a joint. Auntie was close enough to catch a whiff of cinnamon but didn't make the connection. She was worried he was going to light it, perhaps blow smoke rings at Lee, who was no longer staring out the window but stalwartly facing the opposite seat. His hands were neatly folded on his lap as he leaned his head and shoulder into Auntie. She accepted the warmth of his touch and let some of her weight rest against him. How quickly he reached for his Korean-ness, wrapped it around himself like a blanket when the air on the bus thickened and charged. She didn't mind.

And anyway, they were only a few stops from the doctor's office. In the silence that Joyce allowed, Auntie remembered she was arriving an hour early and pictured Lee sitting in the grimy reception room—calm at first, but how long until he lost interest in that germy issue of *Highlights*? Bad news would blare through the cheap television bolted to the wall, and they probably wouldn't let her change it to cartoons or whatever Lee watched. How long until he regretted his decision to accompany her?

Joyce frowned—or, more precisely, frowned back. Auntie exhaled slowly through her nose. It wasn't her fault the seats made them face these people. Joyce's frown—reproachful, full-mouthed— hung in Auntie's mind, the upside-down version of the Cheshire cat's smile. There was a word for how Auntie felt, but she couldn't remember it, even after trawling her Korean vocabulary. There were probably a number of pidgin English words, but she refused to consider them. She wasn't that kind of woman.

What kind of woman was she? The kind who handled things. "We may be at the hospital a while," she told Lee, who was watching Joyce's son, probably checking the teen's waistband for a gun. An inquisitive grunt erupted from Auntie: the bus's rocking must have brought it forth. She twisted her mouth shut, but Lee still didn't respond. "If you want, I can call your mother, have her pick you up." She knew how to explain things to Hae-won in Korean: the honorifics simplified the discussion, made it clear Hae-won should defer to her elder, but the English version was complicated. "Your son skipped school because we . . . had an agreement." The dynamic between Auntie and Hae-won changed as the moral high ground shifted.

The bus slowed a little, and Auntie swayed with it. If the moon raised and lowered water, what affected the tides of language that pulled and pushed on her? Not knowing a word or being unable to recover some essential flavor lost in translation—no matter how long she stayed in this country, this difficulty would circle her always.

Without changing her expression, Joyce stared at the window past Auntie, making a show of not looking at her. "I just don't want you bored or grumpy," Auntie offered.

"Oh, I'm happy to spend the time with you." That's what she expected Lee to say, but he didn't respond. Joyce's son had pulled out a handheld video game and jabbed at the buttons, the volume on full blast. A fuzzy melody and cartoon sound effects sprinkled into the air. "Jealous" wasn't the right word—it was like every part of Lee except his hands reached out toward that shiny plastic toy.

Taking advantage of the distraction, Auntie ran her fingers through Lee's hair, feeling an illicit thrill, as if she'd kidnapped him and made him her own. The bus stopped for an elderly man wearing a gray tracksuit. A white gauze bandage covered one eye. The bandaged man paused hopefully near the front row, but Joyce's son was engrossed in his video game—or pretended to be, and Joyce certainly wasn't moving.

Lee vacated his seat. Auntie scooched over to make room for the elderly man and directed a scowl toward Joyce's son. She hated his jeans, which were comically tight, and his ugly green sneakers. Ultimately, though, his lack of consideration was his mother's fault. The bus suddenly braked, pressing Auntie into the man with the bandage.

"Whoa, sorry. I don't take the bus often," she said to her surprisingly bony neighbor, who didn't respond. Something caught the attention of their fellow passengers: a few stood and pointed toward the windshield. Auntie heard the word "biker" but couldn't see anything. She started to stand—the bus braked again, hard, and a man pitched down the bus aisle, raising his hands defensively right before his face slammed off the windshield with a thud Auntie felt in her chest. "He-a crash! Go light . . ." Auntie realized she was standing, that the bus's momentum had pulled her to her feet, that a spray of pidgin English had burst from somewhere inside her. The impact seemed to vibrate in her spine and belly, and her entire body cringed.

The bus coasted toward the curb, and now Joyce was standing, too. Auntie turned to Lee, who was crouched in the aisle. They made eye contact, and she quickly turned to Joyce. "Went. He went . . . right down the aisle," Auntie said flatly, as if Joyce were the one who needed correcting. Even though all eyes were on the driver as he radioed into dispatch, Auntie felt the passengers' scrutiny rest on her. She was suddenly nineteen again, the phrase "He-a crash!" echoing though the bus. She blushed so hard her glasses fogged up and pinpricks of heat pierced her scalp. Through the windshield, the passengers watched as a cyclist carrying a shiny orange messenger bag weaved through traffic without looking back.

Someone on the bus angrily narrated into her phone, "Some dickhead on a bike cut us off, and when our driver hit the brakes, this poor bastard lost his balance. Flew down the aisle into the windshield." Auntie expected a Rorschach pattern of blood on the windshield, but there was only the driver out of his seat, leaning over a man in a blue windbreaker sitting on the steps, his face in his hands. Passersby on the street and passengers alike had their phones out to document the scene—although, she noticed, neither Joyce nor her son were among them. She couldn't explain the feeling, but a new thrill gripped Auntie: it could have been *her* sailing toward the windshield. A sense of kinship extended toward her fellow survivors in the front row—except Auntie's fish-scented howl was also part of the public record. She imagined the teens mouthing it to each other between giggles. Lee clung so tightly to her arm that it was almost numb, but she couldn't face him. Not knowing what else to do, she sat. "He slide down bus, bang off-a bus into window," she said loudly, exaggerating the accent as if to exorcise it.

"Lawdy!" Joyce said, her eyes gleaming and an odd smile stretching her face. Her eyebrow shot up, as if to say, *How about that, when you bury something but it springs back like a weed? For some of us,* her expression said, *language and shame are universal.* She raised her voice. "What to do, what to *do?*"

"His face red cara but he okay." Picture a pair of boxers leaning into each other near the end of a long bout, one spitting out a mouthguard to whisper to his opponent. Auntie felt tears of gratitude welling but forced them down. She wasn't that kind of woman, either.

Joyce drawled out a sentence that sounded like a single word and ended with "waffalouse." In between, Auntie recognized "bet" and "awl" and could only blink in response. Backpedaling, Joyce twitched her shoulders and said, "Ain't it a shame. Lawd-all-mighty." Her son continued to play his video game.

"Someday, you bit traffic, someday it bit you! I try to say Norma Lee," Auntie said, shaking her head.

"Sure do," Joyce said, pronouncing it "shore." "These kids on bikes got no *sense.* I got places to be," she said, sincerity returning in the last few syllables.

"I'll be late for the pardy, I might as well work there." Other ESL practice sentences swooped in from the past: The red ball is the star of the party. I walk to work. Run a red light and be sorry. A police cruiser slowed beside the bus and an officer emerged. Sensing an end to their game, Auntie tightened her throat and in the most exaggerated pidgin she could muster, yowled, "Lain in sbane falls mainly in the prain."

Joyce leaned back, taking in Auntie's face and hat before donning a somber, inquisitive expression, one eyebrow leaping up. With the flourish of a chef yanking a cover off a platter, she said, "But . . . let me *axe* you." Auntie laughed along—regardless of what she understood, she recognized the hooded expression that passed over Joyce's face with those last three words, the delight that followed. The teens in the middle of the bus tore their gaze from the cop shining his flashlight in the injured man's eyes and stared at the two ladies, each wearing the same ill-fitting Braves hat, cackling so hard they nearly doubled over. The teens' faces were black as rice cakes, and Lee was downright confused, which somehow made everything funnier.

Later that day, Auntie filled out paperwork while Lee stood enchanted by the enormous fishtank in the doctor's office. He'd jogged to it without hesitation, taking his place next to the two white kids—brothers, probably—and struck up a conversation with them. Whatever allowed him to be this comfortably American, it was a blessing, one she'd never understand or possess.

It occurred to her that Joyce never finished her last question. What if she really had something to ask? Auntie set down the clipboard and turned to Lee, who was running his finger along the glass, tracing the path of a blue-and-yellow tang. She thought of the sentence she'd repeated thousands of times her first few years in America: "Walk to work, arrive, party hard like a rock star." The ESL teacher at the church was a young American-born Korean with dyed blonde hair who said "Wow" a lot. Auntie had dutifully wrapped her own ambition around the sentence, accepted it as a familiar nemesis. Today had peeled itself away to reveal something to Auntie, and the blonde teacher's mantra sped through the years to accompany it. This wasn't the party Auntie expected, but watching Lee's content, steady reflection in the cloudy water, she suspected the long, difficult work to be worth it.

SOLITUDE CITY

ALASKA

aura Moon is dreaming about horses when a phone call wakes her. It is her father's voice, but he's speaking Korean, a language she hasn't heard in years. The words tumble in her mind until something clicks, but they still don't make sense. She sits on the edge of her bed, waiting for the news. "Your sister is missing. We know it wasn't foul play and her daughter is fine," her father says. Laura can hear other people on the line. Some of them are speaking but not to her, and she cannot hear well enough to understand. This is a conference call, she realizes. The others are relatives in Korea. Night comes at strange hours in Alaska, which she still isn't used to. The cold air in her apartment assures her this is not a dream.

"Who's going to look after Kacey?" she says, thinking of her niece. An aunt or grandmother begins to ask why she hasn't already volunteered, but Laura's father interrupts.

"Your cousin is watching her for now, but we've chosen you." Of course. She is in her early thirties and unmarried. "I have sent a jet from Midway—it should be there in a few minutes." This is the family's decision. Laura knows it's not up for discussion.

"Very well," she says, taking a deep breath and letting it out slowly. There are two ways to bid farewell in Korean, depending on who stays and who leaves, and she tries to keep her voice free of anger as she uses the appropriate one, "*Annyeonghi kyeseyo.*" Goodbye when you stay and I go. She calls the office and leaves a message. Outside, the fields and hills all look slate and granite. Her apartment is a paragon of silence and right angles: her Humanscale lamp hovering over her glass desk, her Nyatoh coffee table, her vinyl collection (Apollo Records, Blue Note 1962–1980). It took rearranging to perfect this aesthetic unity; it took effort to achieve this kind of balance.

CHICAGO

Laura found it amusing to send Kacey the noisiest toys possible: drums and keyboards, sassy talking dolls. This was mostly to annoy her sister, Jennifer, but she also sent crayons and origami kits and bike streamers, things a little girl might need. These are the first things she sees when she enters Jennifer's apartment in Chicago—a snare drum, an orange paper flower. Displayed on their thick glass shelf, they don't look like toys, and Laura wonders if they've always been there. She peers out the window at the street below.

"Mommy?"

Laura feels a new kind of heartache, something crystalline that spreads. Of course she resembles this girl's mother from behind: slender, with the same shoulder-length black hair. She presses her hand against the window and watches her breath form and fade. The glass is thick, but she can still feel the wind pushing from the other side. She turns around to see the girl's expression change. Kacey, seven years old. And cute—half Korean, half white. It's in the brown highlights in Kacey's black hair, the soft curves of the eyes and nose that deny easy classification. There's a gorgeous blurring of cultures, a metaphor for an American future.

Kacey marches to the middle of the living room and stops a few feet away. Laura knows her niece is doing her best to remain polite, but she can't hide her disappointment.

"I'm sorry," Laura says. She pops the latches to her leather portfolio, tries to smile as she offers a pair of coloring books. Children like presents, and these were always her favorite. Kacey doesn't say anything. Laura can't offer promises or news about her mother. She can only offer coloring books.

PINHOLES

Watch, their father said. This was almost a decade ago and both sisters, Laura and Jenny, stood with him in his den—Laura remembers a long oak table and the smell of hardcover books. The globe was lit from inside and punctured by clusters of brilliant, pin-sized holes. *These are markets we own,* he said, turning out the lights. North America and Asia were brightest, but there were holes everywhere: even Africa and the North Pole. This is where you could find his company's electronics: the globe was bright enough to see his face. *Spin it,* he said. Today, that globe would exist simply as light, and Laura thinks of her sister, who has vanished into it.

It is night and Kacey is asleep. Laura is outside on the apartment balcony, talking through a migraine to her father, the phone cold against her ear.

"I have sent my best people," he says. His voice pops and skips like a vinyl recording. There's a roar in the background—maybe he's on a helicopter. "With things like this, it's best you don't know the details," he doesn't say.

"What about Kahului? It's not a big airport, but."

"It's on the list. All my jets are in motion." He knows more than he's saying, Laura knows, but he's gone. *Signal lost,* says the telephone.

Laura knows her sister is in Hawaii. She's gone to look for Kacey's father, who Kacey still refers to as "Superman," pointing to the tall man in framed photographs on the wall. Jennifer was always quick to point out that Superman didn't really exist, and neither did Kacey's father once she was born—packed up his belongings and left while they were still in the hospital.

It must have been a similar shock when Kacey and her grandfather returned from a weekend in upstate New York to find the apartment empty except for a pile of garbage bags containing Jennifer's old coats and boots, things too heavy to carry. Before she left, she had hung a scroll above the desk. It was from a shop in Albany Park, cheaply painted in Hangul with the proverb *Speak of the tiger and it will come.*

Jennifer had purchased five plane tickets to five different continents. She'd been gone for at least twenty-four hours by that point, and their father didn't have enough time or people. A lesson in humility. Laura heard he'd thrown the bags off the balcony, watching them burst as they hit the courtyard below. She pictures his red face. He breathes heavily, barely able to contain his rage. How could his Jenny embarrass the family like this? He would blame her for this loss of control, his anger feeding on itself. Laura thinks of Kacey's expression when she realized Laura wasn't her mother, and her anger rises until she pushes away the image of her father. Still, it wasn't enough that Jenny left—*she had to be cute about it.*

This phone with its cracked screen and floral case is her sister's. He sends them the same models every month. Laura had just grabbed it off the counter, ordered *Papa* on the voicedial. She imagines the network waking up, glowing paths in circuitry as some cloudy consciousness traces the call. Satellites and dishes turn their faces toward Chicago as she tosses the phone over the balcony, leans to watch it shatter. Her father can buy half the city. Let him buy her a new one.

HIDE-AND-SEEK

Kacey is well behaved. She attends her academy in a dark pleated skirt and white dress shirt, comes home and doesn't say much. Laura figures this is normal given the situation. But there are moments of exuberance, girlishness, which she sees as hopeful. Kacey is in first grade, proud of her ability to locate and label, in feminizing cursive, her home city on a map. Laura hopes the family's explanation is enough: Jennifer has a certain illness, is receiving treatment in a famous Minnesota hospital, and will return soon. Kacey believes this with every ounce of her tiny little heart. Of course the doctors will help Mommy. People go into hospitals and come out better, that's how it works. This unshakable confidence upsets Laura, who still isn't sure of Jennifer's return. She has been missing for five days.

Kacey senses there is something wrong despite everyone's assurances. Sometimes she hides. "One missing relative is enough, thank you," Laura doesn't say when she finds Kacey crouched in the downstairs gym. She's below eye level, at the age where they're all limbs. And she can move quietly and appear suddenly, which Laura finds unnerving. The next day, Laura finds her niece in the lobby's coat-check room as she peeks out as if to check whether the world has righted itself. A coping mechanism, perhaps. Laura thinks about her a lot, mostly late at night when Kacey is asleep in the next room.

. . .

But Aunt Laura doesn't have time for hide-and-seek this morning. Her father called late last night, told her to find a new job. So this morning, she's agreed to a long-standing open request for a meeting. She and Kacey make a deal: Laura will eat an entire octopus if Kacey behaves. Raised on takeout and Hot Pockets, wide-eyed Kacey follows Laura around and chatters the entire morning, which is possibly more distracting than hide-and-seek.

"Does this mean you're going to be staying in Chicago, Aunt Laura?" she says as they arrive at the building. "Have you ever eaten an octopus before?" she asks in the crowded elevator. "Can you eat a pony next?" she asks as Laura sits her down in the lobby and makes her promise to stay. "Is it going to be alive when you eat it?" she says as Laura rubs her temples, thinking of a clever response. The receptionist's phone rings. They're ready when she is.

"No. Remember your—"

"I promise *I won't go anywhere*," Kacey says, hugging the side of her chair. Laura nods and walks into the office. It is large and empty except for a fernlike plant in the corner and a brushed-aluminum desk in the center. Behind her is a window with venetian blinds, through which her interviewer can see the waiting room. He starts to close them but changes his mind. The rod clicks against the blinds as he returns to sit behind the desk. He is Alex, owner of a rival electronics company. Think Apple versus Samsung, Sony versus LG.

"Alopecia," he says. "Bald is beautiful, or something like that. Rare genetic disease. Complete hair loss."

"I see," she says. He's young, not yet forty, sexily ruthless in an old Ivy League sense. Collar stays and a light-blue shirt beneath the suit jacket. Neutral-colored striped power tie, just like the men's magazines suggest. These Mayflower WASPs can smell fear and new money—Laura makes sure he can't smell anything on her.

As he asks the usual questions, "from one CEO to another," Laura thinks about her outfit. It took her only an hour to buy the business suit: blouse, black rayon under a thin black-and-white houndstooth jacket. Skirt: black, knee-length. Her hair is swept to the side today, held in place by a silver plastic barrette inset with a plastic turquoise gem. Kacey picked it out. Trying not to stare at it, Alex asks about the photoshoot for the *Forbes* cover, and she says it was life changing—a paradigm shift, really. The old purse matches her shoes, but why did she wear heels? They had time to shop for a new purse but didn't. She could have taken Kacey along. Something a mother and daughter might do. "How much time do you spend fussing over that fern?" she asks, already bored with him.

"You think I invited you here to learn about your father. About his weaknesses, so I can archive and exploit them," he says, opening a cavernous desk drawer and tossing away the manila folders littering his desktop. This is the "cut the crap" part of the interview. She's used it once or twice herself.

"It looks tropical," she says. "Do you turn up the thermostat when you leave the office?" He does his best to appear patient. They have a proprietary climate control. Speaking of climates, what's it like in Alaska? "If I wanted, I could legally grow up to twenty-four cannabis plants in my apartment. For personal use," she says. He blinks and sits back in his chair. This is the expression she's been waiting for, this buffoon who thinks he can exploit the family by targeting its women. She's about to completely wreck the interview when he leans forward and rubs his missing eyebrows.

"You know, I never liked the man. At least in the role I know him. He has that stone-faced, ruthless-tycoon thing down, but I always wondered if there's anything behind it."

Laura settles a little in her chair and leans forward.

"Like a vast, iron-colored ocean with a few desolate . . . schools of fish swimming through it. Perhaps." This seems like the first unscripted thing he's said and there's something weirdly vulnerable about it.

"What do the fish symbolize in your metaphor?" she asks, picturing her father heaving garbage bags into the frozen pool.

"You tell me."

She tells him about her father's obsession with numerology (a lie). She looks through the window at Kacey, who is holding on to that chair with her arms even as her legs try to drag her away from it, and tells him that her niece was named after KC and the Sunshine Band (the truth).

"Well, it's better than being named after one of their songs," he muses.

Laura hates him a little less. He promises to keep in touch.

EIGHT ARMS TO HOLD YOU

If you're an executive, competitors occasionally test your courage over dinner. On the road to becoming CEO of her consulting company, Laura ate a deep-fried bird skeleton in Japan, blowfish in San Francisco, *balut* in the Philippines—even the awful pizza in Rome, but she doesn't tell Kacey this. She's too thankful for her niece's good behavior and a little nervous before meeting with her father. They're in a contemporary Korean restaurant whose windows shout "fusion food," "bistro," and "phone cards" in Hangul. Bright yellow, blue, and red track lights hang from the ceiling.

They bring the food all at once and Laura slowly eats the pickled egg that serves as a garnish, dips it in her soup. Kacey stomps with impatience and Laura takes the lid off the main dish, which contains udon noodles and a few broiled baby octopi, heads the size of golf

balls. Laura was worried that the size would render them less shocking, but Kacey seems horrified by their miniatureness, like something
grown in beakers by a mad scientist. The tiny suction cups, the texture
of the heads. The smell. Laura carefully picks one up with the blunt
ends of her chopsticks. It's limp, boiled in a red bean curd sauce. Kacey
watches, transfixed, and Laura explains how the tentacles curl when
they're cooked. Kacey puts her hands over her mouth and shakes her
head slowly as her aunt tosses it in the air, where it flips, and catches
it with the thin ends of her steel chopsticks. She offers it to Kacey,
who squeals and pushes back into her chair. Laura tosses it again and
catches it in her mouth by a long tentacle. The rest of the creature bobs
and swings against her cheek. She opens her eyes wide and makes
a mooing noise. Their waiter approaches, then quietly backs away.
Laura bites each tentacle off as daintily as possible and finishes, Kacey
watching through her fingers. Laura dabs the corner of her mouth with
her napkin and leans forward. "I believe I feel like kissing someone,"
she says and Kacey shouts "No!" as she slides out of her chair.

"Kiss him," she shouts, pointing to the waiter as she runs past,
her laughing aunt close behind.

EDWARD MOON

Kacey is calm after lunch, watching her aunt with a newfound
sense of awe—even passes up the opportunity to push the elevator
buttons. They ride in a vacuum of silence to the top floor of her
grandfather's building, and Kacey waits quietly in the lobby. The
skyscraper (although the word doesn't seem adequate for such a
building) is a monolith of glass and steel, designed to intimidate. But
there is another reason behind its design. The building's triangular
structure is practical, of course, gives it strength, but Edward Moon's
Korean name means *deep lake* and the building's shape allows him a

commanding view of Lake Michigan. Laura used to be embarrassed by the building, felt it childishly indulgent. But one can only resist that kind of power for so long, knowing that the rumble beneath your feet is the cold wind parting over the face of the building. She stands before the broad window and watches Lake Michigan.

She's looking through clouds at this height, but she can see Soldier Field and the harbor beyond, white ships in toothy rows. Beyond that is the city's eastern coast; at this distance, you can barely see where the lake meets the sky. To the west is a grid of parks and lesser skyscrapers. From here, the city is a prize to be captured. She moves to the window's edge to follow the river, lead-colored in the early afternoon.

Her father enters the room almost silently and she startles a little. She turns and hugs him, perches on the chair across from the heavy teak desk. "That bald weirdo," he says, rubbing his palm against the desk's surface. Of course he already knows. She glances over her shoulder at his rival skyscraper, also triangular and exactly one story higher.

"He has you figured out," she says.

"This is not what I meant when I said to find a job." He wanted something to get her mind off the situation, something to do while Kacey's in school. "A chance to work for a real company," he doesn't say.

She looks at him, her courage draining. He's a man with heavy muscle beneath his suit, someone who leverages anything to his advantage. He doesn't have to read men's magazines, his power doesn't come from his suit. A sensible tie and a shock of black hair—from a distance, there isn't much to distinguish him from the hordes of salarymen below. Edward Moon is a man of long silences and they steep in one for a few minutes. "I have paid off the apartment"—they both know which apartment he means—"for the next hundred and two years," he declares.

"A bit optimistic, don't you think?"

"You haven't met my scientists," he responds. "That bald fool thinks cloning dolphins and neural bridges are the future. I own the future. What do you think I've been selling all these years?" He calls Kacey in. She has a calming effect on him and the heaviness in the room dissolves. He dotes on her, treats her with a gentleness Laura's never seen, as if he's saved it just for her.

"Tell me what you think," he says, handing her a new cell phone designed for six- to eight-year-olds. She loves it, and yes, she can have it. With Aunt Laura's permission, of course.

"I want you to meet Wyatt," he says, pushing the intercom button to call him in. Wyatt is slim, but his suit can't hide his muscular arms. No ring, she notices as they shake hands. His healthy, thick brown hair, combed to the side, gives him a generic professional appearance.

"Are you a scientist?" Laura asks, mostly to see how he'll respond.

"In a sense," he says, smiling. Her father insists he's not a bodyguard—someday he will be the company's president. Laura's intrigued, at least, wants to reach out and press his crooked nose. She looks to see what Kacey thinks, but she is busy playing with the new phone, which Laura confiscates and puts in her purse.

"Wyatt's a movie buff," Edward says. "You two should have dinner together."

"Of course," Laura says. Find a job, find a husband. She's been in Chicago nine days.

Wyatt walks them to the car, and Laura politely demurs. She's busy, doesn't know how much longer she'll be in town. As she checks her rearview mirror, she sees him staring up at the skyscraper—probably wondering what to tell his boss.

∎ ∎ ∎

The next morning, Laura's phone rattles on the counter. Half-awake, she answers without checking the caller ID.

"Why would one name a child after that particular band?" Alex asks.

"I think it has something to do with the seventies theme party at which she was conceived. How did you get this number?" she says.

"It was on the . . . thingy." She waits. "Internet," he says.

"It's not, though."

"I'm downstairs. Standing under your balcony, actually. Someone threw away one of your dad's phones," he says. Laura sighs. "I never gave you my business card," he says.

"I'll buzz you in."

"My company developed a cell phone that can stop bullets. You strap it over your heart," he says, entering her apartment only after she gestures him in.

"You need something like that more than I do," Laura says. "Especially after my father learns you were here."

"I'll strap them all over my body. Do you think the three of us can have lunch?" Something about "the three of us" gives her pause. "Really?" Laura knows he doesn't have children when he suggests Kacey pick the restaurant. Laura calls to her through the door and Kacey voices her request. Laura agrees, curious to see how this will play out.

TACO BELL

The closest franchise is near the Magnificent Mile, so they park and walk. It was fun dressing up in an orange pantsuit for the occasion, but as they pass through a seedier street, Laura is glad to have this man with them. His lack of hair emphasizes his eyes, which stand out blue against the dirty concrete. There's something unsettling about his presence—the vagrants and panhandlers instinctively move from its charge.

"I really am a huge fan of your work," he says once they've reached the relative safety of Taco Bell and ordered their food. He leans across the table, which has a Formica-like finish and two pastel-blue stripes.

"Do you know what your aunt does?" he asks Kacey, who shakes her head. Her aunt makes breakfasts, packs lunches, and sometimes entertains her. Can there be anything else? He looks over, but Laura motions for him to explain.

"She makes movies," he says, but Laura cuts him off. "In a sense," he protests. He explains product placement, rotating the logo on her cup toward an invisible camera. It's more glamorous the way he describes it. In reality, her firm is hired to alter scripts to create realistic product placement situations. But mostly, she travels, approving projects on airplanes and chatting with clients across the country. There's an almost sexual charge from the constant motion, leaning forward into the interchangeable chaos of business. Despite its Hollywood successes, hers is still a small company. They need her back, she knows, and she feels a twinge as she pictures her quiet apartment in Alaska. She has the occasional date to a movie premiere—no place for children there. *Movies.* The word doesn't seem to fit the product, the confluence of committees and marketing forces. "Now, you're making movies completely based around products," he says.

"TV's been doing it for years and there have been a couple serious Hollywood attempts, but it was hard to get the eighteen-to-twenty-five demographic to pay for it. Now we have all this untapped nostalgia, though."

"What about the movie based on the Skip-It?"

"Canned. Who told you about that? The Skip-It was basically a cleverly marketed torture device. Remember? Well, I guess they were mostly for girls. But imagine the litigation. All those shattered ankles . . ." Kacey slurps her soda and frowns at the untouched food on their trays.

"What's your favorite toy, Kacey?" Alex says. She holds up a coloring book.

SILVER BUTTONS

Laura answers the door around midnight to find a mariachi band in the hallway. There are seven musicians wearing sombreros and purple uniforms, complete with the short *chaqueta*, silver *botonaduras* running the lengths of their pants. The lead singer plays a chord on his guitar and mumbles something. She asks him to repeat it but still doesn't understand. Asking again would be rude, so she just nods. He points to the number on her door and attempts a smile. It is late for them, too. One violinist notices her discomfort—the hall is cold and her nightgown is thin—and they step back a few feet. As they launch into song, she calls Alex to thank him. "They're wonderful." She holds the phone so he can hear.

"What are you talking about?" he says. He is in a meeting, she realizes from his tone. "I seriously did not send you anything." Then he realizes how this sounds and says he was planning to send flowers. "Wait, what's happening?" he asks. He sounds tired, too.

"Never mind," she says. He hangs up reluctantly. Kacey emerges from her room in her long T-shirt and socks. She narrows her eyes, focusing her displeasure at the band interrupting her slumber. "Let me see your phone," Laura says, and Kacey pads off to retrieve it. Laura doesn't like looking foolish and is not about to ask if her niece

is responsible for this musical interruption. The call history is empty
and besides, Kacey seems genuinely surprised. The band, sensing
the tension, plays a festive trumpety song, but nobody enjoys it.
Laura grabs her purse off the counter and hands them five twenties.
Someone down the hall unchains his door and peeks out at them.
The lead singer accepts the money with a sad smile. Laura wonders
how many times a day his band is sent somewhere as a prank. She
closes the door and sends Kacey back to bed.

Now, Laura can't sleep. She wonders who the band was intended
for. She thinks about the shattered phone and her call the first night
in Chicago, wonders who might be tracking her sister's phone.
Figuring it doesn't matter anymore, she grabs another one off its
charger. Telephone. Someday, her father will think of a more fitting
word, she thinks as she sits on the couch and scrolls through the
Options menu. She checks the contacts, then the history. There are
pictures on it, including one of Kacey's father.

Laura's never been with a *pae geen*, a white man, and looking at
Kacey's dad, she idly wonders what he would be like. And he does
look like Superman, especially in this picture where he's wearing
the costume, cape and all. He has a barrel chest and a strong jaw,
someone both men and women could safely call handsome. This
is from a Halloween party (she hopes), back when Jennifer was a
fashion designer. Before she was an interior designer. Before she was
a financial planner. She finds a picture showing both of them and of
course they're the best-dressed couple there. She shuts the phone
off and sets it on the coffee table. Her headache moves to the back
of her skull. *God, Jennifer.*

But she isn't thinking about Jennifer or Superman now. She's
thinking about a man with eyes the color of the IBM logo, whose
bald head contains a coiled, byzantine ambition. The meeting she

interrupted—what were they discussing? Mapping Europa's ocean beds? Nanoshields?

There's a message on her phone when she wakes. His meeting over, Alex wants to buy stock in her company. "I want to take it slow. When you're ready, give us a call," he says. It sounds like he's at a party, Brunori loafers sliding on marble floors, canapés rushing by on crystal trays. Backroom deals even her father couldn't imagine. "There's no hurry."

GLITTER

There's always the possibility Jennifer won't return. Laura feels it again as she helps Kacey write a get-well card. Later, she will pretend to mail it, secretly keeping it to show Jennifer if she returns. *This, little sister, is what happens when you abandon your daughter on her birthday.*

"Glue and glitter was definitely the way to go," Kacey says. Laura sweeps the remaining sparkles onto a sheet of construction paper and funnels them back into the vial. It's only been a few weeks, but Laura wonders whether Kacey's adjusted, whether she considers today to be the new normal. The longing and wondering, the permanent babysitter. Kids are tough, everyone tells her. School, homework, TV, get-well card. Still no word from Hawaii, and Laura's father doesn't seem as confident. She wonders how badly he wants to find Jennifer now that Kacey has Mommy 2.0. Features include improved reliability and role modeling.

"Kacey," Laura says gently, "I want you to know that . . . even though your mother is doing much better, it might be a long time before she comes back."

"I know," Kacey says, her little hand drawing her mother's name on the envelope.

"But, I just want you to know that no matter what, someone will be here to take care of you."

"You." Kacey says, and looks up at her. "You," this time quieter, and it sounds like a question. This is the moment Laura has side-stepped for twenty-two days. Under Kacey's unwavering gaze, Laura feels something ache deep in her chest. She looks her niece in the eye and runs her fingers through her hair. "Of course, honey. I'll be here until your mom comes back." Kacey nods and busies herself with the card, tracing her pencil marks with a pen. Laura feels something calm inside her, and she's surprised by it.

The light on her phone flashes and Laura sits back down. On the screen is Jennifer's shaky cursive: *I've found him.* Laura glances at her niece, who is drawing a heart on the envelope. Laura, no stranger to technology, types in codes to boost the signal, traces the call, and listens to the phone ring. She listens to her sister breathe, contemplating what to say. She turns to the stupid scroll on the wall: *Speak of the tiger and it will come.* And here it is, a silent, fiery messenger of change. The signal fades and it's back to text. *So you like Mexican food now,* Jennifer writes. Mariachi mystery solved. Laura turns the chair around and with her fingernail taps something vicious onto the face of the phone, then erases it. Jennifer's been watching the whole time—she knows the heartbreak she's causing. Laura exits the kitchen. Who knows through which cameraphone, through which telephoto lens she's being beamed to Hawaii. *So what now?* the expression on her face says. She grabs her coat and heads outside, leans against the thick glass doors separating her world from her niece's.

You dont know about Love, comes Jennifer's reply. Laura looks at Kacey, who is resting her head on the table. Resisting the urge to smash the obnoxious gray screen, Laura slides it into a pocket and looks out on the lake, then pounds her palm against the balcony. She leans back against the glass, blows on her hands to warm them.

They weren't twins, of course, but they were pretty, tall, and Asian. Growing up, this was all people saw and they often confused one for the other. This misplaced attention bothered Jennifer, but they still occasionally took tests for each other, never got caught. It wasn't for the grades, of course—there was a thrill in passing for someone else. And now, Laura can see the possibilities of a permanent trade. A long panorama: herself quietly guiding Kacey's life, the family—something folding over to repair itself. Watching the sky, she traces Kacey's future back to the present moment. These past weeks, Laura felt her sister's life as a strange cage dropped on her. But Kacey—will she be able to bear the weight of Jennifer's absence? All this broad architecture about to collapse on one unsuspecting child. Laura's hands shake as she types *Your daughter misses you*. Send.

I cant come back is Jennifer's response after Laura has put Kacey to bed. Laura walks in and looks over the sleeping girl, smooths her hair. Laura could retrace the call and convince her sister to return home. But. She looks at the proverb on the wall: *Speak of the tiger*. She lifts the scroll off its nail and turns it around to let the blank side speak.

SCRABBLE

It is early in the evening and Kacey is with her grandfather for the night. Laura walks out of her bedroom and pauses to watch her computer turn on by itself. It begins updating automatically, text scrolling in a diagnostic window. Everything electronic annoys her nowadays. Her shareholders want answers—her cell phone is so full of messages that it actually feels heavier. She pours herself a glass of chardonnay and sits on the sofa. Alex is sprawled out on the couch next to her, staring at the coffee table.

"That was a good game of Scrabble," he says.

"Scrabble is a verb." Her computer makes a clicking noise and she turns to see a message on the screen. *Call your father.* She does.

"I left you six messages," he says.

"I turned my phone off."

"Kacey has stuck a popcorn kernel up her nose," he says. Laura tries not to laugh, especially when she hears Kacey's little voice in the background saying, "Hi, Aunt Laura."

"I have exhausted all the safe options."

"You need to take her to the hospital," Laura says.

"Are you sure? Because—"

"Stop. Stop. I'm coming. Promise me you won't do anything until I get there." Alex offers to drive. His silver car is streamlined, weirdly silent, and fast. They make it to Edward Moon's high-rise in fifteen minutes. Kacey jumps in the backseat. Edward Moon climbs in next to her. He is wearing a three-piece suit. Alex rubs his arms, somewhat underdressed in an old Gabba Gabba Hey T-shirt and sweatpants. He knows Edward is watching his face in the side mirror.

"They're going to ask why you did it," Alex says to Kacey. Laura knows it was an experiment—Kacey doesn't know why. Every time she exhales, there's a long whistling noise.

"Try breathing through your mouth, honey," Laura says calmly. Kacey nods and the whistling is replaced by a quiet panting.

"I have never seen this before," Edward says, eyeing his granddaughter suspiciously.

"Kacey, don't pick at it. Good heavens."

"Sorry," she says. The gauges turn blue as they pass beneath an el platform. In the window, Kacey traces the glowing white letters of the downtown hospital's sign.

In the waiting room, Edward sits with his granddaughter while Laura ties back her hair and fills out forms. Alex brings them coffee and stands next to Laura, trying to look important. "Are you the father?" the doctor asks him. Laura looks at Edward, who says nothing. Kacey folds her hands on her lap and stares at the ground.

"No," Alex says.

The doctor taps his clipboard. "I'll be right back," he says.

"This stops now," Edward says before the doctor has even left. He looks from Laura to Alex.

"Why?" Laura says.

"Some things cannot be forgiven. You have no idea. This man—" Alex reaches out for Kacey, giving Laura a look that says, *Please, she doesn't need to see this.* She nods. Edward moves to intervene, but Laura stops him.

"Who are you thinking of right now?" she says.

"What?" he almost shouts. Laura tries to smile at Kacey, who stares over Alex's shoulder as he hurries them from the room.

"Yourself or Kacey?"

"First your sister in disgrace, now you. You cannot see that man."

"And there's your answer." Laura looks away. The television is broken, so the patients in the waiting room watch this new drama unpack itself.

"Some things . . . ," Edward says.

Laura raises her face to meet his. "Forgiveness might be in short supply in this family. But I've done nothing to forgive." She sits next to her father and speaks almost in a whisper. "You know that scroll in Jenny's room? *Speak of the tiger?* Well, it's here and I'm dealing with it."

"Please explain more of our proverbs to me. You know nothing of love." Laura stands to follow her niece and Alex.

"I've made my choices. It's your turn," she says. The waiting room is silent.

SUPERMAN'S DAUGHTER

It has been over two months since Jennifer disappeared, but Laura no longer keeps track. She's busy moving her company to Chicago, where she plans to build a triangular skyscraper one story taller than Alex's. But this afternoon, Christmas is on her mind. She's been decorating—and cleaning—Alex's house. It is a rectangular colonial in the northern suburbs, "a perfect Christmas house," Kacey notes. They're visiting for the weekend, and the wide front porch practically begs for lights.

Alex lost a bet, so he's sitting on the floor of his den watching the game on his cell phone. He frowns at the screen, squinting at the throwback jerseys the home team is wearing. "And I thought the new Bengals uniforms were bad."

"I never liked the font on the Bears jerseys," Laura says. She pulls the lever on the recliner to put her feet up.

Kacey walks in. "Why can't people fly?" she demands.

"Oil companies would lose money," Alex says, holding the phone closer to his face. "Touchdown. Wait . . . is there a flag?" Kacey appeals to her aunt.

"The answer requires science, darling, and you don't like science," Laura says, watching Alex watch the game.

"Seven points. Money in the bank," Alex says. He grabs a Nerf football off the coffee table and tosses it at Kacey, who bats it away.

"If I could fly, then I could be Santa Claus."

"You're not fat enough," Alex says, poking at her belly. Kacey glares at them and leaves the room.

After the game, Laura finds Kacey in the kitchen drinking a cup of water so big she has to hold it with both hands. After she finishes, she reaches up to set the cup on the island. Laura explains simple physics and human flight, while Alex interjects from the other room. "Impossible. You don't have wings."

"But why?" Kacey wants to know.

"Maybe you can," Alex shouts back after a few minutes. Which probably means there's another game coming on, Laura thinks. He wants to watch it in peace.

Kacey is electrified by this new possibility. She looks to her aunt for confirmation. Laura thinks for a minute and grabs a red dishtowel hanging from a drawer.

"This is practice. Actual flight comes later."

Kacey seems underwhelmed by the terry cloth. Laura swirls it in the air, then ties it around Kacey's neck. Satisfied with her aunt's explanation, Kacey runs around the kitchen island, turning to see the dishtowel waving behind her. Laura intercepts and picks up her niece, who shrieks, then giggles at this sudden loss of gravity. The doorbell rings, and Laura's surprised at how the vibrating chimes shiver in her chest. She inhales deeply, leaning back a little.

"Who's there?" Kacey shouts.

Laura would like to think it's her father.

There's only one person it cannot be, she thinks, someone with a deep aversion to the cold, someone who's exiled herself to an island, palm trees and sand. Laura ignores the ache in her shoulders and holds Kacey against her chest. She feels Kacey's heartbeat but knows it's really her own. For a brief moment, she wonders whether Kacey even considered Jennifer a possible guest. As the cold and snow rush through the open front door into the kitchen, she's happy to let the possibilities hang in the air, branch out, and fill the room.

In her apartment in Alaska, the black vinyl and steel countertops grow cold. There's something about the perfectly balanced planes of metal and glass, how they yearn for a caretaker. And so it must be with empires. But Laura wishes she could explain to her father that it's Kacey's unsteadiness, like a child on the move, confident someone will catch her. How can one ignore that pull? *Maybe,* she thinks with growing certainty, *he feels it, too.* It's why he set aside his empires of pride and anger. He has two generations to guide, two generations increasingly unafraid of him. Sharing space and time with his archnemesis. She can forgive him for taking so long.

"Your father's here. He brought presents," Alex calls out. Laura pictures the wrens and sparrows, interrupted by the commotion, regrouping loudly in a neighboring tree. She hears the visitor stomp-ing and wiping his shoes on the doormat. The door closes, cutting off the sound of wings and wind.

"Let's say hello," Laura says, still carrying her niece. The muscles in her calves tense as her niece swings forward, already preparing for the next motion.

"Hello!" Kacey shouts as their momentum carries them into the wintry chaos of the living room, where Alex is helping their guest remove his heavy coat.

ACKNOWLEDGMENTS

I'd like to thank my family, friends, and colleagues. I could not have finished this book without Geeta Kothari, Cathy Day, Michael Byers, Chuck Kinder, and Aubrey Hirsch; thank you for your friendship and mentoring. The best thing about being a writer is being reminded how smart, talented, and generous your friends are: I'm especially grateful to my readers Nicole Lobdell, Adam Reger, Sarah Harris Wallman, Salvatore Pane, and Kara Hughes. I'd also like to thank Geeta Kothari, Jeffrey Condran, R. O. Kwon, and Bonnie Jo Campbell for taking the time to read and blurb the collection. Last but certainly not least, special thanks to Paul Yoon for his kindness and support—and to Sarah Gorham and the outstanding staff at Sarabande Books.

"Princeton" was published in *Avery*, "Clear Blue Michigan Sky" was published in *Green Mountains Review*, "Stop Hitting Yourself" was published in *Hyphen: Asian America Unabridged*, "The Thirty-Eighth Parallel" was published in *Papirmasse*, "Rumors of My Demise" was published in *Great Jones Street*, "Dressed in Red" was published in the *Los Angeles Review* with the title "Pockets," "Scenes from the Reverse Metamorphosis" was published in the *Monarch Review*, and "Solitude City" was published in the *Kenyon Review*.

As a Navy brat, **ROBERT YUNE** moved eleven times by the time he turned eighteen. In the summer of 2012, he worked as a stand-in for George Takei and as an extra in movies such as *The Dark Knight Rises*, *Me and Earl and the Dying Girl*, and *Father and Daughters*. His fiction has appeared in the *Green Mountains Review*, the *Kenyon Review*, and the *Los Angeles Review*, among other places. His novel *Eighty Days of Sunlight* was nominated for the 2017 International DUBLIN Literary Award; other nominees included Viet Thanh Nguyen, Margaret Atwood, and Salman Rushdie. Currently, he teaches at DePauw University, located in beautiful Greencastle, Indiana.

SARABANDE BOOKS is a nonprofit literary press located in Louisville, KY. Founded in 1994 to champion poetry, short fiction, and essay, we are committed to creating lasting editions that honor exceptional writing. For more information, please visit sarabandebooks.org.